IN OUR WORDS

QUEER STORIES FROM
BLACK, INDIGENOUS, AND
PEOPLE OF COLOR WRITERS

D1002762

Visit us at www.boldstrokesbooks.com

In Our Words

Queer Stories from Black, Indigenous, and People of Color Writers

Stories selected by
Anne Shade

and edited by
Victoria Villaseñor

2021

IN OUR WORDS: QUEER STORIES FROM BLACK,
INDIGENOUS, AND PEOPLE OF COLOR WRITERS
© 2021 BY BOLD STROKES BOOKS. ALL RIGHTS RESERVED.

ISBN 13: 978-1-63555-936-1

THIS TRADE PAPERBACK ORIGINAL IS PUBLISHED BY
BOLD STROKES BOOKS, INC.
P.O. BOX 249
VALLEY FALLS, NY 12185

FIRST EDITION: JUNE 2021

CREDITS
STORIES SELECTED BY ANNE SHADE
EDITORS: VICTORIA VILLASEÑOR AND STACIA SEAMAN
PRODUCTION DESIGN: STACIA SEAMAN
COVER DESIGN BY TAMMY SEIDICK

CONTENTS

SWEET POTATO

Briana Lawrence

Briana Lawrence is a self-published author and the Fandom Editor for *The Mary Sue*. After analyzing pop culture and de-transforming from her magical girl state, she indulges in an ever-growing pile of manga, marathons too much anime, and dedicates an embarrassing amount of time to *Animal Crossing*.

When I was sixteen, it became a tradition to come to my mama's house after church. Everyone knew she made the best fried chicken and macaroni, and Lord, don't get her started about some collard greens and cornbread. But the best part, by far, was her sweet potato pie. She'd start making 'em on Saturday night to have them ready to go for Sunday dinner. The smell would perfume the house like a department store fragrance counter, and she'd knowingly hide a pie in the microwave just for me to eat in peace once the church crowd left our house.

I was Mama's kitchen assistant. My job was to hand her ingredients and hum spiritual songs with her while she cooked. We'd occasionally bump our hips together when we got to a lyric we liked, Mama managing to dance and assemble a meal as if the two went hand in hand. Mama was a large, dark-skinned woman who dressed in bright colors and let her joy seep into her cooking. I was the spitting image of her—not as heavyset, and with longer, wilder hair. Mama told me that her hair used to be as luxurious as mine, but time had added some gray that made her look more distinguished. It framed her face like a salt-and-pepper globe, and she couldn't be more beautiful even if she tried.

Today was like any other Sunday. Mama was humming a song from the choir, one that had caused all of us to get up and stomp our feet. I'd usually join in with her, but on this particular Sunday, I didn't have it in me.

"What's the matter?" Mama asked as she poured flour into a paper bag, combining it with dashes of pepper and thyme. The *real* way to make fried chicken, according to her. One time she had a fit when I tried to do it in a bowl instead of one of the bags she had stashed in the bottom cabinet.

"Huh? Oh...nothin', Mama."

I don't know why I insisted on lying. She always saw right through me, even if her attention was on an entire tray of chicken. She'd already warmed up the grease in her cast iron skillet and was ready to put any Colonel to shame.

"Come on now, sweet potato," and *ugh*, damn those childhood names that stick worse than gum underneath a table, "you know you can't lie worth a damn."

I could, actually, just not to *her*.

I sighed as I sat at the kitchen table, kicking my stocking-covered legs the way my five-year-old self used to do when I was upset. No wonder Mama knew something was wrong, I normally would've had these itchy things off as soon as service was over. "Kenneth asked me out."

"The pastor's son?" She shook her well-seasoned chicken around in the flour bag. "That's a fine-lookin' boy."

Tall, with light brown skin and dimples for days when he smiled, his church clothes were always pressed to perfection as if he were competing in a sharp dresser contest with the other boys. He always held the door open for women and accepted the cheek pinches of the elderly ladies with grace. "I guess he is...if you into that sorta thing..."

Mama stopped shaking the bag and set it down on the counter.

She watched me carefully, studied me like final exams were fast approaching. "And *is* you into that sorta thing?"

I stared down into my lap instead of her big, brown eyes. When Mama looked at you it felt like the entire world was analyzing every inch of you. I started to count the number of flowers in my dress. Sixteen years old and still wearing floral print to church like a kid.

"Ava Marie, I asked you a question."

It was rude to leave Mama waiting, especially when she threw the *Marie* in my name. I swallowed the lump in my throat and said, "No, Mama, I ain't."

"Well then," she said as she grabbed the bag again, "you best tell that boy no."

And just like that she was back to shaking the chicken. I waited for any sign of hate or disdain, any questions about being sure of myself or a gentle poke to give the pastor's son a chance. But Mama's voice was steady as she went back to humming her song, even throwing a *hallelujah* in for good measure.

I stood up and walked over to her, carefully picking out my next set of words. "You know…Pastor Michael gonna be disappointed. And the other brothers and sisters are gonna talk."

"Let 'em," she said with a shrug. "Kenneth will find some other girl." Then, without missing a beat, "Pull out the eggs and cheese so I can get to cookin' the macaroni."

"Mama…"

"Hush up now, girl, and grab them eggs."

I wanted to tell her that the church wouldn't be as relaxed about it as she was, but she was already humming again, putting the flour-coated chicken into her pan. I did as I was told, even gave in to her hip bump with a tiny smile.

It didn't take long for the kitchen to smell like a proper Sunday dinner. I left the room to set the dining room table, more than happy to leave the kitchen so my mouth would stop watering. We only used the dining room on Sundays. The table could easily seat a dozen people or more if we squeezed in a couple extra chairs. As the Sunday congregation arrived at the house, they all made sure to comment on how good the food smelled. But through the fried meat and copious amounts of macaroni and greens, the sweet potato pie was the most enticing scent. Mama had set several pies on the kitchen counter and wagged her finger at anyone who attempted to get a piece before dinner.

Kenneth was there with his pastor father, a perfect gentleman who was *raised right*, according to the sisters, because he pulled my chair out for me. He sat next to me and smiled his handsome smile. All I could do was offer a weak one in return. Pastor Michael had us join hands and bow our heads in prayer, Kenneth's thumb rubbing against the back of my hand. I prayed for the prayer to end quickly.

With a hearty cry of "Amen" we began to fill our plates with food. Before I could even get a spoonful of macaroni Kenneth said, "So, Ms. Ava, I was wonderin' if you had a chance to think about what I asked ya."

Lord. He just *had* to bring this up in front of everyone, huh? Mama passed the plate of cornbread to me in an attempt to pull me out of the conversation. "Kenneth, maybe wait 'til after dinner."

"Aw, the girl is just shy." That came from Pastor Michael, who patted Kenneth on his back and said, "My boy asked Ms. Ava out today."

The entire table—except for me and Mama—smiled their approval. They began talking about how cute it was, some of the elders even remembering the days when we were children who didn't know what dating was.

"I knew y'all would get together." That was Sister Hazel, the oldest member of the church. All her stories revolved around remembering when we were *this big*—hand held at knee level to indicate our heights as children. "You two always used to play together after service."

That was an overexaggeration. Ninety-nine-point-nine percent of church kids play together. We all wanted to run around because our butts fell asleep in the pews.

"What is you two gonna do for ya date?" Brother Johnson, always loud and boisterous, couldn't help but chime in as he mixed his cornbread with his greens.

"Well, I was thinkin' of just catchin' a movie, maybe grabbin' a bite to eat." Kenneth was beaming, having planned the whole date without me.

"That's a fine date." That came from Brother Wilson, who had already finished two drumsticks and was eyeing a third. His wife nudged him in an attempt to get him to slow down, but he ignored her and grabbed himself another piece. "Sounds like our first date, right, honey?"

"No. Not at all."

"Oops, I meant...n-never mind." Brother Wilson chomped down on his chicken. Apparently, he'd gotten his first meeting with wife number four mixed up with one of the others.

"You gotta take her somewhere nice, though, Kenneth." That was Sister Mary, too busy talking to take a bite out of her food. "And be sure to have her home on time. Don't be out there doin' anything foolish."

"Yes, ma'am."

"Come on now, Sister Mary. Kenneth's a growin' boy! Ain't no harm in a little—OW!" Brother Wilson winced. That nudge from his wife hadn't been as gentle as the previous one.

Kenneth, at least, had the manners to look a bit flustered. He turned to me and said, "We can go anywhere ya want, Ms. Ava. You can pick the movie and the restaurant."

Everyone was watching me, waiting for my response. Maybe I could, at least, share a tub of popcorn with him. And I could certainly pick a restaurant on the cheaper side. "Kenneth, I—"

"Ava don't wanna go out with you," Mama said, finishing my sentence for me as she ate a forkful of macaroni. The thin strands of cheese showed just how creamy it was. Mama knew it, too, because she let out an appreciative *mmm* as she ate.

"Mama," I whispered to her. "You ain't have to do that." I wanted to turn him down politely, not embarrass him during a meal with other people.

"They was jumpin' to conclusions and you wasn't gonna say no, even if you wanted to."

It was true. Mama always spoke the truth. I was willing to go out with someone I wasn't interested in just to spare his feelings.

"Now, what's wrong with my Kenneth?" Pastor Michael's voice always commanded your presence, a voice that would immediately get anyone on his side. No one was eating now, not even Brother Wilson.

"Nothing's wrong with him." Except for Mama. Mama was eating. She was going to town on her macaroni and making her way toward the greens. She'd be getting to the sweet potato pie in no time. "She just ain't interested."

"Hmph. Guess she was too busy makin' eyes at Sister Rita's granddaughter."

Ah yes. There was the *real* Sister Mary, better known as *Sister Gossip*. If you wanted to hear any dirt about the churchgoers, she had you covered. Age didn't matter, she'd rat out the kids, too, just to garner an *oh no you didn't* reaction. Thankfully, Sister Rita wasn't there to comment, nor was the granddaughter I'd been *making eyes* at.

"That...that's—"

"You ain't gotta respond to that," Mama said. "Ava can *make eyes* at whoever she wants."

"She should be lookin' at Kenneth and not some fast little girl."

Said *little girl* was almost eighteen and hadn't done anything scandalous, but I guess me looking at her warranted that kind of response from Sister Mary. The others at the table seemed to agree, whispering to each other as I tried my best to convince the floor to swallow me whole.

"Now, now, Sister Mary, it's all right," Pastor Michael said, always trying to be the voice of reason. "She's just confused, is all." Voice of reason...until he dropped that tidbit of wisdom.

I knew better than to talk back to adults, especially churchgoing adults. I sat in my chair and listened to them all let out a chorus of *yeah, that must be it* with a dash of what the devil must've done to get to me.

But Mama wasn't having any of it. She was a full-grown adult who didn't have to bite her tongue. "What she confused about? You the one tryin' to get her to date someone she don't even like."

"God says—"

"No." Mama was the type of woman who only raised her voice when someone was about to do something supremely stupid. It was to get them to stop, immediately, like scolding a child who was about to touch a hot stove. When it came to true anger, though, her voice got low, *dangerous* even. It was the uncomfortable calm before the storm, the only warning you got before she decided to act. That was her voice right now, those gentle eyes that had comforted me earlier now sharp and narrow. "You don't know God the way I do," she said, stopping the good pastor from dragging God into this.

"With all due respect, Sister—"

"Ain't no respect in this house right now," Mama said, cutting Sister Mary off before she could add more fuel to the fire.

"Maybe we should just go." Pastor Michael stood and brushed the dinner crumbs from his suit, his expression still annoyingly calm as if he hadn't done anything wrong. Kenneth stood up with him, and everyone else followed suit, Kenneth avoiding making eye contact with me.

"What about the pie?" Brother Wilson, of course. His wife switched from elbowing him to slapping him upside the head. Brother Wilson winced and accepted defeat, but not before taking a drumstick for the road.

"We'll see y'all next Sunday, yeah? After you've simmered down a bit." Pastor Michael smiled at Mama and headed for the door. "Oh, and thank you for the meal." His best attempt at ending things on a good note.

"Take some time to read the Good Book," Sister Mary added, her lipstick-covered smirk showing remnants of red on her teeth.

Once our guests were gone all I could think to say was, "I'll help clear the table." I hadn't finished my dinner, but my appetite had left faster than the congregation had left our house.

I stood up to take some plates back to the kitchen. Mama didn't respond. She just sat there, stewing in her anger, her fist wrapped tightly around the fork she'd been eating with. I could feel the heat radiating from her, but after a couple of deep breaths she decided to finish her meal. I'd never seen anyone eat a piece of chicken so ferociously, and when she was done, she slammed the bone down on her plate and spoke a soft, "How dare they."

"Mama, it's fine. It—"

"It ain't fine," she snapped as she stood from her chair, finally helping bring the plates into the kitchen. "And to think I made sweet potato pie for them close-minded bigots."

"Mama, we can eat the pie ourselves." Several pies, in fact. Sweet potato pie could easily become my new favorite breakfast. "I don't care what they think."

There I was, lying to her again. What I should've said was that I'd already known how this would play out, so there was no point in caring. We'd go to church on Sunday and everyone who was at dinner would give a play-by-play to those who'd missed out on Mama defending her no-good daughter. Sister Rita would be appalled, and Sister Mary would conveniently leave out the part where she called her granddaughter *fast*. Then Sister Rita's pretty little granddaughter would sneer at me, along with the other teens and especially Kenneth. Pastor Michael would give a powerful sermon on forgiving *the misguided* because *they don't know no better, Lord, they just don't know.*

Praise them. Amen. Then we'd have dinner and go about our business.

Mama was still angry, though, aggressively scraping the leftover bits of food from people's plates into the trash. "They got the nerve to call themselves children of God. Ha! God would be ashamed of them."

It was a statement I'd heard before whenever someone had done something wrong, but I'd never heard it said so passionately. "You talk like you know Him personally." I laughed, grabbing Tupperware out the cabinets. We'd most definitely be having chicken again tomorrow.

Mama just stood there, motionless, so still that I thought she'd stopped breathing. She was looking out the window, her eyes fixated on the graying sky. I waved a hand in front of her face to try and get her attention, but her eyes didn't waver. They looked glossy, like watercolor droplets hitting a canvas to swirl together in a picturesque formation. Finally, I placed my hand on her shoulder and gently shook her. "Mama? It was a joke, Mama."

She blinked a couple of times before her lips curled in an almost playful smile. "Of course, sweet potato." Then she kissed me on my cheek, humming to herself as she went about cleaning the kitchen. "Make sure the door is locked, okay?"

"Okay…"

I wasn't sure how to describe it, but something about the exchange felt off. Part of me couldn't decide what'd upset Mama more: Sister Mary and the pastor belittling me, or the pastor accusing her of not being familiar with God. Whatever it was, I was certain that we could calm down over some relaxation and pie.

When I went to the front door, I noticed that the sky was a strange color now, like someone had smeared a greenish paint within the clouds. How had it taken such a turn so quickly? In the kitchen it had been a typical gray, a sign of potential light showers and maybe a lightning bolt or two. I couldn't help but step outside to make sure I wasn't seeing things and made a face when I felt the air against my skin. It was warm, muggy, like I'd stepped into a sauna with all my clothes on. "What the—"

"Come on inside now, Ava."

I looked back at Mama, her smile large like that of a mischievous child who was up to no good. The wind was starting to pick up, the clouds moving together and headed away from our house and in the direction of where the others had gone. "What's with this weather?" I asked as I stepped back inside, Mama closing the door and locking it.

"Nothing to worry about. Now, let's go and have some of that pie."

We went to church that following Sunday, just as Pastor Michael said we would. There wasn't any gossip before the sermon, though, and his words held a somber note. We were asked to keep Sister Mary and some other folks in our prayers. Their houses had been devastated by a tornado, of all things, an anomaly in our city as we usually only had to deal with rain or snow. After the service, Mama approached Pastor Michael and asked if we could do anything to help. She even suggested a bake sale and offered to make a couple of her pies. "No one got to have any last week," she said. "We could raise some money to help Sister Mary and the others."

"That's mighty kind of ya," he said. "I'm sure they'd appreciate it."

"Is your house okay?" Mama asked.

"Ah, we was lucky. Just a little bit of damage to the house. How about you?"

Mama shrugged her shoulders. "Nothing. We was just fine." There was a confidence in her voice, a tone that was reserved specifically for bragging rights. I'd only heard Mama sound like that when I brought home a good report card or when she correctly identified the killer in one of her crime shows.

"I see," Pastor Michael said, nervously shifting from one foot to the other. There was something about the way Mama was looking at him, a glint in her eye that put the man on edge. "That is fortunate. I suppose God really does work in mysterious ways."

"God?" Mama chuckled, sounding insulted at the suggestion. "This wasn't God, Pastor Michael. This was Mother Nature."

"Well, I suppose technically—"

"Yes, you do suppose."

I watched Pastor Michael carefully. He looked like he was shrinking under her gaze, like a child who knew they'd upset someone who held their entire life in their hands. "Anyway…I do appreciate your offer, Sister—"

"Mother," she corrected. There was a rumble in the sky, a low sound that whispered of a storm approaching. Before, when we'd been in the kitchen together, I thought that Mama's eyes looked off. As she leaned in toward Pastor Michael, her eyes electric and wild, I understood.

More importantly, so did he.

"Don't come at my baby again." Such was the declaration from Mama, *my* Mama.

Sunday dinner never took place at our house again.

WASH AND SET

Mason Dixon

Mason Dixon lives, works, and plays somewhere in the South. She and her wife enjoy grilling, traveling, and fighting for control of the remote. Her books include *Charm City*, *21 Questions*, and Lambda Literary Award finalist *Date With Destiny*. Writing as Yolanda Wallace, she has won two Lambda Literary Awards for Lesbian Romance. She can be reached at authormasondixon@gmail.com.

Aundrea Arsenault set her cell phone down and let out a silent scream of frustration. Chad Millar constantly wreaked havoc with her schedule; he was at it again. Because they were both VPs, she couldn't call it pulling rank. Because his father was president and CEO of the bank they both worked for, she could call it pulling strings.

She had been about to log off for the day when her phone had rung. Part of her had said to let the call go to voicemail—it was past eight p.m., after all—but she prided herself on giving her clients the personal touch. Unfortunately for her, Chad had been on the other end of the line instead of the burgeoning entrepreneur she had expected. He wanted Aundrea to attend a virtual conference in his stead because he and Daddy were going on a golf trip to Puerto Rico with some of their cronies. Never mind that it was mandatory for the operations officer to attend the meeting, and he was head of operations. Never mind that she had several vacation days coming up and nonrefundable plane tickets for a long-planned and often-delayed getaway.

She felt her blood pressure rise a bit more each time she pictured Chad and his father sipping cocktails and making deals on the back nine while she tried not to fall asleep in front of her computer screen during the deadly dull series of presentations.

Resisting the urge to throw something at the nearest wall, she checked the time instead. She had less than twelve hours to unpack for New Hampshire, cancel her reservations at the quaint little B&B she always visited when she needed to recharge her batteries, and update the registration for the online conference. If she didn't kill Chad first.

Before all that, though, she had to get her hair done. She'd been putting it off for days because she couldn't find the time. She had even less time now, but she could no longer delay the inevitable. She had to represent the bank in an official capacity, and she wanted to look her best even if it was only during a three-day series of Zoom meetings.

She reached for her cell phone and pressed speed dial with her thumb. "Suzanne," she said into the receiver, "I know it's late, but can you squeeze me in tonight?"

"We were about to close. The last customer just left, and Latoria is locking up right now."

"I'm sure she is, but I've had an unexpected change of plans and I need to be camera-ready in the morning. If you could somehow see me tonight, I would be sure to make it worth your while."

Long accustomed to giving orders and having them followed without question, Aundrea found it difficult to beg for an hour of her hairdresser's time. She probably wasn't the only client asking Suzanne for special treatment these days. Most of the salons had been slammed since they reopened for business. Suzanne's place was no different. Thanks to its stringent safety protocols, Aundrea didn't feel like she was putting her health at risk each time she paid a visit.

"Most of my stylists—Barbara included—have already gone, and the rest are about to," Suzanne said. "What's that?" She began a conversation with someone Aundrea couldn't hear. Aundrea heard a muffled "Are you sure you don't mind?" then, clearer, "Désirée's here. She says she doesn't mind waiting for you."

Aundrea sighed with relief. The mall was open until nine, but she didn't want to get an assembly line hairdo or be surrounded by a bunch of people who refused to wear masks in public. She had an understanding with Barbara, Suzanne's main stylist. When Aundrea sat in the chair, Barbara always knew exactly what she wanted and never tried to freelance, experiment, or take shortcuts. With Barbara gone, Aundrea would have to take her chances with someone else. Her hair didn't look like a rat's nest yet, but it was beginning to take longer and longer each morning to bend to her will. One day she was going to cut it all off and be done with it, giving her one less thing to worry about in her harried life. Until then, it was monthly trips to Clean Cuts, the best Black-owned beauty salon in DC.

"Tell her I'll be there in fifteen minutes."

Suzanne snorted. "Take a look at the traffic outside, honey. You'd better make it thirty."

Aundrea pulled into the half-empty parking garage that serviced the customers of Clean Cuts and the rest of the businesses on the block. After she found an open spot, she killed the engine of her SUV, set the alarm, and headed up the street. She ignored the admiring wolf whistle of the parking attendant as he checked out her legs. She was half a decade short of forty, but she was often told she looked ten years younger. "Black," as her mother constantly reiterated during their weekly phone calls, "don't crack."

Aundrea checked her watch. Five past nine. It had taken her the full thirty minutes to make her way across town and then some. As she regarded the salon's locked doors and darkened windows, she thought with a flash of panic that Désirée had given up on her and headed home. She had spent most of the crawl through traffic not listening to the latest installment of her favorite podcast but trying to remember which one of Suzanne's styling specialists Désirée was.

She knew most of the salon's employees by name—Cynda handled the kids, Latoria the high school and college crowd, Barbara the thirtysomethings and professionals, and Miss Beatrice the churchgoing habitués of Amen Corner. For the life of her, though,

Aundrea couldn't remember Désirée, and it was killing her. Was Désirée the one with the gold tooth and blond-streaked hair who saw most of the club-hoppers, or the one with the dusty wig, bad attitude, and sour expression who saw only the most desperate? Aundrea searched for a crack in the drawn shades but found none. She reached through the bars and knocked on the bulletproof glass door. She kept one eye on the street to make sure no one was painting her as a potential target. When she turned back to the salon, the shade had been pulled a little to one side and a pair of sparkling, almond-shaped hazel eyes were staring at her. Aundrea finally had a face to put with the name.

Désirée was the new hire. The graceful, long-limbed sister with the mile-high turban who saw the incense-burning, ankh-wearing Erykah Badu devotees. She reminded Aundrea of her niece, a Georgetown junior who seemed to think that rebellion and Afrocentricism hadn't existed until her multi-culti generation had come along.

Aundrea's brother's daughter had changed her name from Makayla to Nefertiti after her freshman year and constantly sent her aunt essays and poems she thought Aundrea should read so she wouldn't be tempted to sell out and forget her roots. Funny, Aundrea thought, how it was often the lighter-skinned sisters who were always lecturing the rest of their race on what Black was. She was dark-skinned and unashamed of it. Being proud of the face she saw in the mirror every day wasn't something she needed to be taught.

Désirée unlocked the door and ushered Aundrea inside. "I called Barbara so she could give me the 411 on you," she said, locking the door again. "She said you're a week late for your wash and set. Would you like to have that done today, or would you rather go ahead and have a touch-up instead?"

Aundrea unbuttoned the double-breasted jacket of her designer skirt suit and draped it across the nearest chair. Even though she, like most of the bank's staff, had been working from home for months, she preferred to dress like she was still heading to the office every day. Tonight, though, she couldn't wait to get back home and slip into a T-shirt and a pair of boxers while she plotted her revenge on Chad.

She didn't feel his behavior stemmed from a gender bias or even a racial one. At work, the only color that truly mattered to him was green. He acted the way he did because he knew he could get away with it. Plain and simple. She hated when he exuded an air of unearned privilege. One day, she was going to call him on it, whether it cost her the job or not.

Aundrea warily regarded the flickering line of vanilla-scented candles surrounding Désirée's station. Sure, they provided delightful ambiance, but they were the only light in the room. How was Désirée going to be able to see what she was doing? Aundrea couldn't sit in front of her webcam for the next three days looking like a five-year-old had styled her hair. "I don't want to hold you up any longer than I already have."

A sly smile slowly creased Désirée's angular face. "Your time is my time," she said as she tightened the band holding her clear plastic face shield in place.

Aundrea laughed. "Apparently, Barbara also told you that I tip well." The compensation she left behind was often more than the bill itself.

"I think the words she used were '*very* well,' but let's not quibble." Désirée glided across the room. Her sandaled feet moved noiselessly, but the clattering of the cowrie shell bracelet around her right ankle announced her presence. She gestured toward the freshly sanitized chair in front of her.

Aundrea settled into the chair. "When you called, did Barbara offer to come back down here and relieve you?"

"Of course, but she's got a man at home to answer to. I don't. Is there someone you're rushing to return home to," Désirée asked, reaching to unbutton the top button of Aundrea's silk blouse, "or am I allowed to take my time?"

Aundrea felt Désirée's long fingers lightly touch the back of her neck as she turned Aundrea's collar under once so it wouldn't stick out above the top of the black plastic smock and be drenched by the torrent of running water when they reached the shampoo sink. "I'm in your hands."

"Not yet, but you will be soon."

Aundrea checked herself. She and Désirée had done the harmless flirting thing and it had been fun, but it was time to get serious. She was there to get her hair done, not hook up with someone she was still getting to know. Besides, she never mixed business with pleasure. No matter how tempting the prospect.

As Désirée gathered the bottles of shampoo and conditioner and prepared the chemicals she would need, Aundrea took in the way Désirée's full hips stretched the material of her ankle-length African-print wrap skirt. She visually tracked the long, straight line of Désirée's back from her narrow waist to her broader-than-expected shoulders. Her gaze went up, up, up the long neck and examined the dips and swirls in the three yards of olive material that had been painstakingly wound around and around itself to form a majestic wrap atop Désirée's head.

In the mirror's reflection, Désirée caught Aundrea looking. Their eyes met. Neither looked away. The moment felt electric. But it was just that. Only a moment.

"I was beginning to think you didn't like me," Désirée said as she flipped on the overhead light.

Aundrea blinked as her eyes adjusted to the sudden brightness. She was grateful the mask covering the lower half of her face hid the look of surprise she was certain was etched there. "Why do you say that?" She had never been anything but cordial with Désirée or anyone else in the shop.

"I've been working here for three months now and you've never made an appointment with me. Until tonight, though that was hardly by choice."

"What can I say? I'm a creature of habit." Aundrea felt the tension drain from her shoulders. Obviously, the candles had achieved the desired effect. Or perhaps Désirée was responsible for her relaxed state. "Are you new to the area? I haven't seen you around the city."

"I doubt you and I run in the same circles."

"Perhaps not, but DC's a small town. Everyone knows everyone else. Those circles often intersect."

"True." Désirée parted Aundrea's long, thick hair in the middle and combed out the tangles. "I grew up here," she said, finally answering Aundrea's question. "I moved away for college and came back after I graduated."

"Which college did you attend?"

"Columbia."

"That's a good school. What was your major?"

"Political science." Désirée unscrewed the lid on a tub of relaxer and shoved her hand into the thick white mixture.

As the cream was applied to her roots, Aundrea felt its initial coolness followed by its sting as it began to do its job.

"Before you ask, I'm working here until I decide what I want to be when I grow up." Désirée divided Aundrea's hair into sections with her comb and applied more relaxer. "It's not burning anywhere, is it?"

"No."

"Good."

Désirée began to work the mixture into Aundrea's hair with her gloved fingers. Aundrea sighed. Simple human contact was the one thing she missed most during the pandemic. Being touched was like heaven, even if it wasn't skin-to-skin.

"I'm going to tell Barbara she doesn't know you as well as she thinks she does," Désirée said. "She tried to convince me you never talk while you're in the chair. She says you like to get in, get done, and get out. Are you that way about everything?"

"Only the necessary evils," Aundrea said, settling into the shampoo chair. As she rested the back of her neck on the lip of the basin, she felt her professional façade begin to fade away. Instead of playing her cards close to the vest like she did when she was at work, she wanted to display them for all the world to see. "If it's something I *want* to do instead of something I *have* to do, I like to savor every moment. If not, then I just want to get it over with."

"In that case," Désirée said, turning on the water, "should I speed up or slow down?"

Was it just Aundrea's imagination, or did every question Désirée asked sound like a double entendre? "I'll leave that up to you."

❖

Aundrea usually kept her eyes closed while she was getting her hair done. She didn't know where to look, otherwise. There was only so much to look at in the salon, and she considered it impolite to stare.

"You're not falling asleep on me, are you?" Désirée rinsed the suds out of Aundrea's hair for the third time, then squeezed another dollop of shampoo into the palm of her hand.

Aundrea lifted her lids and was treated to a glimpse of Désirée's breasts, which hovered tantalizingly close as she leaned to lather her up again. Aundrea wanted to bury her face between them, wet them with her tongue, take them into her mouth and hear Désirée moan with pleasure. "Hardly," she said, trying to regain focus.

Désirée smiled down at her. "Just checking."

Tired of playing games, Aundrea came out with it. "Is all this leading somewhere?"

Désirée's smile broadened. "I certainly hope so."

While she waited for the conditioner to soak in, Aundrea imagined attending company gatherings with Désirée on her arm, introducing her to her colleagues at industry functions. She had begun to contemplate what her family would say about her dating a younger woman when she stopped and scolded herself for jumping the gun.

"Hold up," she told herself, "your name isn't Stella, and Terry McMillan isn't plotting the details of your life. Just because she seems to have an interest in you doesn't mean you should start planning the best time to back the moving van up to her apartment."

Across the room, Désirée was bent over in front of the full-length mirror. Olive material collected at her feet in a growing pool as she slowly unraveled the intricate head wrap. Anxious to see what kind of hairstyle was hidden under there—trendy, simple, or sophisticated—Aundrea lifted her head for a better view.

Désirée straightened with a tired sigh and tossed her hair over her shoulders. It fell in a wavy cascade that ended midway down her back. As she combed through it with her fingers, she spotted Aundrea watching her again.

"I see you, Becky with the good hair," Aundrea said.

Désirée flashed a playful smile, acknowledging that she was all too familiar with the nickname for people with the kind of hair that didn't have to be permed or pressed into submission.

After she put her face shield back on, Désirée rinsed the

conditioner out of Aundrea's hair and squeezed the excess water from it with both hands. "Okay," she said, indicating Aundrea could move to the styling chair. She raked through Aundrea's hair with the regular comb, then snapped the comb attachment onto the blow dryer.

The hair dryer provided more body and curl, but unless it was a special occasion, Aundrea didn't have the time or patience to spend two hours roasting underneath it while she waited for her hair to dry. The handheld version took only a fraction of that time to get the job done.

When Aundrea's hair was nearly dry, Désirée parted it in several places and applied grease to her scalp. Then she picked up the blow dryer again, drying Aundrea's hair and moisturizing it at the same time. When that was done, she parted Aundrea's hair on one side and reached for the flat iron.

Aundrea had a conservative, low-maintenance hairstyle. She slept in a silk head wrap to protect her edges, woke up, combed her hair, and went to work. Easy peasy.

"We seem to have hit a lull in our conversation," Désirée said, nearly finished.

"I was giving you some space. I thought you were back there trying to decide what you want to be when you grow up. A political pundit, perhaps? If there isn't a current time slot available on cable TV, I'm sure there will be as soon as another anchor gets caught up in a scandal of their own making."

"I love arguing, especially when I know I'm right. Getting paid for it would be a bonus. On the other hand, though I love the idea of the political process, I'm not fond of either the players or the game."

"A banker, then," Aundrea suggested. The cynical part of her wondered if Désirée was being so flirtatious because she was angling for a job.

"No, thanks. The entry-level positions at most financial institutions don't pay enough to live on, and I don't want to go broke while I'm trying to work my way up the corporate ladder." Désirée reached for the setting spray. Aundrea closed her eyes while the fumes swirled around her head. "I'll be starting law school at the University of Virginia in the fall. I have a few more years to decide what I want to do after I pass the bar."

"You don't sound very excited about it."

Désirée shrugged. "When I applied to UVa, I tried to be realistic about my chances of getting accepted. Now that I'm in, I almost don't want to go. Not when I might have found a reason to stay."

Aundrea couldn't ignore her body's reaction when Désirée gazed deeply into her eyes. She couldn't deny wishing the words Désirée had uttered were true. Despite that, she was a realist, not a hopeless romantic. "Aren't you being a bit presumptuous?"

"Presumptuous? Perhaps, but I prefer prescient." Désirée removed Aundrea's protective smock with a flourish.

Aundrea's fingers trembled as she reached for her collar. She felt unsteady. No surprise, given how thoroughly Désirée was sweeping her off her feet.

"Stop." Désirée playfully swatted at Aundrea's hands. "That's my job." She unfurled Aundrea's collar and pressed out the wrinkles with her hands. "There you go. All done."

"Thank you." Aundrea slipped on her jacket and handed Désirée a hundred-dollar bill. When Désirée headed to the register to make change, Aundrea pulled a business card out of her pocket, wrapped a fifty around it, and dropped it into Désirée's tip jar.

Digital tablet in tow, Désirée returned with the change. "Same time next month?"

Aundrea, who had been too busy over the years to think of LTR as anything other than an initialism that didn't apply to her—like NRA or GOP—began to grow more comfortable with the idea. Maybe a long-term relationship wasn't a pipe dream after all. "Actually, I was hoping for something a bit sooner."

Désirée looked at the available dates on the appointment app on the tablet in her hands. "How soon?"

"Do you have plans this weekend?"

It took Désirée a moment to realize Aundrea meant personally, not professionally. When she did, her smile was the most dazzling she had flashed all night. "As a matter of fact, I don't."

"Have you ever been to New Hampshire?"

"No, I haven't."

Aundrea stepped out of her comfort zone and moved closer to Désirée. "Would you like to go?"

"If that's where you're going to be, yes, I'd love to."

The words were whispered. Like she and Aundrea were exchanging sweet nothings across a shared pillow.

Okay, so maybe exacting revenge on Chad wasn't such a good idea after all. The next time Aundrea saw him, she might have to thank him instead. She pointed to the tip jar. "I left you my number. Give me a call, and I'll fill you in on the details."

"Is there anything I need to pack?"

"Just your imagination and a sense of adventure. Everything else is optional."

"Clothing, too?"

This time, Désirée's smile was wicked, and Aundrea was suitably tempted. "Especially that."

"Sounds like the perfect long weekend."

And tonight felt like the beginning of a shared journey meant to last much longer than that.

ART APPRECIATION

La Toya Hankins

Hankins resides in Durham, NC. Her work includes novels *SBF Seeking, K-Rho: The Sweet Taste of Sisterhood*, and various short stories. She is working on her third novel, exploring the relationship between mothers and daughters. Readers can savor her blog *Pate and Caviar: Memories of a Flavorful Childhood* at www.latoyahankins.com.

"Can you believe she said, 'You know you look different wearing clothes?' Who does that?" Alana leaned against the kitchen counter and considered the unusual start to her day. She sipped her morning ritual of ginger tea with vanilla cream and waited for a suitable reply to her musing.

"That does sound strange. But like I said when you told me—all after the fact, I might add—about posing nude for a bunch of strangers, that kind of behavior would lead to some wild situations." Fatima's eyes remained focused on her textbook. "In all the years we've been friends, I never would have figured that would be your kind of thing. Hell, I really can't think of anyone in our circle who would get down like that. Wait, maybe Claudette, but not you."

"What do you mean, that didn't seem like it would be my thing?" Alana sat down across from her fellow graduate student. "I did it because it paid seventy-five dollars a session, and we both know finances were tight last semester. I had to do something to supplement."

Fatima looked up at Alana. Her eyes transmitted her struggle to express herself tactfully. "I'm not knocking you for doing what you needed to do." She paused and shifted her size 6 bottom in the wooden chair. "It's just that I have trouble imagining you, of all people, being a nude figure drawing model. You just don't seem like the type."

You of all people.

Alana was overweight. Some would say she was shapely, voluptuous, or thick. For others, the terms included morbidly obese, fat, or healthy but not in the right way. She had heard all the words. From her ten-pound, six-ounce arrival to the present, she had always been a "chunky monkey," her grandfather's pet name for her. She grew up in a family where love meant second helpings, and brownies treated boo-boos. While her family saw nothing wrong with an elementary school student weighing in the triple digits, the outside world had other thoughts.

She ingested society's view that her size marked her as undesirable and throughout her adolescence struggled to emulate the self-acceptance displayed by her similar-sized sisters and aunts. She grew comfortable with people seeing only her size instead of her. Alana had her circle of friends who heralded her as "the smart one" or "the funny one." She knew her girth blocked her designation as "the pretty one."

Alana's attitude toward her body began changing when she attended college. It wasn't a single event that sparked her awakening. Instead, it was enrolling in a women's studies class that examined how views of women's body shapes often minimized accomplishments. She became friends with a self-described "fluffy femme" who served as president for the university's chemistry club and found herself in a circle of friends who didn't let their clothing size define them.

Slowly, Alana began to realize she had to let go of the idea that her full figure was flawed. She started small. First, it was sleeveless shirts and shorts in the summer. Then it was shopping trips where she allowed her lover to buy her outfits that hugged her curves like a kindergartener clutching a parent on the first day of school. The shapewear she used to torture herself began making fewer and fewer appearances as part of her daily wardrobe.

Alana began claiming her curves as a way of capturing her power. She even worked up the nerve to embrace her lesbian identity in her junior year. She left college with a newfound appreciation of her abundance.

She carried that confidence with her when she moved to Delaware to pursue her graduate chemistry degree. Still, with all her newfound body appreciation, the flyer asking for art models challenged her. It was one thing not to swathe herself with fabric when she moved around campus, but was she ready to reveal all? She wanted to lay bare her insecurities, yet she questioned if this was the best way.

Each week Alana gazed at the ad. The forty words seemed to offer an opening to advance her journey toward self-love. But even after she walked into the art office and signed up for a class, she wasn't sure she could do it. The day before her first assignment, she arrived thirty minutes early and walked up and down the hall. Each step away from the door felt like retreating into her old mindset of shame.

She bore no false hopes that shedding her clothes would rid herself of all the bad memories of feeling less-than because she was plus-size. Still, the feeling that washed over her during that first class defied words. The tension constricting her lungs evaporated, allowing her to inhale with satisfaction of the choice she made.

Alana's decision to take her clothes off elevated her to an almost transcendent level. She floated above her body and looked down on a woman unashamed of her coffee-colored curvy landscape. Shedding her clothes, she'd freed herself from the shackles of not being seen as a woman because of a few extra pounds.

Because she was nude, she couldn't use her sense of humor or intelligence to hide behind or distract others from her proportions. Honestly, she was still processing the experience. Alana knew if she had to do it over again, she would. She just doubted if someone who had never struggled with how society viewed plus-size women would fully understand.

"I guess we all have our reasons for doing what we do. But regardless, the fact this chick recognized me after all this time just caught me off guard." Alana selected a banana from the bowl on the table.

"You didn't think after being buck-ball naked for about three months, people would remember your face to be able to say, 'Hey, how are you doing?' if they saw you on the yard?" Fatima looked doubtful.

"Honestly, no. I would go in after the teacher called the class to order and then go directly behind a screen to take off my clothes. The teacher explained what the class would be working on that day while I changed. I came out when the teacher finished giving instructions, dropped my robe, and assumed the position. I posed for about fifteen minutes at a time with a five-minute break in between. I would sit there thinking about things like what I needed to work on for my classes, what I needed to get from the store, or I just zoned out and listened to the music the professor played. When the timer went off, I would get up, get dressed, and leave before he dismissed the class for the day."

"Sounds like a good escape. I would love to get a job where I can sit on my ass and get paid. Only, wearing clothes." Fatima sat back in her chair and tilted her head. "But again, weren't you scared you were going to run into anyone outside of class? I mean, the campus is big, but I don't think it's that big."

Alana threw her banana peel in the trash. "You have a point, but the only people taking the class were declared art majors, all of them undergraduates. Typically, the paths of undergrad art majors and master's level chemistry students don't cross, so I figured my secret would be safe."

"Well, at least one person didn't get that memo. So, tell me again what happened this morning."

Alana's raspberry-tinted lips parted into a gap-toothed smile. "I'm standing at the elevator in Austin Hall, wondering why I agreed to teach an intro chemistry class first thing in the morning. Anyway, this girl with platinum hair comes up and stands beside me. She was about your height, dark-skinned, nose piercing, and she had some weight to her. She was giving me this whole Storm vibe. I'm talking from the comics, not the movies."

"Yeah, yeah, I get it. So, the two of you are standing there."
Fatima's expression encouraged Alana to get to the good part.

"She looks at me for a minute, then asks if I had any classes
in the art building last year. I told her no, but I did pose for a figure
drawing class. She replies, 'I thought you looked familiar.' Then she
hits me with the line about me looking different with my clothes on."

"Now, that's something I have never heard. Points for creativity."
Fatima snorted.

"It does sound odd, but she sounded like she was startled to see
me, but in a good way."

"What did you say?" Fatima closed her book and leaned forward.

"The elevator doors opened at that moment. I got in and asked,
'Which way do you think looks better, with or without?' My words
jooked her so bad she couldn't think of an answer or move to get on
the elevator. I pressed the button and left her standing there." Alana
chuckled.

"I have to give it to her that she managed to remember you
from last year. Hell, I've gone on dates with dudes who struggled to
remember my name after spending three hours with me when I've run
into them two weeks later."

"Hence the reason I like ladies. We tend to have better memories.
On that note, I will let you get back to your reading. I'm going to my
room to start grading the tests from this morning's class."

"Cool, it's time for me to head back to campus anyway. I have
a meeting with the chair of my department in thirty minutes. Check
you later."

Alana walked across the slate-colored carpet to her bedroom,
intending to put the morning's encounter out of her mind. Still, her
mind kept pivoting back. Her decision to pose was in order to move
her along the path toward acceptance of her body. She certainly didn't
expect to have a stranger come up to her and make an odd comment
first thing in the morning almost a year later.

Two hours later, Alana's grumbling stomach alerted her to take
a break from her academic endeavors. The cupboard and fridge were
close to bare, and she didn't have time to order delivery. There was
a new coffee shop within walking distance of her afternoon seminar

that offered an eclectic vegetarian menu and a waitress that was a dreadlocked vision of perfection. Alana figured she would savor some soup and a sandwich, do some people watching, and be in her seat in time for her afternoon class. She grabbed her keys, her hat, and her coat and headed back into the winter weather.

Well, this is a surprise, she thought moments after crossing the restaurant's threshold. The platinum-haired African American woman who'd mentioned the difference in her clothing that morning sat solo at a table inches from the entrance, focused on a sketchbook in front of her. Alana considered just passing her to avoid breaking her concentration. Then her curiosity kicked in.

"So, you never answered my question. Which one do you like better?"

The woman's head jerked up and she met Alana's teasing glance with surprise. Alana recognized the effect of her interruption and cursed inwardly for potentially creating an awkward situation. Then a slight smile crested the woman's face.

"I guess both of them are beautiful." She paused. "Listen, I'm sorry if I offended you this morning. Sometimes my mouth moves faster than my sense of appropriateness."

"No worries. It was a high point of my day. I'm Alana, by the way."

"I'm Rome, like the city." She gestured for Alana to take a seat. "My parents met in Italy. My mom was part of a college exchange program. My dad was stationed there in the Air Force. When I was born, they decided to name me after where they met."

"Well, I think Rome is a cute name. Anyway, I'll let you get back to enjoying your lunch. I just popped in to get a bite before my four o'clock class."

Rome placed her hand over Alana's, then quickly retracted it after a curious look from Alana. "I feel so bad about being an ass this morning. I realize I sounded inappropriate, and I want to make it up to you. Allow me to buy lunch."

Alana thought the gesture was a little excessive, but far be it from her to turn down a free meal. She lowered herself into the cushioned seat and shrugged off her coat. The grip of the chair felt familiar. Since the class, she decided to view tight fits as hugs, not hindrances.

For a second, she questioned her casual attire then realized, *What's the point? She's seen me naked.*

Rome flagged down a waitress to bring the table a menu, but Alana was already a step ahead. She rattled off her order from memory. She questioned the look on Rome's face but shrugged off any possible negative connotations. A bossa nova song Alana recognized played in the background as they made light conversation about their respective majors and hometowns.

"So how does an art history major end up in the science building this morning?"

"My neighbor and I carpool to campus, and he grabbed the wrong backpack when he got out of the car." Rome took a sip from her mug. "I agreed to meet him in the lobby by the elevator so we could switch. He was on his way down when I saw you this morning, hence my reason for not getting into the elevator. I always wanted to say something to you last year but never worked up the nerve. When I saw you this morning, I took it as a sign. I admit it sounded different out loud than in my mind. You would have thought after months of thinking about what I would say if I had the chance, I would have had a better way of putting my thoughts out there."

"It's fine. It did catch me off guard, but I wasn't offended." Alana acknowledged the waitress bringing the food. "Oh, this looks yummy. You'll have to try their gumbo. It's not as good as my Ya-Ya's, but it will do in a pitch."

In the past, Alana had avoided eating in front of strangers. She always felt people judged her portion size. But sitting with Rome was different. They chatted and chewed like old pals instead of women who'd only shared a brief conversation hours earlier.

Good food and good conversation. Alana took a sip of iced tea. *I like this feeling. It's good to not focus on what everyone around you is thinking about you. It's nice to focus on what you're thinking about the person in front of you.*

"Did you ever see any of the drawings from the class?" Rome asked between bites of her chicken salad wrap.

Alana shook her head. The thought of seeing how she looked in charcoal never crossed her mind, but hearing Rome's query had her curious.

"Then you're in luck. My workspace is around the corner, and I would love for you to check out my sketches," Rome said. "I have to warn you, it's a little crowded and messy."

Alana checked her watch. She still had an hour, and the professor was usually late. Why not?

"I would like that. I'm ready if you are."

Rome radiated in response to Alana's acceptance. She reached into her pocket and pulled out her card to pay the bill. Alana insisted on leaving a tip, and within fifteen minutes, they headed to Bearden Hall.

"I hope you don't think it's weird I have your pictures on my wall. I keep them up there for inspiration." Rome stood self-consciously beside the framed renditions of Alana's naked form.

The studio resembled a broom closet with a large desk and two metal chairs. A flicker of self-consciousness sparked within Alana about how much space she occupied. Then it flamed out as she basked in Rome's aura of pride.

"Until you, all the female models were just a collection of right angles, nothing inspiring. They all seemed to blend, with only their hair color changing. Then you showed up. It was like going from being offered chicken nuggets to coq au vin."

Alana looked sideways at Rome.

She stammered out a better explanation. "Most of the other models we had didn't look like you or me. Nothing is wrong with being thin, but I appreciate women who look like women, not girls. I'm talking women who carry the power of the world in their hips. When you showed up, you challenged me to take my art to the next level. I didn't get a chance to follow up with you until today, so now that I have the chance, I would like to say thank you."

Alana fell silent, amazed at how with just a few lines and shading, Rome had managed to capture so much of her. The passages of the drawings seemed to chart her initial reluctance by showing her nude form to the full-frontal display of her bountiful beauty.

"I am speechless. If I didn't know this was me, I would have thought it was someone else, if that makes sense." Alana couldn't stop smiling. In the back of her mind, all the taunts and stares withered away as she basked in the beauty of her body, depicted as classic art.

"Thank you. I always say the artist is only as good as her inspiration. You were a great muse last year. I saw your form as very Rubenesque but updated for our times. The way you carry yourself with such power and grace made me proud to be a woman. You radiated confidence, and frankly, it made me step my game up when it came to my work. I mean, it takes ovaries to pose with no clothes on in front of people, and you did that."

Yes, I did, Alana thought. *Yes, I did.*

They stood shoulder to shoulder, silently admiring Alana's naked form.

"You know, I would love to sketch you again…that is, if you have the time," Rome said. "I know my space isn't as polished as the art building, and I can't pay you, but it would be a great honor for me."

Alana considered the request. She'd decided to pursue becoming an art model to assert her feeling of comfort with her size. Through a chance encounter, she had connected with someone who confirmed that her satisfaction with her size resonated with them and made them challenge themselves to do better. It would seem taking her clothes off was a good idea.

"Rome, I think we can work out a schedule because I like what you've done, and I'd love to see what you can do. But so you know, the nude thing was part of a journey I was on last year that I don't foresee traveling again anytime soon. Any posing will be with clothes on."

Rome's face lit up. "I have no problem with that. Just because I said you look different with your clothes on doesn't mean I see you as anything less than stunning. We can start tonight, if you like."

Alana declined the offer. One could only take so much art appreciation on a wintery Wednesday.

LAST CALL FOR LOVERS:
AN EXCERPT FROM LIGHT UNDER THE STAIRS

Akil Wingate

Akil Wingate is a BBC Writers Room–shortlisted writer, filmmaker, and explorer currently based in Paris. His literary work has been serialized and published on platforms and publications that include *Crave*, *Graze*, *Devilfish Review*, *Afro Myths Volume 2*, *Starset Society*, *Travel Mag*, *Savvy Explorer*, *Writers Weekly*, and *Writing Tomorrow*. He currently presents the game show *Live Casino Show* for Channel 5 UK and the innovation series *EHLLO TV* for Euler Hermes. His latest documentary *The Write Room* has been officially selected by The Lift Off Sessions Festival for screening at Pinewood Studios in London.

Light is oddly like a dancer flitting in and out of the nooks and crannies where shadows nestle, spinning them round, dipping them, then leaving them to perish all by their lonesome on the periphery of the dance floor. Light moves in its own swim. Sometimes monochrome waves. Sometimes tidal waves of rainbow backstroking through the sleepy parts of the house. Waking up every snoring corner. Drowning every lumbering squeaky door to open and close and rolling fearlessly down every creaking star. Light is a dancer.

I sit at the other end of the breakfast table. Solomon is casually lying at my feet. Jason is buried behind the black and white print of the *New York Times*. "I don't read that toilet paper called the *Washington Post*," he once told me. I think it was nothing to do with the political drivel pouring from its pages on the conservative bent. No. I think he's always been in love with the idea of tenure at NYU or Columbia. Some university in the heart and soul of the big bright city. Maybe it's my fault we never took that step toward a brownstone in Brooklyn. A flat in Queens. New York is overwhelming. We both agree on that front.

The newspaper trembles and his boyish laughter comes sailing through its pages. Solomon snorts, clearly unimpressed. I stab at my eggs, force myself to eat. Force myself to scrounge down another bite. But sometimes eating is a chore. Eating is a routine…I tend to rebel against routine. But I'm ramming down scrambled eggs, pushing my toast from one edge of the plate to the other with my fork.

He giggles again and the newspaper flaps and rolls and vibrates in his hands. I look up and the light coming in through the dining room windows is dancing around the room.

There is a small jar of jam. Just to my right. Strawberry jam with no sugar added. Just what the doctor ordered. I have my fits, days when I crave savory items and days when my mouth waters for sweet. This recent spate of days sees me wavering between the two. Sometimes even mixing the two at once. Dark chocolate with sea salt. Roast chicken seasoned with lemon and black pepper and cayenne and dribblings of raspberry. Fromage blanc with muesli and banana and avocado. All swirled together.

So I spread the jam across the toast. It crunches when my knife smooths it out. I lick my finger. There, where a dollop of jam leapfrogged the knife and stuck there.

"Mmm," I remark.

"Tastes good?" Jason asks from behind the curtain of the newspaper.

"Yes."

He cackles with gleeful laughter, head buried farther down into the dunes and black and white sandstorms and dust devils of his newspaper. Then just like that he looks up and out over the horizon of the *New York Times* and says, "What do you think of settling down?"

"Settling down in what sense, amore mio? Are you telling me to behave myself?" I ask.

"No. But you probably should behave…" He smirks. I smirk back. His eyes twinkle. The corners of his mouth are watery. He's salivating, almost. Something on the tip of his tongue has gotten him an appetite. "I mean to say, what do you think about making it official… You and me?"

"Are you asking my opinion?"

"Sort of."

"Well, if you're asking my opinion, I love the idea of settling down, as it were. And making it official is what I dream of doing…"

"Okay," he says. Then the wings of the newspaper outstretch again, covering his face in the feathery down of black and white print. Scandals with the American president. Waves of populism undulating across Europe. Tennis star berating a line judge. Et cetera, et cetera, and blah blah blah.

"Okay?" I say and let my fork fall onto the plate with a hard clank. "Okay, mister?"

He chuckles. "I'll keep you informed."

"You cheeky—"

"Language," he says.

I can see him smiling behind the veil of the newspaper. I don't actually see him smiling. But I can visualize him smiling behind the newspaper. Pleased with the epic tease he just put me through, I feel myself getting hot. Flush. But it's not for lack of eating. It's the idea that he and I might finally take this thing we have together to the next level. I suppose that means growing up. If we ever have.

"Don't make me put a spell on you," I say.

He drops the newspaper. "You can do that?" he asks.

I chuckle to myself, sensing the dark curiosity rising in him. "Don't test me," I say quietly, amusedly.

He lifts his newspaper, then slyly says under his breath, "Where's Dorothy when you need a house to fall out of the sky?" He laughs.

"What?"

"Nothing, my love. Finish your breakfast. You'll need your strength for later," he says, holding back laughter.

❖

Sundays are like hymns waiting to be sung. Waiting to be plumbed from the depths of your soul and bellowed out into the waking world. They come slowly. Sometimes jubilantly. Sometimes like rivers that flow through dying wood, sweeping with them every last trace of debris and decay. Washing the forest floor clean of any dying residue. Preparing it for what comes next. Monday. A new week. Reflection. Awakening.

Sunday is like scrubbing down inside and out. Resting your batteries. Rejuvenating. Mindless entertainment. Distraction. Slow cookers. Thawing out. Exfoliating.

But for some reason, today I can't imagine any of those things. My fingertips smell like cigarettes. Like they have ruthlessly and mercilessly been burned to the nail by Marlboros with no filter. I bring them to my nose, and the smell is definitely a cigarette smell. But I don't smoke.

"Jason," I call. He's coloring into the lines of a coloring book. It keeps him Zen, he tells me. Choosing between sky blue and rose magenta crayons for the colors of a peacock's feathers is beyond my pay grade. But if he likes it, I love it.

"Yes, my love?" he says mockingly.

"Smell this." I pinch my fingers together. He stares at me with a look floating somewhere between bad boy and dark curiosity.

"What am I going to be smelling?" he asks tentatively.

"You tell me." I plop my fingers directly under his nose.

"You've been smoking?" he asks.

"No." I feel a wave of heat rush over me. Brush across my face and crawl down my back, disappearing somewhere into the chestnut floorboards beneath our feet. He looks at me with a question mark drawn between his eyes. He bites his lip. He does this when he's confused. When he's worried. And when he's horny. He might be all three at the moment. Sitting there in his shorts and tank top and slippers. He's ready for bed or for beach. But he can read me. He can read my expressions like I can read between the lines of the living and the dead. Some of our best and worst attributes rub off on our partners in a spiritual sort of frottage, imbuing them with the kinds of gifts and curses that we often take for granted.

"So, you're telling me you didn't pick up a smoking habit in your sleep?" He smiles. His jokes are second rate.

"No," I say. "I'm going to wash my hands."

He grabs my arm. "Wait." And he stands up to meet me eye to eye. The heat from his body is intense, like a sunburst exploding into the cosmos. But here it radiates against me. Envelops me, even. Then he kisses me. "I'm serious about settling down," he says softly.

And a cold chill ripples through me. I'm distracted. But I'm here. I'm present. I'm listening. Trying to hear him completely and read things around me at the same time.

"I am too," I say, looking deeply into his welling pools. Those boyish eyes. What color are they? Green and blue. I heard Bowie had one green eye and one blue eye. He holds me, gripping my arms firmly, pressing his heat deep into my linen shirt. The lines and muscles and contours of his body insinuate themselves against mine. Sharing secrets and bedtime stories that only our two anatomies would know.

"I love you," he whispers. Then he smothers me with another kiss.

"I love you sweetly," I whisper back. I'm transported between the soft wetness of his kiss and his strong, fiery embrace and something else in the back of my mind. Something I said I have to do. What is it? I can't remember suddenly.

Then he lets me go and I stand there staring blankly at him. I'm searching for something. Maybe a Sunday hymn. What am I supposed to be using this day for? What am I supposed to be getting ready for that's approaching? I can't honestly remember.

Then he says gently, "You gonna wash your hands?"

Ah yes! That's it. Brain fog burns off. Like his voice melts through that haze of questions. Slices through it and completely evaporates this amnesia that took hold of me. Why am I forgetful? "Yes," I say softly. Then I pad into the downstairs hallway bathroom.

Here it smells like rain in the wood. Like fresh sweet moss and wildflowers. Like bark. And like sage and vanilla. Everywhere you'll find sage and vanilla in this house. It's ever present. My choice. I'd put it in Jason's breakfast cereal if it were palatable.

Cold water. Then hot water. Scrubbing with industrial-strength soap. Then with sage soap. And then again. Scrubbing until I lose feeling in my fingertips. Scrubbing until I feel raw at my fingertips.

"That'll do," comes the voice. But it's not my voice. It's a voice, yes. It's a baritone voice piping through the mirror. I look up at myself in the reflection. My eyes look wild. My skin suddenly white. Pale. Ghostly. Almost translucent. My hair is wild, like branches from a dead tree sprawling outward. Stretching outward. Bereft of waves and green sprouts and fruit. No. Not quite dead yet. But skating on its edge. Have you ever seen someone slowly dying without them knowing they were dying? This is that look. My lips black with ash and maybe soot. My brittle nails yellowed like my wild eyes. Yellowed with some inner…some inside…How do I say it? Soiled or sanguine. I don't know.

"That'll do," he says. Then he wipes his wrinkled hand across his mouth, staring back into the mirror. Trembling. Smelling like strong, suffocating cigarette smoke and whiskey. But Japanese whiskey. Not some gas station behind-the-counter brand. Something special bottled in a dark black bottle and kept in a red silk bag. His hair falls across his face. Streaks of gray and black midnight intermingle. And he brushes it back with that trembling hand of his.

There's a knock at the door. He turns, switches off the faucet quickly. Smooths his hair back. Takes a deep breath. "That'll do," he whispers again.

"Geronimo?" Jason's voice comes swimming through the door. "You okay?"

I look down at my hands trembling under the faucet. Dry now. That cigarette smoke? It floats away. I look back at my reflection. No wild eyes. No wild hair or blackened lips and white skin.

"Who were you?" I ask quietly into the mirror, not expecting a response. So I don't get one.

"Yes. I'll be right out," I say to Jason through the door. But I'm staring back into the mirror. I'm trying to will him to come back. Willing the reflective glass to open that door again.

Think, Geronimo. What did you see in the mirror? Details.

He was wearing a dark shirt. Was it a T-shirt? Um, yes. Yes. A Grateful Dead T-shirt with a long list of concert dates printed down its face. Faded red and orange colors. He had on a necklace…made from…cowrie shells…and…what is it? A tattoo on the side of his neck. No, a scar. No. No. A tattoo. Cut and etched and inked deep into his skin like a scar. What is it? It has long wings and a tail, spiraling around the side of his neck. Something with scales. A mane. Fleshed out in green and red ink. Talons? A lion's head…Hooves? Ah yes. A chimera…

And there behind him. What did you see? Stalls. Empty urinals. Green dirty tiles on the wall. Posters. Band posters. A blacked-out window. Can you smell this place? Try. No…no…

Yes. It smells thick with piss and shit. Rife with cigarette smoke. And marijuana. And other things. Burned things. Chemical. Organic. Natural. Unnatural. Things that don't come back from a blaze. Things that when permeated by the frost or fire, never again are what they were before. Blood. I know that metallic smell. People have bled in these urinals. In this sink. Graffiti. Everywhere. Painted on. Sharpied on. Markers and spray paint. Phone numbers. Anarchy symbols. Fuck the police. Or fuck John. Or fuck me for a good time. A lot of fucking going on here. And more bleeding. From needles. From sex. From fighting. From bleeding out. Dying. No, not here? Yes. Yes. Oh yes here. Lots of bleeding out.

He'd touched the sink counter for a fleeting moment. What did it feel like? Brittle. Sticky. Rough with scrapes. Raised surfaces. From paint and graffiti and band stickers. Fluids. Substances. Vomit. Caked on the edge of the sink. Spit. Chewing gum that's turned hard like clay. And hot white light bulbs blazing overhead. But here everything is washed yellow in this strange green-tiled bathroom that reeks of piss and shit.

But him. His skin is so pale. So beyond white. Who were you? I ask again.

I pull away from the sink. His sink. I close my eyes, and I let the smell of the fresh wood wash over me. Sage and vanilla hug me. Take me in their soothing arms and caress me back to life. Massage the blood back into my joints and veins. Then I go.

I pad gently out into the hallway. The house is quiet. I can't even hear birds outside. Or ambulances roaring through Georgetown. It's serenely quiet, so I can hear drums pounding. Toms. Kick. Snare. Again. Toms. Kick. Snare. Pounding over and over again.

"That'll do. Can I have percussion now, please?" I hear his cigarette-washed baritone come careening through the thick swim of instruments tuning. Playing. Crackling over a sound system. Then bongos play. Rumble even. "Guitar now, please."

Then this wailing shred of guitar slices right down to the jugular. Plays with this line of shreds and runs that sound like fire. Feel like fire, even. "Okay, vocal mics."

Then the sound goes. Nothing more. No. Not really nothing more. Sunlight is spilling into the hallway. Leaping over my feet. And I place my hands along the wall to steady myself as I walk into the front living room. Solomon has moved to the front door.

"Where's your father?" I ask him. "Where's Daddy?" He barely lifts a brow. Grunts something. "Jason?" I call. But no answer comes pummeling back at me through the quiet and sunlight. "Where'd he go, boy?" I ask Solomon.

Then he leers up at me and he grumbles, "He went for a jog." Breath sizzling with fire and flame.

"Why are you so grumpy? Do you need to go for a walk so you can take a poo?" I ask.

He lifts his head. "I don't need to poo. We don't only pee, poo, and bark, you know."

"You fetch things too," I say.

"Now you're being provocative," he grumbles and lays his head back down.

"I knew I should have gotten a cat…" I say.

"Bring a cat around and see how that turns out for you," he says. Then he closes his eyes. Disappears behind those fleshy, wrinkled veils. And then snores some. So, he's gotten the last word this round. And he put an exclamation point on it with a grunt and a belch of snores.

I turn back toward the interior of the house. It's calling out to me from every nook and cranny. Poking at me. Telling me to look closer. Sundays are for cleaning. Yes. That's what it is telling me. Clean between the shelves in the study. Wash down the soft and hard surfaces in your office. Scrub the dishes, again, in the kitchen. Change all the sheets and bedding. Do a nice walk-through burning sage. Lighting candles. Open windows to let fresh air in. Stale air out.

Play Mahalia Jackson. Sarah Vaughan. Shirley Caesar. Albertina Walker. Aretha Franklin. Dinah Washington. Ella. Billie. Nina. Lena. Drink green tea. Let it sit in the sun on the front porch. Nibble dried Italian tomatoes. Rifle through old photos. Mom and Dad. Brother. Sister. Iron sheets. And shirts. And trousers. Steam suits and curtains and polish shoes. Steam-wash the hardwood floors. Vacuum the carpeted ones. Pull all the curtains open. Let sunlight pour in from every orifice. *Let it shine. Let it shine. Let it shiiiiiiiiiine.*

This house will be clean.

Opening doors and closing them. Opening bathroom doors and listening for cracks and squeaks. Office and study doors and checking for things that fall through the cracks. Front and back doors and lingering around for any stealthy scents that might have assumed I won't catch whiff of them. Upstairs doors and downstairs doors for things that go up or down, hiding in the dark. Closet doors. Looking for lost and found. Forgotten objects, things tucked away. Smelling the outside world on my favorite winter coat. A pea green wool Navy pea coat that falls all the way down to my knees. Running my hands down its coarse fabric. Feeling sensations tingle like sparks at my fingertips. Then I see the vision of Jason.

"You coming in or not?" Jason says. Peeling off his winter coat, a leather jacket. A motorcycle jacket, at that. Then his red Christmas sweater. His khakis. And boots. Socks. Then his boxers. Then he screams gleefully, dashing barefoot across the snow. Then dipping a toe into the hot spring. He looks back over his shoulder, up the dunes of crystalline white snow. Back through the line of pine trees and footprints to me on the cabin porch. Me cradling my thermos of Swiss Miss hot chocolate with marshmallows. The very same hot chocolate that my mother adores. Biting my lips hard against the brunt of the winter breezes. Sheltered like an Eskimo in my pea coat. And I don't say anything at first.

Solomon sidles up against me on the cabin porch. His warmth rejects the cold. Thumbs its nose at winter. Like he's saying to the seasons, "Don't you know what I am?"

"Come on!" Jason calls from the spring. He's up to his shoulders in bubbling hot water. Jets of steam shoot up around him.

"Okay," I say reluctantly. And I place the thermos down near

Solomon's head. "Not for you," I tell him. Then I peel off my pea coat, letting it fall onto the snow-dusted cabin porch. And off goes my black turtleneck, trousers, and all.

And the snow bites viciously into my bare feet. But I'm running. Tasting the steam mists as I get closer and closer to the spring. Pine needles smell fresh. Clean. The air is lashing out at me, trying to make me turn back. Scream for my warm clothes and hot chocolate. But I've got news for it. I'm not turning back. I'm plowing deeper and deeper into the snow. Nearly falling forward. Losing footing. Finding my balance. Feeling the cold and the heat battle for front seat in my invisible car. And then I jump right in. I go cannonballing right into the spring. Not even dipping a toe. Not even hesitating at its lip. Just launching right into its depths. Then right into Jason's arms. We go under. His hands are squeezing my buttocks. My lips are locked on his. We're exchanging breaths. His body is trembling against mine.

He's struggling to keep his eyes open underwater. But maybe it's ecstasy. Maybe it's heat. Maybe it's make believe. Something compels him to close them. And close them he does. And I'm holding him, feeling every ripple and undulating wave rise up through his body. Freeing him of every last remaining trace of cold. Every last touch of fear. And then I take his sex in my hands. Still never coming up for air. And his trembling instantly stops. And he opens his eyes. Underwater. We kiss. And again. And again.

"Your father's going to have questions…" Mama's voice cascades over the bubbles and steam. Carries itself fearlessly through the pine wood. Sails across the not so anonymous footprints and scattered bits of clothing in the snow. And it lands casually on our watery rooftop. Jason goes up for air.

"Hi, ma'am," he says.

Then I slowly float up to the surface. "Will he now?" I ask.

"He will," she says. She's standing there on the porch in a rose-colored T-shirt and leggings, her gray hair cut short in a small Afro looking like it's been dusted with snow. She's sipping from my thermos of Swiss Miss hot chocolate. And then she dips her fingers in it and bends down to Solomon. He ravenously licks from her fingers.

"That's mine, by the way," I say casually.

"Is she not cold?" Jason whispers to me.

"No," I whisper back. "Runs in the family."

"Except for you," he says.

"Skipped a generation."

"Stop talking about me like I can't hear you," she says. Her eyes burn bright even from this distance. Twisting in their sockets like spiraling shooting stars. "Anyway, dinner's ready." And she turns to go. "Come on, Solomon. I've got a nice steak for you." He growls with satisfaction and clicks across the porch with his humongous paws, following happily after her back into the cabin. "You don't need to see any of this tomfoolery, boy," she says, sliding the door behind her to a close.

"What tomfoolery?" I ask Jason.

"You and me…" He winks. "We're naked, in case you forgot."

"I didn't forget." And I pull him back underwater.

I pull away from my pea coat in the closet. Then I spy my father's vintage trench coat. I procured it. Okay, I stole it from his closet. He can't wear it anyway. It's one too many sizes small for him. Hovering around in the days of his roaring twenties. I touch its sleeve. It feels smooth. Waxen. Warm. Smells like cinnamon and black licorice.

"I bought that in Poughkeepsie," Dad says, swilling a glass of pinot and leaning back into his recliner in his study.

"I love it," I say, slipping into its sleeves. It falls across my body perfectly. "Looks like I'm just right."

"Don't get any ideas," he says.

"No. Just checking out the merchandise," I say back.

He places his glass down and then he licks a finger. Thumbs through some pages in a book.

"What are you reading?"

"Teaching of James," he says.

"Brother of Jesus."

"The one and only."

I sit down in front of the fireplace. It's crackling occasionally.

Belching out small sparks and flakes of ash that float down to the floor. I'm staring into the flames, watching them turn over like waves in the ocean. Watching them rise and fall.

"What do you see?" he asks.

I look back up at him, sitting there at his desk, book on his lap, glasses at the edge of his nose. And me seated cross-legged on the floor like I was a little boy so many ages ago at my father's feet while he worked.

"Ghosts," I say. "So many ghosts."

He chuckles to himself. "We all do, son." He takes a strong sip. Then he breathes. "Some of us choose to ignore them."

I look away. Then I can't compel myself to continue looking into the fire. I get to my feet, still wrapped in my father's trench coat. And I reach over him, taking his glass. Then I sip.

"Good, isn't it?" he asks.

"Yeah."

"Your mother and I bought a case of it when we were in Aix-en-Provence."

I nod. I remember that trip. Evenings with pasta and spritzer. Or fish and Riesling. Or bourguignon and any sort of gentle red. Lots of baguettes. Day and night. Visits to countryside restaurants and village shops and horse stables. Long walks to clear your head. Phone calls with the grandkids. Sometimes video calls when the time permitted. Lots of cheeses. Driving slightly inebriated. Wearing sandals or loafers and shorts and T-shirts with a pullover draped over our shoulders. That summer was magical...

"I remember," I say. Then I place the glass back down on his desk.

Then I pull away from the trench coat. I rub my fingers together and smell them. I can still smell the cinnamon. I can still smell the pinot. I can even hear the fireplace.

"You hate snow and the cabin," Solomon growls from the hallway.

"I love that cabin," I say wistfully.

"Then you should visit them more," he says.

"Go back to sleep," I say.

I run my fingers across Adidas jackets, bomber jackets, more trench coats, wool coats, big coats, slim coats, leather jackets. Then I stop at Jason's motorcycle jacket. His favorite. A Harley-Davidson motorcycle jacket he bought when he was living in Gangneung, South Korea, teaching English to young Korean kids. He was late twenties at the time, struggling with his Hangul and jumping from one continent to the next during each of his paid vacations. The leather is smooth. Sublime. Ageless. Timeless. Unaffected by anything the elements throw at it. It smells like him. Humid citrusy cologne. Balmy deodorant. Unassumingly fresh aftershave. Bread crumbs. Strong Italian coffee. Probably Lavazza or Illy. Shampoo. I run my fingers down the sleeve. Across the breast pocket. Down the zipper. Closing my eyes, hearing his laughter fill the house. Then down to his right pocket. My hand stops there. I hear his laughter again. Filling my space. Filling my head.

"Stop laughing," I say out loud. Laughing myself.

But his laughter is joyful. Contagious. Sexy. And I hear it pour over everything like sweet honey. Like thick maple syrup.

"Another?" he asks.

"Sure," comes the other voice. Male. Younger. Lighter. Full of spice.

I hear glasses clink.

"Congratulations on the thesis," Jason says.

I close my eyes. I can see a flash of dim orange lamps and chandeliers. A bar made in the fashion of a French brasserie is busy with punters. Tables, nicely appointed with their own lamps and candles, are weighed down with platters and entrees. Businessmen and women. Couples. Families. Casual to well-dressed.

Then I see Jason pouring from a bottle of pinot into another glass. He's wearing a black pullover...No. That's my black turtleneck he's wearing. And his motorcycle jacket is hung simply on the back of his chair. He hands the glass over to his guest. Their hands briefly touch when passing the glass from one to the other. His guest's hand is smooth. Young. Gentle. Not rough. Not exposed to the rigors of manual labor. Manicured. And he pulls the glass up to his perky lips. He sips. His eyes are bright. Enthusiastic. Beaming with a rare sort of giddy youth that we all eventually lose after a certain age. And I can immediately tell that he hasn't yet reached that certain age.

"Thank you," he says. "Mmm, this is good."

"Pinot," Jason says.

"So the thesis was really tough to get through…But I'm glad you didn't let me quit."

"I'm glad you didn't quit either." Jason smiles back at the kid. Then he looks at his watch. "Sorry, I've gotta dine and dash," he says.

"You can't stay a little longer?"

"No, I gotta get home. G will be worried."

"Ball and chain?" he asks.

Jason doesn't answer. Instead he gives him a smirk, a knowing look that says, *I know what you are trying to do.* Instead he puts down a few bills on the table and gets to his feet.

"Finish the bottle. But take a taxi home…See you in class on Monday."

"See you," the kid says. Almost moping with dejection. And Jason goes.

I pull back from the motorcycle jacket. But something is there in the pocket. I know it. I can feel it. I reach inside. A crumpled-up piece of paper. A receipt. La Croix Restaurant. Of course, I know it. Not far from the National Gallery. Sort of fancy. But more of a stomping ground for political hacks and lobbyists and journalists and even some of the symphony and theatre set near the Capitol building. Not the kind of setting for extreme luxury or romantic window dressing. And families with kids won't find chicken nuggets, fries, or coloring books on the menu.

One bottle of pinot is forty-six dollars. Rip-off.

I turn the receipt over. It reads, "Eric. 202-555-1278." I slip the receipt back into the pocket. I can see Eric's face. Lonely, handsome grad student. Sits in the third row of the auditorium lectures. Takes notes on his laptop or tablet. Sometimes rides a Vespa around campus. Plays tennis and swims. Likes Kylie Minogue. Not Madonna. Thinks tanning beds are both overrated and overpriced.

Suddenly the doorbell rings. I turn around, jolted from my visual eavesdropping. I quickly pad to the front door. I open it to a man, forties, pouch, gray-black mustache. Yankees cap and a light jacket. He has his big bear paw of a hand on the shoulder of a boy. Young teens. His son, I imagine. The son's eyes are cast downward. His hands are in his pockets. He's wearing shorts and Chuck Taylors. A Green Lantern T-shirt. And his shoulder-length hair falls across his forehead.

"Are you Mr. Geronimo?" the father asks.

"Geronimo," I say. "It's my first name."

"Okay. I'm Richard and this is my son Christian."

"Nice to meet you." I take Richard's hand, shaking it firmly. He's nervous. Hiding something. But before I can read deeply into what that something is, he pulls his hand back.

"What can I do for you, Richard?" I ask. Solomon comes along clicking. The boy, Christian, lights up at the sight of the dog. Smiles. Solomon looks up at the boy. Studies him.

"He...we, have a problem. I was told you can fix this kind of thing."

I stand there silently. I look back to the boy. He's transfixed by Solomon. I don't know what he sees. Sometimes kids just love dogs. Sometimes kids just love big awkward Solomon. And then sometimes kids see what I see. And they can't hold still.

"Well, why don't you come inside and tell me all about... your problem," I say. And I step aside to let them in. The boy pets Solomon's head as he passes by him. Then I close the door and I stand there. Opening front doors and back doors. Trying to catch a whiff of scents that don't expect me to linger. Don't expect me to sniff them out and see what hides. What lurks beneath.

So I hover there by the front door for a moment. And then it comes blasting by. Very quickly. But slow enough for me to catch it try and sneak by. Cigarettes. Strong suffocating cigarettes with no filter. *I know you.*

I turn back to the father and son. Smile so as not to betray my sense of worry. Then say, "Can I get you anything to drink?"

"No thanks for me," Richard says. Then he taps his son's shoulder. It's not a violent tap. But it's not a gentle tap either. It's the kind of tap that says, "What did we talk about in the car?"

And the son looks up and says with a small voice, "Orange juice?"

I smile back at him. His voice is musical, like a boy soprano that hasn't yet transitioned fully into his puberty. "Orange juice it is," I say. "Why don't you make yourselves at home in my office there." I nod toward the two big sliding parlor doors that open into the office. I push gently past them and slide the doors open. Solomon pads past me into the office. It's as if he's given a signal to the boy that everything will be okay. And the boy follows after him. Then his father slowly goes in.

"I'll be right back with that orange juice," I say. Then I quickly pad to the kitchen. I'm doing it unconsciously. Rubbing my fingertips together and smelling them for cigarettes. But there are none. This smell is imprinted somewhere on my brain. Burned somewhere into my retina. It left its dirty fingerprints on my spotless bathroom mirror. And this house will be clean.

I open the refrigerator and pull out a carton of orange juice. Then I think for a moment. I grab a tray and three glasses, and I pour for each of us. Even if only the boy asked.

I hear the front door open. Then close. Almost slamming closed.

"Babe," Jason calls loudly from the front door. He's probably swimming in his own musical fog with his earphones plugged deep into his ears, listening to Miles or Coltrane or NPR at 100 million decibels. "Babe," he calls loudly again. And I can hear him peeling off his running shoes and letting them plop down with two thumps by the front door.

I quickly head to the lobby with a tray and glasses filled to the brim in hand.

"For me?" he asks.

"For our guests," I say.

"Guests?" he says loudly, still speaking over the din of the music in his ears.

I mimic pulling out his earphones, and he does.

"What guests?" he says softly, sweat pouring down the front of his tank top.

"In my office." I hand him the tray. "Why don't you take this in to them and you can treat yourself to one of these glasses."

He kisses me as he takes the tray from my hands. Then he slides the parlor doors open with his butt. "Effective," I mumble. And I watch him go in to the boy and his father. Solomon's lying at the boy's feet. "Everything is fine here," I tell myself. And I pad back into the kitchen. I really wanted a glass of orange juice. So I pour one more for me. But I don't go just yet. I'm standing there in the kitchen, holding the cold glass in my hand. Letting the sunlight dripping through the kitchen windows douse me in a rain of yellow and gold light.

But what am I looking for? I'm sniffing the air. Distinguishing between things. My father taught me that.

"Fruity. Dry. Woodsy," he says, swilling his glass. Putting it down. Pondering it for a moment. Picking it back up. "Definitely woodsy." Putting it back down. Thumbing through his book. Mouthing the word *woodsy* over and over again as he reads.

"Woodsy," I say out loud.

But I don't find catches of woodsy scents. I find car exhaust. Road tar. Fresh cut grass. Pollen. Sweat. Traces of Jason's cologne mixed with his sweat…and cigarettes. These two things aren't related. This I am sure of. The former comes from his run. Sprinting through Dupont Circle. Making it all the way down to the Smithsonian and back. The other could be any dive bar club from here to Tuscaloosa. They don't live in the same spaces. And yet for the moment they do.

Jason slowly pads into the kitchen finishing off the last gulp of orange juice. He looks at me with the wry kind of smile he gets when he's tempted to speak without a filter.

"Say it," I say.

"Friendly guests," he says.

I don't say anything just yet. I watch him finish off his orange juice. Then he peels off his tank top. His muscles animate themselves as he does. Light pouring into his lines and creases. Disappearing into the fabric and form of his skin.

"Good run?" I ask.

"Yeah."

"Why don't you hit the shower and we'll chat later."

He winks, then goes. And I turn in the direction of my office. "Woodsy," I say again out loud. Then I pad gently down the hallway into the office. I slide the doors closed behind me and I sit down across from Richard and his son with my drink in hand. Occasionally swilling it like it's a glass of pinot.

"So, Richard," I begin. "Why don't we start from the beginning?"

He's finishing off his glass. The boy has barely touched his.

Instead his eyes are darting around the room. Studying things. My books. My plants. My candles. Solomon.

"Well…As you might have noticed, Christian is special…"

I nod.

"He's autistic."

I nod again. I don't know any of these things. But I'm nodding to encourage Richard to keep talking.

"But lately he's been having nightmares or sleepwalking fits."

I look over at the boy. He's smiling. Then mouthing something. Stroking Solomon. Then looking up at the ceiling. Then smiling at me. And back to the ceiling.

"What kind of fits?" I ask.

"He says he sees something. He says he sees something come into our house and move around."

"When you say he sees something, has he described what it looks like?"

He takes a deep breath. "Well. He says it looks like a shadow. A shadow man."

I don't say anything. I look back to the boy. He's mouthing something again. Then he's stroking Solomon.

"I didn't believe him at first…"

"Why?"

"Well, because…he's, you know…"

"Special?" I ask.

"Yeah, special." His voice cracks with a New Jersey kind of rust. And it sprinkles itself all over my coffee table.

"Well, what made you change your mind?" I ask.

He looks down into his empty glass. He doesn't say anything for a long moment.

I ask, "Would you like some more orange juice, Richard?"

He looks up suddenly, like I've jolted him from his sleep. Fear and confusion are burning in his eyes. What do fear and confusion look like? Like a gray wolf and a white wolf running together through the snow, chasing a small white rabbit. Darting after it when it leaps down through holes. Camouflages itself in drifts of clear white snow. Scurries behind big, tall trees. Cowers behind a bush.

"I saw it," he says.

"You. Saw. It?"

"I saw it," he repeats. Voice trembling. Betraying his deep thick alpha male timbre. "It looked like it was seven feet, eight feet tall… My wife and I were sitting on the couch, watching the game. And something told me to look up. And when I did, I saw it go across the living room. It crossed from one side to the other so fast I didn't trust what I saw at first. But then it crossed again. Disappeared into the wall."

"And your wife?" I ask.

He swallows hard. "She didn't see it," he says slowly.

"Or she says she didn't see it," I suggest quietly.

"She didn't see it," he says firmly. I watch him. He's gripping the glass hard. I'm worried he'll crush it in his big hands. But it resists. It resists remarkably.

I look back to the boy. "When was the last time any of you have been visited by this…shadow man?" I ask.

"Two nights ago," he says.

"What happened?"

"Christian woke us up screaming in the middle of the night. So Deb, my wife, told me to go in and check on him. So I did. And he was hiding in the corner looking up at something on the ceiling."

"What was he looking at, Richard?"

"I don't know. It had left by the time I got into the room…But I know it had been there." He looks down into his glass again. As if he's fishing for something down in the trace lines and puddles of orange juice all the way at the lowly bottom of his glass.

"How's that?" I ask.

He looks up. His eyes are racing back and forth, wet with tears. But more than tears. The same clump of fear and confusion, the same sweat and madness and anger and adrenaline that mats itself to the pricked-up fur on that white wolf's back. That runs out like foamy spittle at the corners of that black wolf's mouth. That trembles and undulates in waves up through that rabbit's whiskers and equally its nose and mouth and eyes and tufts of fur. This is what that is.

"Huh?" he asks.

"How did you know something had been there?" I ask.

"I could smell it," he says. "Like cigarettes."

I sit up straight in my chair. I resist bringing my fingertips to my nose even though they're tingling. Buzzing. Instead, I swill my glass again.

"Christian," I say calmly, softly. He looks up at me. Mouthing something. Stroking Solomon gently. "Do you remember what you saw? What scared you?"

He looks past me. At the wall, searching for it. Trying to locate it in the room. But he can't. He tries to shape it with his hands. Etch it out with his fingers. But he can't. Then he looks back at me and says, "Man."

"A man?" I ask.

"Big, tall, dark man."

"Did this man say anything to you?"

He shakes his head no.

"Do you know what this man wants?" I ask.

"He's looking for something he lost."

I think about this for a moment. "Do you know what that thing is?"

He shakes his head no again.

"Okay…" I say. He strokes Solomon some more. Studying the room.

"What do you think?" Richard asks.

"I don't know just yet…" I look back to the boy. "I need to see for myself."

"You talking about coming to our home?" he asks. Maybe there's some shock there. Maybe some disgust. I can't quite distinguish it. It's on the tip of my tongue. Swilling in the bottom of my glass.

"No. Hopefully that won't be necessary." I see a flash of relief in his eyes. Then I get to my feet and walk over to Christian. He's stroking Solomon gently. I kneel and stroke Solomon too. Our pairs of hands are gently coursing over his smooth fur.

"His name's Solomon," I say.

"Solomon," Christian repeats.

"You like dogs?" I ask.

He shakes his head no. His father cuts his teeth.

"But you're petting one now, Christian," Richard says. But the boy shakes his head no again.

"Not a dog," Christian says quietly.

Richard throws up his hands in frustration. I look briefly over at him. Not for long. Just long enough to take him in. Tough exterior. Big commanding voice. Strict rules. And inside jelly. Scared. Scared for his son. Scared for his home.

"Christian, do you trust me?" I ask.

He looks at me for a moment. Then he nods his head yes.

"Good," I say. "I want you to do something for me." He nods yes again. "I want you to close your eyes. I want you to close your eyes and go into your room. Okay? Can you do that for me? Can you close your eyes and go into your room? But don't be scared. Solomon is your friend. And if anything happens, he'll protect you."

He nods his head again yes and slowly closes his eyes.

"What are you gonna do?" Richard asks.

"Shh," I tell him sternly. Then I close my eyes. Slowly stroking Solomon's fur wherever Christian's hands once were. Plumbing for the residue of his touch matted into Solomon's fur. Trying to catch glimpses of the boy's touch until—there, yes there—I find something.

I can see the rose-colored wall. Comic book posters: Green Lantern, Blue Beetle, Nightwing, Flash, Shazam. And a bookshelf stacked to its brim with comics. DC Comics. New ones. Old ones. Vintage. Present day. His bed kitted out with Green Lantern sheets and pillows. A small desk with a computer. A basketball hoop over his door. And a bright window that looks out on the neighborhood street. Sun shining in.

And then there, I smell it. Wafting across the room. I turn, tracing the burning smell. Following its creep through the cracks of the bedroom door. Watching it inch its way up the wall. Slink along the ceiling. And drip down the corner into the floor.

"Who are you?" I ask.

But it doesn't answer.

The room feels cold. Dank even. And there's another smell here. Mildew. This is new. This is now. Maybe because I'm here. Eavesdropping. This isn't part of the past. No. This is present.

"Who are you?" I ask again. I'm fixated on the corner. There, where the smell of cigarettes hunkered down and didn't budge. I know I am not alone in this room. I know it is there in the corner. "Come out," I say. "I see you hiding."

And the wall trembles for a moment. Then like that it unfolds itself. Up from the gray carpet. Peeling back the soft plush carpet fibers in the corner. Lifting its hood and revealing its face. Arching its long black back. Then getting up from its knees. Leaning against the wall. Inching upward. Ever upward. Until finally I see it. Head bowed under the ceiling. More than seven feet. The whole height of Christian's room and then some. This long, towering mass of shadow. Standing in the corner. Not moving. Watching me, watching it.

"Who are you?" I ask again. But it says nothing. But I remember what I heard in that dirty bathroom. So I regurgitate it. Vomit it back up like the pablum and spew and liquor and crank vomited over the sink, graffitied and stained with the lives of all those club divers who did or did not live to headbang another day. "That'll do," I say and then it trembles. Scared. Flustered with fear and confusion. Reeking of cigarettes. Blackened lips and translucent skin. Hands trembling. Eyes racing. Trying to understand.

"You are not welcome here," I say. It recedes back into the wall. "No!" I say firmly. "You will not hide here...You will go. Now!" It trembles at the sound of my voice. "You are not welcome here!" I yell. And its trembling, shivering tendrils of black milky shadow disintegrate into a million pieces, falling like sparks into the carpet. Evaporating as they impact.

I open my eyes. Christian is giggling. "You can open your eyes, Christian," I say.

He smiles. "Gone."

"Yes. I think so too," I say.

"What...what happened?" Richard says nervously, still clasping the glass.

I reach over and take it from him. My fingers gently brush his. He recoils. I see it. But I quickly ignore it. And I place the glass down on the coffee table.

"This thing, this shadow person is gone for the moment. Maybe he won't come back. Maybe he will in some weeks. Some months. If it does, you tell me...and we'll do a cleanse."

"A cleanse?"

"Yes. Of your home…if that doesn't bother you."

He sits there quietly for a moment. "No…of course not." Trying to awkwardly manage his lie. Flirt with the truth on his lips. But I don't care. He's archaic. An old idea. He's the one who's scared. Not me.

"Woodsy," Christian says suddenly.

I whip around to look at the boy. He's stroking Solomon again, mouthing the word as I had done.

"He *is* special," I say softly to Richard.

Sometime later. Much later. Maybe thirty minutes later after formalities and awkward stares, I accompany them to the front door.

"If anything returns, let me know," I say.

Jason appears up at the top step. He's changed into a button-down and some khakis. Richard sees him, then quickly looks away. Maybe repulsed. Maybe confused. I can't read it, to be honest.

"Thanks again," he huffs. But he's rushing Christian out the door.

I hear Christian manage one more "Woodsy" before they disappear down the sidewalk.

"See," Jason says.

"See what?" I ask.

"Friendly guests."

Pale Moon Rising

Celeste Castro

Celeste Castro, she/her, is an American Mexican from small-town, rural Idaho, where most of her stories take place. She grew up with learning disabilities, though she always kept a journal. In addition to fiction, she's a staff writer with *Hispanecdotes*, an online magazine for Latinx writers, where she publishes essays and poetry.

The shrill buzz of the cicadas acted as a prelude to the sun, which peeked over the horizon, announcing another day, although I had no idea what day it was. I was blind to time. I let the moon guide me as did most people like me—Gemini with a Pisces moon rising. Though I did have some sense of time. I knew that I'd been camping and working on location in northern Mexico for over a month researching and banding great crested caracara, a gorgeous wide-winged black-and-white falcon, commonly seen on the Mexican flag. A symbol representing the Aztec legend of Tenochtitlan and my people.

"Something just occurred to me," Rocío, my coworker, said through a yawn. She poured us both a cup of instant coffee.

"Care to enlighten?" I asked, settling my sunglasses against my nose. The sun bathed me in light, but it could never truly warm me.

"It's the summer solstice."

"It feels like it," I said. The days, the nights, and the birds ran together. I stretched and an awful crack echoed in the thick morning air. I hung my head forward and rolled it from side to side. My black curls fell forward and impeded my vision.

"You poor baby," Rocío said. She began massaging my neck. "We got to stop doing, you know, that thing."

"No. Never. It's not that, it's the ground." I moaned the deeper she pushed into my tendons. "That feels so good. You're a miracle worker." She had such brilliant fingers.

"You should try the hammock, it's like sleeping on air."

I caught movement from my peripheral. The hammock swayed to and fro in the steady wind as if seconding Rocío's suggestion.

"But then I wouldn't get to sleep with you." I sat upright and turned toward Rocío to kiss her.

Summer flings in bird banding fieldwork weren't uncommon. Three to four months of work in far-flung parts of the world, pretty girls came, and pretty girls went—why not have fun?

"Well then, you're going to have to suffer." Rocío laughed and wiggled her eyebrows.

I loved Rocío's laugh. It was as gentle and easy as the desert wind and one of her best features. She was so different than me. I was a self-proclaimed plump-cum-voluptuous, short woman with a head full of curly black hair, with dark features, big eyes, and big lips.

Rocío, on the other hand, was a tall drink of water, with long flexible legs, a juicy backside, and hard muscle. I wasn't purely attracted to her for her physical attributes. Rocío was strong as hell, one of the best cliff climbers I'd worked with. Birds didn't stand a chance, and neither did lusty women. I was going to miss her at the end of the season when, inevitably, we'd have to say goodbye.

I leaned in for another kiss and almost suggested taking it back to the tent when one of our colleagues made their presence known.

"Morning, glories," Jam said, busting from their tent like a whirlwind, bringing a plume of dust as well as Eleni, their girlfriend, in their wake. The pair, both members of our field team, joined us. They settled into their respective chairs reaching for the pot of coffee at the same time. "Whatcha two lovebirds talking about?"

"Today's the summer solstice," I said.

"It's all downhill from here."

"What the hell are you talking about? This is the best part of the year; all the good holidays are coming up." Rocío held up her fingers and started counting. "There's Halloween, Día de los Muertos, Thanksgiving, Christmas…" Rocío went on about her favorite Thanksgiving dishes and traditions.

"Holy shit." Jam slapped the arm of their chair and stood, rattling the contents of the breakfast table.

"Jesús Cristo," Rocío said, spilling coffee down the front of her. "Dude. Warn me the next time you're going to freak the fuck out. You owe me a clean shirt." She leaned forward and pulled the fabric away from her skin, shaking off the liquid.

"Sorry."

"Well?" Rocío said. "Why the outburst?"

"This is the year of the pale moon," Jam said.

"Oh! Why didn't you say so? The pale moon. Yes, of course. What's the pale moon?" Rocío deadpanned.

I squinted skyward, barely making out the faint outline of the moon juxtaposed with the rising sun. It was a beautiful sight to behold. Two celestial beings blessing our day. A memory flashed into my mind's eye. A lush field. A fence. The images disappeared before I could process what it meant. I shook it away and took another sip of my coffee.

"The pale moon," Jam said, their eyes wide as if the pale moon was as common a holiday as the ones Rocío had mentioned. "Every three years, right around the summer solstice, give or take a week, a pale moon is said to rise, and that's when the Peuchen feeds."

"Oh. Okay. The Peuchen. Why didn't you say so? What the hell is that?" Rocío asked.

"How do you not know? It's huge around these parts. I thought you were Mexican?"

"I can't possibly know all things Mexican." Rocío laughed. She held out her hands.

"A Peuchen is a shapeshifter. Sometimes it takes the shape of a flying snake or a huge bat that sucks your blood." I sucked air between my teeth just like Hannibal Lecter in the movie *Silence of the Lambs*. My comment gained me a hearty laugh from the team.

"Sounds like a vampire," Rocío said.

"A Mexican vampire." I ran my finger along the soft skin of Rocío's neck, feeling her vein throbbing underneath.

"And does the Peuchen convert its prey into sexy, hot vampires?" Rocío asked, settling her eyes on my lips. "If so, convert me now."

"C'mere, then," I said, leaning toward her.

"Nope," Eleni piped in, her voice flat, her face somber. "It pretty much sucks your blood and leaves you to rot. No romantic ending whatsoever."

"And you know this because, why?" Rocío asked, dragging her attention from my lips to Eleni.

"We saw one…well, we heard one." Eleni looked at Jam. "It was the year we met, remember? Three years ago, almost to the day."

It was sweet that she remembered the exact day that they met. I searched my memory and reviewed all of my bird research jobs. I couldn't remember where I was last year, let alone three years ago.

"We were banding birds in Bolivia and we heard the creepiest, most eerie-sounding scream, like the kind of scream that makes you wonder if you've heard an actual murder." Eleni's brow furrowed. She looked to Jam, who gave her a concerned smile.

"We didn't think anything of it," Jam said, "because cougars can sound like that, fucking freaky cats. But then, later that week, when Eleni and I went into town, everyone was in shock. People were telling us to watch our backs. There were camping restrictions. Special agents were asking questions, interrogating everyone. The stores were closed. The whole town was at a standstill. We asked around and learned that a local woman had died."

"Some poor rancher woman had been found dead, all of her blood drained."

"We did the math and figured that it happened the night we heard that crazed screaming," Jam said.

"The freaky thing is, we don't know if it was the woman screaming or if it was the Peuchen. I'll never forget the sound for as long as I live." Eleni closed her eyes and shook her head. She shivered.

"Wow. That would be hella creepy if it were true." Rocío snorted and then laughed.

"It's true!" Eleni gasped. "It's totally true. Look it up. Seriously. Three years ago. Google it. Vampire, rancher woman, Bolivia. It's all there."

I seemed to remember a similar story from my time in South America but didn't know enough to offer anything useful. Stories like this were common in small towns across the world. Every region had its version.

"Get outta here. Do you believe this?" Rocío asked, while turning toward me.

"You're asking someone whose idea of a good time is binge-watching *Unsolved Mysteries*." I accepted a high five from Jam. We nodded at our shared appreciation of the unexplained.

Rocío rolled her eyes. "Do you also believe in Big Foot?" she asked.

I gasped. "He's my favorite cryptid of all time. He and I go way back." My comment got a round of laughs and another high five.

Rocío knitted her eyebrows and crossed her arms.

"Are you scared?" Jam asked.

"Scared? What? No."

"Oh, this is going to be fun." I leaned into my chair and folded my arms behind my head. I loved messing with Rocío. She was easily disturbed and highly emotional, which made her so good at sex and fun to tease.

"You know what's fun?" Rocío poured herself more coffee. "Fieldwork. Banding birds. Research. Science. That's fun. Creepy Mexican vampires, not so much."

"I'm with you, Rocío," Eleni added.

"Thank you!"

"I like creepy American vampires." She leaned toward Jam and kissed them on the cheek, eliciting even more laughter.

Rocío rolled her eyes. "So long as the Peuchen stays in Bolivia, I'm cool."

"It's not just in Bolivia," Jam said, pulling out their phone and scrolling through it. "Before Bolivia, it was sighted in Peru, and before that was Quincy, Washington."

"Where the hell is Quincy?" Eleni asked.

"Hey, I'm from Quincy," I said.

"That's a random location."

"It's the perfect place for blending in." I brushed my fingers against Rocío's. She pulled away as if I had burned her.

"Well," Rocío said as she stood, "as much as I'd like to talk about huge-ass blood-sucking snake-bat whatevers, we have birds to band." She stood with a huff and took off toward the work tent.

❖

I spotted Eleni approaching in the distance. Her form took shape bit by bit as she drew closer to our banding tent. She wavered like a mirage in the blistering heat. Ripples of her existence danced against the backdrop. The sun's rays shrouded her in an orange glow. One wrong move and she'd disappear completely. It looked as though she limped slightly when she walked. I pulled myself from my chair, the entire effort a feat of strength. The power of the late afternoon sun restricted my movements. I trudged to meet her, hoping she was okay.

"Easy," Eleni said as she handed the caracara to me. He still bore the brown shades of a juvenile, but hints of black coloring peeked through. "He did not like being woken up. Wore himself out, but still has a lot of fight left."

The bird squawked, grumbled, and wiggled in my grasp. "Good, that's good. He's a good strong bird," I said as I secured him in my hold, careful to avoid his bone-breaking beak. His eager heart thumped against my fingertips. I held him to the side, looked him over, and met his piercing gaze, which seemed to calm him. "Hey, bird."

"Got him, bird whisperer?" Eleni called me by my nickname. I had a way with birds, they seemed to trust me.

"I got him." The bird relaxed completely in my grasp. We shared a deep breath. "You okay?" I asked, finally noticing the blood trailing down Eleni's knee.

"I fucking tripped on a rock helping Jam after this little guy scratched them to shit."

"Damn. Do they need a first aid kit? Want me to send Rocío?" I asked, motioning with my head toward the tent to where Rocío waited.

"We're good. I think we're done for today. What's for dinner?" she asked.

"Tacos."

"Rad." Eleni scurried off, leaving a trail of dust behind.

With the bird secure, I walked the short distance to our workstation and Rocío. Together we weighed, banded, and recorded the bird's information. When I returned to the tent after freeing him, Rocío was on her phone.

"I found the story that Eleni told us this morning about that rancher woman in Bolivia."

I pulled the bandana from around my neck and used it to wipe sweat from my brow. I polished off what was left of my water bottle.

"It's true, she was found dead with half her blood drained. That's fucked, right? I mean, if it's real."

I dropped the bottle onto the ground, not bothering to expend the energy to pick it up even though it was within reach. I sluffed into the camping chair. "It's definitely fucked."

The hum of the cicadas and intermittent flapping of the nylon canopy of our work tent acted as a lullaby. Swirls of wind greeted us from time to time, bringing fresh layers of dust with it. The desert's way of claiming what it thought belonged to her. I closed my eyes while Rocío obsessed over the story.

"You know what's creepy?" Rocío said a short time later. "This rancher woman died with a smile on her face. Who the hell would include that in an eyewitness statement?"

"I've seen you pass out with a smile on your face."

Rocío laughed. "Seriously, though."

"Can I see the article?"

"Trigger warning, the website includes photos." Rocío handed me her phone.

I scrolled through the webpage and grimaced at the images of the rancher woman. My neck began to ache along with my back. I arched forward, trying to work it out. A feeling of familiarity washed over me. Had I been there before? This would drive me nuts!

"Does the website predict where it'll turn up next?" I handed the phone back to Rocío.

"Good question." Rocío furiously scrolled through the webpage. "I don't think so. It only tracks where attacks took place. There doesn't seem to be any rhyme or reason for what location it chooses next. Oh! And get this, the Peuchen paralyzes its victims by staring at them."

"Like this?" I asked, lifting my shades and leaned toward her. I opened my eyes as wide as I could, staring at her, latching on, holding her in my embrace, searching, remembering.

Rocío's eyes widened. Her smile faded.

I couldn't hold it together. I looked away. We erupted in laughter.

"Are you making fun of me?" Rocío smirked and then cleared her throat.

"Kinda." I took the opportunity to kiss the smirk right off her face, frustrated when Rocío pulled away.

"I believed everything about the Peuchen until I read that whole paralyzation by staring bit."

"Why was that the deciding factor?" I asked.

"Well, as I said, according to 'the legend,'" Rocío said, using air quotes, "the Peuchen stares at its prey to paralyze it and then sucks its blood." She tossed her phone onto the table, where it clattered. "How would anyone know that? Every story I've read is about someone who died. There's not one eyewitness, victim, or any other account from someone who's lived through an attack to tell the story, thus, how would anyone know that the Peuchen paralyzes its prey before sucking their blood?"

"Autopsies can tell if there are toxins in the body before death, that's probably how they know."

"Does an autopsy tell you if the toxins were administered via someone staring?"

I pursed my lips. "You have a good point. Or maybe someone's interviewed an actual Peuchen. Ever think of that?"

"Hello, Mister huge and scary bat, impressive wingspan and fangs you have," she said in what I thought sounded like a decent impression of Barbara Walters, "is it true that you can paralyze—" She froze in place.

I started laughing.

"Want to know what I think?" she asked.

A bug landed on my forearm. I sent a blast of air between my lips, sending it on its way. "Of course."

"A deranged, ritualistic serial killer is on the loose and hiding under the guise of an ancient legend."

"Brilliant, if you ask me."

"Right? A man was ripped in half. Oh, it's nothing. It's just the Mothman. A woman was found strangled to death, oh, just the Snake Headed Dog. It's a serial killer, I know it."

"That has been killing people the same way for hundreds of years?" I asked. "That's a damn old serial killer."

"He passes his craft on to his progeny."

"So, a vampire?" The same bug circled me again. I swatted at it this time.

"Do vampires usually kill their prey?"

"It's about eighty-twenty, creating new vampires and killing innocent people."

"Where'd you come up with that math?"

The camping chair creaked when I leaned against the back of it. I folded my arms behind my head. "*Interview with a Vampire.*"

Rocío let loose a single-syllable laugh. "You kill me."

"What if," I found my tobacco and rolling papers, "serial killers are in fact cryptids, ancient legends manifested through evil people?"

"That's deep." Rocío rolled her eyes.

"Thanks."

"And also disturbing."

"Thanks." I rolled my smoke, licking the gum of the paper to seal the deal. I struck three different wooden matches against the table before it lit—darn wind had picked up over the last hour. I blew the first drag at the pesky bug, sending it away for good.

We shared a hand-rolled cigarette while we waited for Jam and Eleni. Caracara floated in the breeze that blew against the sand and blue colored backdrop. A couple of intense gusts of wind threatened to carry our canopy tent across the landscape, but it never did. It was fun watching it try.

"Can you imagine having a superpower where all you do is look at someone and they freeze?" Rocío asked.

"Actually, yes."

Rocío turned toward me.

"My mom can do that," I said.

"I think mine can too."

❖

I moved effortlessly, gliding to and fro. Sagebrush graced against the tips of my wings as I narrowed through canyon walls. Moonlight, my sustenance, illuminated every inch of night. Movement caught my eye. I spotted my prey. Its bleats echoed against the stone canyon. I smelled its blood. I felt its fear even before it registered I was coming. I roared with laughter when I went for it.

"Jimena. Jimena!"

I jolted awake. Something moved me with the force of a bulldozer. I couldn't draw a deep enough breath. I realized my predicament. Rocío had both her arms wrapped around me tightly, as if I wore her like a backpack.

"I heard screaming," Rocío whispered directly into my ear. Her voice was hot and raspy.

"Rocío? What's going on?" I squirmed free and sat up. I rubbed my eyes, my vision coming into focus. I yawned. "You interrupted a flying dream. I love flying dreams. I was about to eat a goat." My stomach growled, surprising me.

"A what? Be quiet. Listen." Rocío held up her finger.

I strained to register clues through the din of the desert at two in the morning. The chorus of night sang in my ears. A melody of croaking, screeching, shuffling, scratching, hunting, and hiding filled my brain. I'd always had an impeccable sense of hearing. This time I heard nothing that would warrant Rocío's distress.

"I swear to God I heard screaming. The Peuchen. I heard it. It's real." Rocío crawled into my lap.

"Dios mío," I groaned as I held Rocío and rubbed her back. Her skin was damp and hot. Rocío's entire body hummed. Her heartbeat pounded against my chest like a percussion and I the drum. "Did you stay up late reading more of those gruesome eyewitnesses and have another nightmare?" This was the third night in a row of interrupted sleep courtesy of Rocío.

"This wasn't a nightmare. This was real." Rocío got to her knees, crawled to the window, and unzipped the fabric window just enough to peek through. A gust of cool night air rushed in and fluttered the nylon walls of our tent, giving them life. They billowed and breathed, feeding Rocío's paranoia even more. She looked every which way, her movements chaotic and twitchy.

"What are you doing?" I dropped back against my pillow and rested my arm over my eyes.

"Hey," Rocío whispered, "did you guys hear that? Jam. Eleni. Jam. Hey." She pressed her face up against the mesh as she reached.

I jabbed Rocío with my foot. "Stop looking out there. If it's truly the Peuchen and it locks eyes with you, game over, remember?" I knew I shouldn't tease, but what the hell, I was awake.

"Shit." Rocío zipped the window up so fast that she ripped the tent.

"Hey, easy. I'm just kidding."

"That's not funny."

"You know what's not funny? Waking up like this fifty times throughout the night."

"I'm sorry, but it was so real." A shuffling sound came from outside the tent, causing Rocío to jump on top of me again.

"Rocío, what the hell? I just bit my tongue."

"Something. Is. Out. There."

"Nothing. Is. Out. There. Seriously, you need to stop reading those stories for the sake of our health, for the sake of the birds. Think of the birds. Think of my tongue. I know you like my tongue."

"I do like your tongue. I'm sorry." Rocío sighed and closed her eyes.

I pulled Rocío closer. She trembled against me. "Hey. You okay?" I kissed her.

"It sounded so real and so close...like, in the tent close. Sorry."

"Don't feel bad. I get it. You're scared. Want to know a secret?" I ran my fingers through Rocío's hair.

"What?"

"Cryptids aren't real." I hated lying, but I had to get some sleep.

"They're not?" Rocío's body deflated.

"Nope." I squeezed my eyes and bit my lower lip, hoping Rocío believed me.

"In your opinion. I think they are real. All the evidence I've found online says otherwise. What if, hear me out, what if, Jam and Eleni are, you know, in disguise and here to eat us?"

"Well for one, Peuchen, don't eat people, they suck blood," I reminded her.

"Jimena, I'm being serious."

"Me too."

"Maybe they're outside right now, waiting for the pale moon to rise so they can strike. The moon has been bigger every single night, and it's bright, but is it pale?" Rocío shook her head. "Think about it. They're the ones who brought it up in the first place. They're plotting. They're *so* plotting. We hear you! We're on to you!" she shouted. "Think about it, Jimena. They've been so grouchy every morning over the past week, and rude, if I'm being honest. Why, Jimena, why? Come to think of it, so have you."

"Maybe because you've been waking everyone up at all hours and we have this semi-dangerous job searching for birds with huge-ass talons and sharp-ass beaks in hundred-degree weather along jagged rocks with said large birds in tow, and doing it on zero sleep is, I don't know, dangerous."

"Are you ever serious?" Rocío groaned.

"I'm as serious as a heart attack. You're being paranoid."

"I'm being paranoid?" She pressed her hand against her chest. "Me? Come on. What are the odds that Jam and Eleni just happened to be in Bolivia the last time that the Peuchen killed someone? And both magically heard the bloodcurdling scream, and both are here, as in right over there." She pointed toward their camping area.

Rocío swallowed a scream and jumped against the wall of the tent, threatening to pull it from the ground when a shriek from outside startled us both. "Did you hear that? I know you heard that," she whispered. Her eyes lit in horror.

"Dios mío!" I said as I sat up. I found my boots, stuffed my feet inside, along with the laces, and unzipped the door to the tent.

"What are you doing?"

"Investigating."

"Like that? Naked?"

"Time is of the essence," I said before crawling out of the tent, muttering to myself. I wrapped my arms around my body to ward off the chilly night air, but then I realized I wasn't cold at all. The silver moonlight blanketed me, enveloped me. I relaxed completely. I looked at my arms, loving the color of the moon against my skin. It felt safe and familiar. I brought my flashlight, but I didn't need it. The power of the moon showed me everything. A current of wind carried scents of both predator and prey, of adrenaline and fear.

I circled the tents and rounded the grouping of trees that kept our camp shaded during the day. Something moved in the distance. The hammock. A shape filled it out. The shape of nothing and everything. It swayed to and fro, the wind enjoying a plaything.

A blaring screech drew my attention skyward.

"Rocío, darling?" I said.

"Y-yeah?"

"Open the window."

"W-why?"

"Open the damned window."

"O-okay."

I used my flashlight's beam to motion toward the trees. Two glowing eyes shone back.

"Oh, ha. Yeah, a screech owl."

"And what sound does a screech owl make?"

"They screech."

"Good girl." I tromped back into the tent, and despite Rocío's annoyance, she was also incredibly sexy, sitting with her legs folded to the side, her body glowing in the light of the moon as it shone through the tent's window. Her chest rose and fell with each breath. Her beautiful brown nipples were hard and pointed toward me as if asking for a tongue-lashing. "So?" I said while crawling toward her, wanting to take her in the light of the moon.

Rocío pursed her lips.

"Rocío?"

"I still can't get over the fact that Jam and Eleni were there, at the scene of an attack." She bit her lip and shook her head. "What are the odds?"

I hung my head dramatically. "I'd say the odds are pretty high. I was there too—yes, that's it!" I finally remembered that something that had been nagging me all week. "The summer of...wait..." Shit. Maybe I didn't remember everything.

"What?" Rocío pulled away to the safety of a shadow. Her eyes were huge black masses. "Why didn't you say anything when we talked about earlier this week?"

"Because I didn't remember I was there until now. It was three years ago, and besides, I wasn't there in that town with them, but I was in Bolivia."

"What were you doing in Bolivia?"

"Andean condor."

"What?"

"That's where the bird jobs are."

"Ho-ly shit. And where were you the time before that? Where were you when it last fed?" Rocío snapped her fingers repeatedly.

"Where was I six years ago?" I squeezed my eyes shut. "Shit, I don't know. Like I can remember every single year of my life in the blink of an eye. Come on!"

Rocío backed away from me as far as she could in the two-person tent. "You were in Peru, you told me that when we met. You were, weren't you? Holy shit." She pointed a finger at me.

"Oh my God. Really? Okay, yeah, I was in Peru, I guess. I don't remember." I looked up, searching for my memories. My neck started aching and my shoulders tensed. "Where were you six years ago?"

"I don't know." Rocío's forehead knitted.

"See? It's hard."

"Oh! I was in La Paz. La Paz!"

"La Paz, Bolivia?"

"I was on vacation with my parents!"

"Isn't that convenient that La Paz happens to be a little town on the border of Peru. Ha," I pointed my finger at Rocío, "you're just as guilty as I am."

"Well—well," Rocío huffed, "where were you before that?"

"Rocío? Must we?"

"This isn't looking good for you, Jimena, if your name truly is

Jimena. The Peuchen feeds every three years on or around the summer solstice, and you have been present or have lived in the country where it strikes. Oh my God! You're in cahoots with Jam and Eleni, aren't you? You're part of a coven. You can't deny it."

"You are so, so very wrong. Covens are for witches! Vampires live in coffins. Do I look like the type to sleep in a coffin? Besides, I can function during the daytime. Vampires burn in the sun! Do I combust into flame when I'm in the sun?"

"Maybe the Mexican vampire is different because of your dark skin, and you have the right amount of melanin that allows you to function and live a seemingly normal life. And, and you always wear sunglasses, literally, you always wear them. Tell me why and I'll drop it."

"I have no words," I groaned.

We sat in silence. I thought that maybe Rocío had worn herself out.

"Holy. Fucking. Shit. The time before that was Quincy. You're *from* Quincy. You said so yourself. Why you would offer up that little tidbit, I don't know, but well played. Good idea putting yourself at the scene of the crime like it's no big deal." Rocío placed her hand over her mouth.

"I don't know what to say except—nope, I have nothing to say," I admitted.

"You've been working bird jobs everywhere there has been an attack. How convenient is that? A serial killer that floats with the birds, easy to hide, easy to blend, a bat among birds, a wolf among sheep. What a perfect cover. Brilliant. How old are you, anyway?"

I opened my mouth and shook my head. Rocío's determination near had me believing that maybe I was a Peuchen. "No," I exclaimed. "This has gone too far, and I'm just as guilty as you for teasing you, and for that, I am sorry, but I don't have time for this nonsense. I'm sleeping in the hammock." I rounded up a blanket, casting bags and bedding every which way. I zipped open the door and began crawling out.

"No, Jimena, please. Don't go. Don't leave me," she pled. "I'm scared. I'm sorry."

I turned toward Rocío. "Then you need to stop. Seriously."

"Do you have to be so damn grouchy about it?"

"You just accused me of being a bloodthirsty vampire! You've woken me up for the past four nights at three in the morning, and guess what, work starts at five, so yeah, I'm going to be a little bit grouchy, because I'm exhausted."

"I'm sorry. I'll stop reading the articles."

"Promise?"

"I promise."

"Come here."

We lay back down. Rocío snuggled against me. I breathed a sigh of relief and closed my eyes.

"Jimena?"

"Hmm."

"I read an article that says that if a Peuchen can be trapped, it can be sent back to hell by a machi."

I tried to keep my voice as steady as possible, but I wanted to scream—to show Rocío the meaning of a bloodcurdling scream. "Yes, I remembered you telling me that already," I said through clenched teeth.

"So that means there's a lot of them, right, because if one's been sent to hell, why are there still killings?"

"You promised you'd let it rest."

Rocío's drawn-out sigh sounded as if she finally and truly gave up. A few more minutes passed, and it felt as though Rocío's tirade might be over for good.

"Jimena?"

"Oh, my God, what?"

She shifted to her side, draping her leg over me, half lying on top of me. She ran her hand along my stomach, traveling between my legs. I bucked against her and opened. "Are you mad at me?"

She tickled her fingers between my legs, easily sliding through my wetness. She captured my nipple between her lips and began to suck. It felt divine.

"So mad at you." I smoothed my hand through Rocío's locks of hair, holding her in place, encouraging her.

"Then I suppose I should make it up to you." Her hot breath tickled my skin.

"My God, woman. I can't keep up." I spread my legs wider, arching into her touch, losing myself at each pass and smooth motion, finally taking her inside me.

❖

"I saw another one! And another." Rocío pointed skyward, her eyes never leaving her binoculars.

"Me too!" I echoed. "Make that seventeen meteors that I've counted."

"Oh, we're keeping track?" Rocío's laughter filled the air.

I loved Rocío's laughter. It was easy and contagious. I was going to miss her. I hated this part. The inevitable goodbye. I reached for her hand and pulled her to my lap. I placed my hand behind her head and urged her downward. Our lips met. We shared heat and longing.

"Where do you think you'll go next?" Rocío asked when she pulled away. Our job of banding crested caracara had come to an end. Jam and Eleni had already packed and left for another job in Oaxaca. We stayed behind one more night to watch the meteor shower before going our separate ways.

"I don't know," I mused. A vision of sand and cattails flashed into my brain along with the smell of brine and marine air. "Probably somewhere where there's water. What about you?"

"I don't want to think about it," Rocío admitted. "I only want this night, the sky full of stars, a meteor shower, and you. I want to remember our last night together, forever."

"I think I can arrange that."

Rocío climbed off me, grabbed her flask of tequila, took a swig, and started dancing in circles. Her laughter ricocheted off whatever surface it found.

I lit a cigarette, took a drag, and watched Rocío's seductive dance. I was incredibly aroused. She was so free, so languid as she moved. Her wristwatch reflected the light of our small campfire and gave her away when I lost her movements to the dark.

Something stirred inside me. The memory I'd been searching for lately became clearer in my mind, but still, I couldn't place it. I licked my lips and awaited my muse, la lunato, to tell me the rest.

As if on cue Rocío stopped dancing. She pointed skyward. "Look! The moon!"

I met the giant shining orb with an open mind. It climbed onto the scene, consuming the black of night and illuminating the sky with the power of a million candles. Nothing could escape it. A tremor shot through me, raising the hair on my skin, waking me from a groggy and pointless slumber. I ran my tongue against my teeth, tasting memories. My body no longer ached.

I flicked the remainder of my cigarette into our campfire, where it sizzled and popped. I joined Rocío, whose body seemed to glisten in the blaze that the moonlight had inspired.

"The moon is so clear, so bright," Rocío said as she hung on the brilliance of the celestial wonder. "I can see every peak and valley on its surface."

"It looks almost pale, doesn't it?" I asked as I came up beside her.

"Ha ha, very funny." Rocío turned toward me and rested her arms on my shoulders, twining them around my neck. "I'm so sorry about the past few days, the whole shape-shifter drama, keeping you awake and being so damn paranoid." She found my lips and nibbled and licked.

"Don't be," I said between kisses. "It was actually kind of fun."

"Fun?" Rocío said.

"I learned a lot about you."

"Such as?"

"You're a true believer."

"A believer?" Rocío laughed and looked toward the rising moon.

"A *true* believer. Seriously, I'm being serious. Look at me." I tucked my finger underneath her chin, directing her toward me, forcing eye contact.

Rocío kissed me again before giving me her undivided attention.

"You are someone who believes that there are unexplained forces in play all around us. It takes an open and eager mind, a special person." I leaned in, taking Rocío's face into my hands, kissing her hard. I pulled back and searched deep into her glimmering moonlit eyes, swimming through to her very soul. "It's a good thing."

"Oh, yeah? Why's—" Rocío's easy smile froze on her face, and she stopped moving.

"True believers taste better." I sank my teeth into Rocío's neck and drank. My laughter, my screams of pleasure, filled the air and mingled with the moonlight as I drained her. I remembered everything.

THE DEPTH OF LOVE

Anne Shade

Anne Shade is the author of *Femme Tales, A Modern Fairytale Trilogy* and *Masquerade*, a historical romance. Anne lives in West Orange, NJ, and when she is not writing about love, she reads fantasy novels and helps make couples' wedding dreams a reality.

The sound of the waves crashing along the shore outside Lindsey's window would normally lull her right to sleep, but her mind raced with grief that she'd been holding back, concern about how her father and sister were holding up, and guilt about lounging at a resort instead of looking for a job. Lindsey threw off her covers and walked from the villa she was staying in down to the beach. It was the middle of the night and no one was about. She found a spot and plopped dejectedly down on the sand. If she had been home, she would have turned on her television to some silly late-night show to distract her, but she wasn't home, there was no television in her room, and something drew her to the beach.

Lindsey watched the waves crash against the shore and let the grief come. Wasn't that why her family had conspired to get her here? To grieve and heal? Once the tears began, all her locked-away emotions suddenly crashed over her like one of those waves.

"Why?" she yelled at the waves that seemed to grow higher in the moonlit distance as her pain grew.

"I just want the pain to end…I just want the sadness to go

away…I just want to understand why?" She moaned as her heart broke all over again.

"Please…please…please make the pain go away," she pleaded to the stars, the moon, the ocean, the heavens above, anyone who might be listening.

❖

Ebele swam just ahead of her sisters as they raced to see who would make it home the fastest. She was so focused on beating them that she almost missed the sound of crying drifting toward her in the waves.

"No, not now," she said in frustration.

She and her sisters were just returning home from assisting a small village in Nigeria with an unknown illness ravaging their people. They hadn't been the only spirits and deities who had shown up to assist, but it had been a heart-wrenching task all the same. All she wanted to do was go home and swim freely amongst her people to clear away the darkness the task had brought on. Ebele kept swimming, but she couldn't outswim her duty. She slowed to let her sisters catch up.

"What's wrong, Eb?" Ayodele asked as Deka looked on in concern. They were attuned to each other's emotions.

"Do you hear that?" If her sisters heard it as well, then at least she wouldn't be alone in whatever task Mami Wata was sending her on now.

"I hear nothing but the sound of the waves crashing above," Ayodele said.

"I don't hear anything either," Deka said.

Ebele sighed. "I hear a woman crying out in grief."

"Ah, well, you are a spirit of compassion," Ayodele said as if that should have been obvious to her.

"I know. We've just been away from home for so long," Ebele said with a frown.

Deka gave Ebele a knowing look. "You're not thinking of ignoring it, are you?"

"I'm sure there are others who hear it that can help," Ebele said, despite knowing otherwise.

"Do you still hear it?" Ayodele asked.

Ebele sighed. "Yes."

Ayodele gave her a sympathetic smile. "Then you must answer it. The fact that we don't hear it also is proof that it's something special meant for you."

Ebele knew this. The waters surrounding the islands of Jamaica were Ebele's family waters, so the humans on these islands were solely her family's responsibility.

Deka smiled and kissed Ebele's cheek. "We'll see you when you return home."

Ayodele pulled her into a tight embrace. "Although I don't hear the call, I feel this one is different. That we may not see you for some time," she whispered in Ebele's ear, then placed a kiss on her cheek.

Ebele looked at her worriedly. "Am I in danger?"

"No, quite the opposite. Be happy, sister," Ayodele said with a mischievous wink before taking Deka's hand and swimming away.

Ebele shook her head. Ayodele had the gift of foresight, and Ebele hated when she left her with riddles like that. She watched her sisters disappear amongst a pod of dolphins, then swam upward until she broke the surface.

Please make the pain go away. The woman's plea was clear.

Ebele's heart ached with the woman's grief. It was so deep Ebele wondered how the woman had managed it this long. She saw a shoreline in the distance and a lone figure sitting on the beach. With a swish of her tail she rode the waves toward the shore.

Lindsey felt as if she had turned on a faucet that couldn't be turned off. Although she no longer wailed and moaned, tears still ran down her face. She looked around, surprised no one had come out while she sat there sounding like a wounded animal for the past fifteen minutes. Using the bottom of her nightie she tried to wipe her tears and mucus-covered face, but she was only replacing what she wiped off with sand, so she gave up. With a sigh she decided to go back to her villa before someone *did* come out and find her wallowing in her misery, but something in the water caught her attention. She gasped at the sight of a dolphin breaking the surface and riding a wave toward the shoreline. She stood and walked slowly toward the edge of the water. When the animal broke the crashing waves again, Lindsey's eyes widened.

"Okay, I must really be suffering from serious sleep deprivation because now I'm seeing things," she said to herself as the silhouette of what she had thought was a dolphin looked like a woman's figure with a fishtail.

Lindsey watched in fascination as the dolphin, woman, or whatever it was swam closer to shore, then disappeared under one last wave before reappearing several yards ahead of her. As a beam of moonlight spotlighted the water, she saw a woman walking toward her. Lindsey knew her tired mind must have been playing tricks on her when she thought the woman had a tail. It was probably a play of the shadows on the water. Then her mind kicked in on the fact that the woman was completely naked. Her wet copper-brown skin glistened, looking as if it were covered in diamonds from the moonlight playing on the water droplets. Her hair was in thick long dreadlocks. She had a narrow waist that curved softly to a flat stomach and generous hips. A chain with a large turquoise stone was wrapped around her waist and lay temptingly just below her belly button as if it were an arrow pointing toward the smooth V between her thick thighs.

Lindsey managed to tear her eyes away from that tempting sight to look at the woman's face as she slowly walked out of the water, reminding her of Halle Berry in that James Bond movie. It was as if the moonlight was her spotlight, giving Lindsey a detailed view of her beauty. She had light golden-brown eyes, perfectly arched brows, the cutest upturned nose, and the reddest Cupid's bow lips all set in a soft oval face. Lindsey was mesmerized as the woman stopped just a foot in front of her and looked her over curiously.

"Hello," the mysterious woman said.

Lindsey took a step back, unsure whether this was real or a hallucination from lack of sleep. "Uh, hello. Are you real?" she asked, knowing how foolish it sounded.

"I'm very real. What makes you think I'm not?"

"Because I'm exhausted and it's the only explanation for why a beautiful, naked woman just walked out of the water like some goddess in a mythical tale."

The woman laughed, and it was like a soft caress along Lindsey's body.

"Thank you for the compliment. You've never gone skinny-dipping before?" the woman asked.

"No."

The woman swept her dreads over one shoulder to squeeze water from them, giving Lindsey a generous view of her full breasts. She quickly looked back up only to meet the woman's knowing grin.

"You should try it sometime. It's so rejuvenating," the woman said as she laid her hair along her back.

"Are you a guest here? I haven't seen you around."

"No, I live nearby. I was swimming along, heard crying, then saw you on the beach. Are you all right?" the woman asked.

Lindsey knew she had been loud, but she didn't think she had been loud enough for anyone out in the water to hear her. "I'm fine. It must have been a wild animal or something."

The woman reached up to gently wipe away something on Lindsey's face near her eye. "You almost had sand in your eye. That could be quite uncomfortable."

Her light touch felt strangely soothing. "Thank you."

The woman shivered and wrapped her arms around her body. "I didn't expect to stop, so I don't have a cover-up. I should probably head back home." She turned back toward the water.

Lindsey found that she didn't want her to leave. "Wait, I have a cover-up you can use. Since you live nearby, you can return it tomorrow."

The woman turned back with a beautiful smile. "Are you sure? I could just swim back the way I came. My home is fairly close to here."

"Don't be silly. There's no sense in going back into the water and catching a chill. I'm staying there." Lindsey pointed to her villa.

"You're very kind," the woman said, placing a soft hand on Lindsey's shoulder. Once again, she felt soothed by her touch.

❖

Ebele gave the woman beside her a quick glance, then looked ahead again as they walked along. The moment she had made eye contact with this woman, she was drawn to her in a way that had nothing to do with the call that brought her here. It was as if something clicked within her soul and made her feel a completeness she hadn't felt in over a century. A feeling she had vowed never to feel again with a human. Deka always told her that you couldn't control what the heart wants, but her sister had never fallen in love with a human. She'd never had to watch them grow old before their soul was released from the broken shell of what body was left. Ebele would help this woman get through whatever was causing her grief and then move on, like she always did.

The woman unlocked and opened the door to let them in. Ebele was familiar with the resort. It was a very spiritual place for humans to come and heal, so she had answered many calls to assist. Ebele thought the woman being here was a good sign, as it meant she was open to healing, which would make her task much easier.

"I'll be right back," the woman said, walking toward the bedroom.

Ebele looked around the room and noticed the recently burned incense on a meditation altar, a few books sitting on the coffee table with the titles *Practicing Mindfulness*, *Healing After Loss*, and *What Color Is Your Parachute?* Proof that the woman was trying to take her healing seriously, but it must not be enough, or Ebele would not have been called.

"Here you go," the woman said as she walked back into the room moments later, offering Ebele a soft cotton caftan.

"Thank you…" She hesitated for the woman to give her name.

"Oh, Lindsey." She then offered her hand in greeting.

Ebele accepted it and was rendered speechless for a moment by a warmth surging from their clasped hands throughout her body and gathering at the center of her being. She could see from the surprised look in Lindsey's eyes that she must have felt it also.

"I'm Ebele."

"What a beautiful name. Does it have a special meaning?"

"Thank you. Yes, it means compassion, kindness, or mercy."

They stared at each other for a moment before Ebele looked away to don the caftan. It smelled of Lindsey, crisp, bright, and clean, like sunshine the morning after a rain. The word *home* whispered through Ebele's mind.

"Have you been at the resort long?" Ebele asked.

"A week and a day," Lindsey said with a sigh.

"You don't sound like you're enjoying it."

"It's not that. It's just that I have a month-long package, and I'm not sure I can take staying that long."

Ebele grinned. "A whole month? Did you book that on purpose?"

Lindsey chuckled. "It was a gift from my family to not so subtly get me out of their hair."

"Why would they want to send you away for a month?" Ebele asked, then recalled that she had just met Lindsey moments ago. It was too soon to be prying. "My apologies, that's none of my business. I should go and let you get your rest." She turned to leave.

"No, I don't mind the company, unless you're in a hurry to leave," Lindsey said.

Ebele could hear the loneliness in Lindsey's voice, and it pulled on her soul like a rope tethering them together. She turned and gave Lindsey a smile. "I couldn't sleep now even if I wanted to. Swimming is like coffee to me. Gives me a wonderful boost of energy."

A happy smile lit up Lindsey's face and made Ebele's heart skip a beat.

"We could sit outside in one of the cabanas. I found a wonderful bottle of homemade rum punch during a trip to town yesterday," Lindsey said.

Ebele smiled. "That would be nice."

Watching Lindsey walk into the kitchenette, Ebele couldn't help but smile appreciatively. Lindsey was just a few inches taller than her with a beautiful, full shapely figure that recalled paintings and statues of Oshun, the river goddess of love, that Ebele had seen over the centuries. She had changed into a white tank top and loose black cotton shorts, her complexion was a smooth deep brown, and her thick, naturally curly black hair was piled atop her head and tied up with a black headwrap. After grabbing a glass bottle from the refrigerator and filling two glasses, she looked up briefly and gave Ebele that bright smile again. *Goddess, she's beautiful.* She studied Lindsey's round face, thick eyebrows, catlike, deep brown eyes, broad nose, and full lips. She had to give herself a little shake to break the spell this woman was casting over her.

Lindsey walked over and handed Ebele a glass. "Shall we?" she asked, leading them out of the villa and back toward the beach.

There were several covered cabanas with daybeds scattered along the beach. The daybed was wide enough for both to sit and keep a respectable distance between them.

"Whew, this seems to have gotten stronger sitting in the refrigerator overnight." Lindsey fanned herself.

Ebele was no stranger to the beverage, which barely affected her after so many years no matter how strong it was. "It's an acquired taste. You become immune to it after a while." She took a long drink, raised the near-empty glass to Lindsey in salute, and placed it on the small table beside her.

Lindsey chuckled. "I guess so." She looked out toward the ocean with a sigh. "For as long as I can remember, I've loved being near the water."

Home whispered through Ebele again.

"Water is a source of life. It symbolizes purification, renewal, and transformation," Ebele said.

"Renewal and transformation? I could use some of that."

Ebele turned to her side to look at Lindsey. "Is that why you're here?"

Lindsey hesitated in answering, and Ebele could feel the internal battle waging within her. She needed to talk, needed to release her pain, but she'd held it for so long she didn't know how.

"Sometimes talking to a stranger can help us find the answers we're searching for." Ebele didn't want to rush Lindsey's healing process, but fear of what she was feeling for the human had her pushing sooner than she normally would.

Lindsey picked up her glass, took a long drink, then set it down. She told Ebele everything that she had been going through the past year. The bad breakup with her ex-girlfriend, the loss of her job, and the even more devastating loss of her brother, his family, and her mother in a matter of days. Ebele could feel all the pain and confusion sitting on the surface of Lindsey's heart and soul. When Lindsey began to cry, Ebele moved closer to her and took her in her arms. It was her duty to take on that grief and pain. It was how spirits like her helped humans to survive and move on.

❖

Lindsey didn't know what it was about this woman, but Ebele had managed to get more out of her in less than fifteen minutes than a month of therapy probably would have. She felt deep down that she could trust Ebele. That somehow, Ebele could help her. She also felt a strange connection with the mysterious woman. Weirdly enough, like she had been waiting her whole life for this very moment. Lindsey felt comforted and soothed in Ebele's embrace. She felt her heart lightening and her dark mood lifting.

As her tears subsided, Lindsey shifted and met Ebele's gaze. The golden brown of her irises sparkled with the moonlight, and Lindsey felt as if she could see the universe in the darkness of her pupils. She was mesmerized, lost in their depth. She reached up and placed her hand along Ebele's face as she drew nearer to kiss her. She held her breath as she expected Ebele to push her away, but Ebele sighed and returned Lindsey's kiss. Lindsey felt as if she had been starved and was finally being given a feast as their kiss went from tentative exploration to hungry passion within seconds. They broke apart at the same time, resting their foreheads against one another, both panting and gasping for air.

"Wow," Lindsey said when she was able to speak.

"I think I better leave," Ebele said, placing a soft kiss upon Lindsey's head and moving off the daybed.

"Ebele, wait."

"Yes?"

"Will I see you again?"

Ebele looked over her shoulder and gave her a smile that made Lindsey want to give her the world if she could just see that smile forever.

"I have to return your clothes, remember? I'll come to you tomorrow night at sunset."

Lindsey nodded. "See you then."

Ebele gave her a wave in parting, then turned and walked back along the beach away from the resort. Lindsey gathered their glasses, walked back up to her villa, put them in the sink, then went to bed. For the first time in months, no dark thoughts clouded her head and kept her from sleeping. She was asleep moments after her head hit the pillow.

As soon as she was out of sight, Ebele stood along the shore, letting the water wash over her toes, wishing she could trade them back for her aquamarine tail to make her way back home to her family. Home. That one word had whispered through her entire being while she was with Lindsey. Thoughts of home now recalled Lindsey's beautiful smile and passion-filled eyes.

"I feel this one is different. That we may not see you for some time," Ayodele had said in parting.

Lindsey was going to be there for three more weeks. Maybe that's what her sister meant. Three weeks was nothing for a being who had lived for centuries. Three weeks to give the beautiful Lindsey her smile, confidence, and light back. Remembering their kiss, Ebele touched her lips and smiled.

"Mami Wata, what mischief are you up to?" Ebele called to her goddess and heard the faint sound of deep feminine laughter in response.

With a sigh she turned and walked up a nearby embankment, where she found a quaint whitewashed cottage surrounded by a waist-high picket fence. She walked through the fence and up the walkway, and found a key under the seagrass welcome mat on the wraparound porch. Whenever she and her sisters were called to do something that required them to stay on land for an extended period, there was always a comfortable home waiting for them. She never questioned how it got there or how it managed to have everything they could possibly need while they were there. She walked over to the refrigerator, opened it, and found fruits, vegetables, and fresh seafood. She grabbed a handful of grapes and ate as she explored her temporary home. When she reached the bedroom, she opened the French doors and sat on the porch listening to the music of the sea as she muddled through what to do about Lindsey.

❖

For the first time in months Lindsey woke up feeling rested. She looked over at the nightstand clock and was surprised to see it was almost nine o'clock in the morning. She had overslept, missing her sunrise meditation and the morning yoga class, and would soon be missing breakfast if she didn't hurry. Instead, she chose to lie there gazing out the bedroom's screen door at the bright blue sky and clear blue ocean in the distance, thinking of Ebele. Like some beautiful sea goddess, she'd walked out of the ocean and into Lindsey's life, bringing a sense of calm and lightness to her troubled heart. Lindsey touched her lips, closed her eyes, and sighed at the other feelings Ebele had given her. Lindsey hadn't had a desire for something, or someone, in so long she'd almost forgotten what it felt like. Things had been so bad between her and Rita those last few years that their lovemaking sessions had been few and far between, with little passion. As if they had just been going through the motions. Last night's kiss with Ebele had burned through her like a raging fire that Lindsey would have willingly allowed to consume her.

"Jeez, it was one kiss. Get a grip on yourself, girl," Lindsey reprimanded herself.

She slowly got out of bed and made her way to the kitchenette. While she had been in town the other day, she'd bought some fresh fruit and nuts from a farmers' market. Since she knew she wouldn't make it in time for breakfast, she made herself a fruit platter and a bowl of mixed nuts to start her day. She carried her meal out to the deck and enjoyed the solitude for the first time since she arrived. She watched the early morning swimmers and returned waves from her fellow retreaters.

She felt energized. Deciding she needed a little adventure to keep the feeling going, Lindsey finished her breakfast, showered, dressed, and made her way to the office to find out what excursions still had space available for the day. There were only two, surfing and snorkeling. She chose snorkeling, since she had done it before and it seemed far more appealing than spending an hour falling off a surfboard. A shuttle took them to a location about ten minutes from the resort. After the instructors learned that all but a few from the group had some experience with snorkeling, they separated them. One instructor took the beginners aside for a lengthier instruction while the other stayed with Lindsey and the other experienced snorkelers for a brief reminder about the equipment and the do's and don'ts to help preserve the environment and sea life during their time underwater.

Once Lindsey was fully enveloped by the warm Caribbean water, she felt a comforting sense of peace. She remembered her first trip to the beach, wishing she were a mermaid so that she could live underwater forever. She had become obsessed with mermaids, covering her bedroom walls with posters, paintings, and pages ripped from books. One framed poster of a beautiful Black mermaid her Aunt Josephine had given her for her thirteenth birthday still graced her bedroom. Lindsey found it a couple of years ago in her parents' basement and had it reframed to fit her grown-up room when she bought her house.

Thinking of that mermaid brought Ebele to mind and what Lindsey had seen just before Ebele came out of the water. She thought she had seen a human form with a fish's tail, and then Ebele appeared. There were always dolphins in the area. It was probably a dolphin swimming near where Ebele was, and her tired brain, along with a trick of the moonlight and shadows, had her seeing things. After all, as much as Lindsey had wished they were real when she was a child, she now knew mermaids were creatures of myth and legend. She smiled to herself, then focused her attention on the beauty and wonder of her surroundings. She continued to swim and explore, not paying attention to where her fellow swimmers or the instructors were until she suddenly looked around and realized she was alone. With her experience she knew that it was best to stay in groups because you never know what dangerous sea life you could encounter. Lindsey popped her head above water and saw that she had been so lost in her own thoughts she'd gone farther out than the rest of the group, who were frantically waving, pointing at something behind her, and yelling at her to come back. When she looked behind her, she could see why. Dark storm clouds were quickly rolling in, and the middle of the ocean was the last place you wanted to be during a storm. She waved back to signal she understood and began swimming toward shore. Too late, she realized it probably would have been better to stay underwater as she swam because her arms quickly got tired, slowing her down.

Lindsey still had a way to go when the first drops of rain began pelting her. She ducked back underwater, turned to her side, and began to fish kick her way toward shore. A flash of light several yards to her left surprised her, followed by relief that she had chosen to continue her swim underwater. If she hadn't, her body would have acted as a lightning rod for the storm raging above. She tried not to panic, tried not to think about how long it had been since she had done a long-distance swim, tried not think about how her lungs ached and how tired her body was getting.

Suddenly, movement out the corner of her eye caught her attention. *Please don't let it be a shark*, she thought. She turned her head slightly and saw an unbelievable sight. Swimming up from beneath her was Ebele. That wasn't the unbelievable part. What was so unbelievable was that the bottom half of her body was a beautiful, iridescent aquamarine fishtail. Surprised, Lindsey stopped swimming and simply stared at the vision in shock.

"Don't be afraid. Take my hand and I'll get you to shore," Ebele said.

It took a moment for Lindsey to realize Ebele's mouth hadn't moved. Her voice had been in Lindsey's head. Fear and disbelief had Lindsey frozen in place as Ebele offered her hand.

"Lindsey, we don't have time for this. The storm is getting worse, the waves are picking up, and you could be pulled farther out with the riptide if you don't let me help you."

Another flash nearby snapped Lindsey out of her shock, and she grabbed Ebele's hand. Ebele pulled her close and wrapped her arm around Lindsey's waist. They stayed underwater as she quickly swam toward shore. When Lindsey felt sand beneath her feet, Ebele released her and stayed underwater while Lindsey ripped off her snorkeling mask and stumbled up the shore and into the waiting arms of one of the instructors, who picked her up and ran toward the waiting shuttle van. Lindsey glanced back over his shoulder, but there was no sign of Ebele.

❖

By the time they returned to the resort, the storm had passed and all Lindsey wanted to do was go to her villa and try and wrap her head around what happened. Instead, her snorkeling group was intent on making sure she was okay before they let her go, and then the resort coordinator insisted on personally escorting her to her villa and making sure she was wrapped in a blanket and had a hot cup of tea before she left her alone. Lindsey wrapped the blanket more securely around her, carried her tea out onto the deck, and curled up on the lounge chair to stare out at the ocean.

She could no longer deny what she'd seen the previous night. She also couldn't use the excuse that she was tired and hallucinating. Yes, she had been worn out from swimming at that point, but not enough to hallucinate a mermaid talking in her head, wrapping her arms around her waist, and swimming faster than humanly possible toward the shore. Thankfully, no one asked how she got back to shore so quickly. They had been more concerned about her well-being in that moment.

As a child she'd desperately wanted mermaids to be real. To believe that deep within the ocean was a secret city like Atlantis where merfolk lived, people who swam the ocean saving drowning sailors and swimmers. Then she had read some story about mermaids not saving but seducing and tricking humans to fall in love in order to lure them to their deaths beneath the ocean. After that she wasn't too sure about wanting mermaids to be real.

Until today, when a real-life mermaid saved her life.

"Excuse me, Miss Thomas."

"Jeez." Lindsey jumped at the sudden appearance of one of the resort staffers. "Yes?"

"I'm sorry, ma'am, I didn't mean to startle you. The chef thought you might be hungry but not up to coming out to eat after your morning, so he made the salad you always order and asked me to deliver it." The young woman offered Lindsey a tray with a covered bowl.

"Thank you, that was very kind of both of you." She wasn't that hungry, but she smiled and took the tray anyway.

"You're welcome, ma'am," she said with a friendly smile in return before she walked away.

Lindsey looked down at the lobster salad on a bed of kale greens, and her stomach growled hungrily. She chuckled. Okay, maybe she wasn't too traumatized to eat. She took one bite when she remembered that Ebele was supposed to be coming over at sunset. Would she still come? Would she have legs or a tail? Well, of course it would be legs. She wasn't going to come flip-flopping up the beach like a fish thrown in a bottom of a boat. Lindsey laughed out loud at that image and found that she couldn't stop laughing. When two women walked by and looked at her as if she'd lost her mind as she sat stuffing food in her mouth and laughing until tears were running down her cheeks, she thought maybe she had. That this was possibly all a dream, and she was actually locked up in some looney bin. For what other reason would she be seeing mermaids?

"Okay, Lindsey, get a grip, girl, before they send people in white coats and a straitjacket over here," she mumbled to herself as she got up and took her crazy self into the villa.

Mermaid or not, if Ebele didn't show up tonight Lindsey decided she would go looking for her, because a conversation was going to be had. In the meantime, a shower and nap were her current game plan. Almost drowning and being saved by a mermaid was tiring.

When Lindsey woke up it was still a few hours before sunset. Too anxious to wait and see if Ebele would show, she made the decision to go find her. She stood before her wardrobe wondering what you wore to stalk a sexy mermaid who saved your life. Since this was supposed to be a retreat, she didn't have much to choose from. She decided on an ombre aquamarine sundress with a high-low hem and low-cut rounded neckline, wore her hair loose rather than tied up, and put on a little tinted lip gloss. Looking at herself in the mirror, she had to laugh. She looked like she was going on a date instead of a mermaid hunt.

"You know this is crazy, right?" She shrugged her shoulders and left the villa.

She walked down to the beach in the direction she had seen Ebele walk the night before. It was late afternoon, so many of the guests from the resort were lounging in the cabanas or frolicking in the water. She smiled and nodded but didn't stop to chat with anyone. About a half mile down the beach she saw a lone figure dressed in a white sundress, standing hip deep in the water, head down, hands slightly raised in supplication, and a basket floating strangely still in the water beside her. To Lindsey's amazement, the waves and tide crashed and pushed everywhere but in the circle of water where Ebele stood. Feeling as if she were intruding on something, Lindsey turned to leave.

"Please, don't go. I'll be finished shortly," Ebele's voice said in her head.

"Would you please stop doing that?" Lindsey said out loud, more annoyed than afraid that Ebele was in her head again.

"My apologies, this will be the last time. Please stay."

"All right." Lindsey walked up to a grassy embankment to avoid sitting in the sand.

As she reached the top, she noticed that several yards away stood a cottage straight out of a storybook.

"Of course, where else would you live but in a fairy-tale cottage." She shook her head and sat down.

Lindsey watched as Ebele finished what she was doing, picked up the basket, and set it in front of her. With a gentle push the basket floated out several feet in front of her, then seemed to be picked up and carried off by a wave going in the wrong direction, and then the basket was gone.

"I wasn't sure if you were ready to see me again," Ebele said as she climbed the embankment and sat beside Lindsey.

"I wasn't either. A part of me swears I'm in a really long dream and the other part of me believes I've known something like this was true since I was a child."

"Are you referring to your mermaid obsession?" Ebele said with a knowing grin.

Lindsey turned toward her. "How…"

"Mami Wata sees all when it comes to her children. She's been watching you since you were four years old and you saved one of our younglings."

Lindsey was confused. "I did what? Also, who is Mami Wata?"

"The first question I can help you remember. In answer to your second question, Mami Wata is Mother Water, the spiritual mother of all sea creatures, land serpents, and water spirits."

"Of course," Lindsey said sarcastically.

Ebele laughed. "I can tell you more later. For now let's get to your lost memory and the questions you have for me."

Lindsey frowned. "I don't remember any strange sea babies or saving anything."

"Close your eyes," Ebele said.

Lindsey did as she was told and felt Ebele's fingertips at her temple. A warm light appeared at the back of her eyes and a memory came, as clear as if she were experiencing it in the moment.

It was her first trip to the beach. Her family was in Gulfport, Mississippi, for a family reunion. She and her cousins were playing along the shoreline when Lindsey wandered toward a cluster of rocks. She heard what sounded like the noise the aquarium lady said dolphins make. She walked closer to the rocks and saw a little girl like her with a fishtail tangled with seaweed and caught in the rocks.

"You stuck?" Lindsey asked.

The little girl cried even louder as Lindsey climbed down the rocks toward her.

"Shh…don't cry, I'll help you," Lindsey said, trying to soothe the fish girl.

As Lindsey began to untangle the seaweed, the girl stopped crying, watching her warily. Once she got the seaweed off, Lindsey sat beside her, put her feet up on the rock, and pushed with all her might. Just when she didn't think she could push anymore, the rock shifted enough for the girl to pull out her fin and shoot out into the water. Lindsey quickly turned around to see where she went, but she was already lost among the waves. Just as she was about to get up, Lindsey heard the dolphin noise again, but this time it sounded happier. She turned and saw the fish girl do a couple of flips out of the water, then smiling and waving happily at Lindsey before she disappeared underwater.

Excited about her little adventure, Lindsey ran back to her mother to tell her about the fish girl she just saved. Her mother patted her on the head and told her how sweet that was, then went back to talking to Aunt Josephine. Lindsey's aunt was the one who told her later that day about mermaids.

Opening her eyes, Lindsey looked at Ebele in wonder. "How did I forget something like that?"

"You didn't forget, it's just the memory changed to something that your human mind could readily accept," Ebele explained.

"My obsession with mermaids."

Ebele grinned. "Exactly."

"And why I seem to be able to accept this much easier than I would have thought."

Ebele nodded.

A thought came to Lindsey. "That baby wasn't you, was it?"

Ebele laughed, a sexy, husky sound that gave Lindsey a warm feeling in the oddest places. "No, I had come into my maturity long before that."

Lindsey looked at her curiously. "How old are you?"

Ebele smiled. "Later. Ask me your other question."

"Did you know about all of that when you came to me on the beach that night? Is that why you came to me?"

"No and no. I came because you called."

"I called?"

"Your grief called to me. Remember the meaning of my name?"

"Compassion, kindness, and mercy."

"Water spirits like me, or mermaids as humans like to call us, have the ability to take on humans' pain, troubles, and worries as our own in order to help them get through a difficult time. In many cultures they believe praying and making offerings to Mami Wata

THE DEPTH OF LOVE

will favor men with fortune, gift barren women with fertility, and give love to the lonely," Ebele explained.

"So, the night we met when you said you heard crying and I told you I was fine, you knew the truth."

Ebele nodded, then told Lindsey what she'd been doing when she'd heard her, and about her sisters and their gifts.

"So, if all or one of your other sisters had heard me, then they would be here instead of you?"

"Possibly," Ebele said with a shrug. "Our calls are at the whim of Mami Wata. She sends her children where she thinks they're needed. We never know why she does what she does, and to question or go against it could cause you to lose favor or bring her wrath upon your head."

Lindsey still found it amazing not only that she was having this conversation but that it seemed to be completely normal that a water goddess had sent a mermaid to help her get over her grief. She still had so many questions, and she started to speak but Ebele placed a finger over her lips.

"Tell me about your family, about you and your life," Ebele said, removing her finger from Lindsey's lips and taking her hand.

Warmth radiated from the point of contact where their palms met, to spread throughout her body and surround her heart. She closed her eyes and gave herself a moment to take a deep breath and feel not only the comfort of the warmth but the feelings it brought forth. She saw her brother's big cheesy smile, felt the joy of seeing Constance holding her nephews for the first time, felt her mother's shea butter–scented hug wrap around her, and she knew they were all there with her right now in Ebele's touch. Lindsey talked about her happy childhood surrounded by a big family on both sides and two parents who openly adored not only each other but their children as well. Her mother was a teacher and her father a bus driver, so they spent most of their life just getting by. The one thing they did have that Lindsey treasured was a deep love for each other, which got them through some pretty difficult times. She talked about how her family embraced her when she told them she was gay, something she knew many of her gay friends never experienced. She talked about her career and the successes she had accomplished because of it.

As she talked, Lindsey realized that her grief was no longer for the loss of her brother, who had been her best friend, or her mother. It was for the loss of herself. So much of who she was had been wrapped up in her job and relationships with her mother and brother, and now that they were gone, she felt as if she'd lost herself.

"But you're not lost," Ebele said. "A part of your life may be gone, but you're not. You must find the strength to carry on the same way your father and sister have. There is still much love in your heart and so much more life for you to live. Don't do it drowning in sorrow and pain."

Lindsey looked at Ebele and felt at peace for the first time in months. "So now you've saved me twice from drowning."

Ebele smiled and wiped a tear from Lindsey's cheek. "All I did was offer you a hand. You did the rest."

There was that smile that made Lindsey's heart skip a beat. "Is it true that mermaids seduce humans and lure them to their deaths?" she asked only half-jokingly.

"Not on purpose. Merfolk just coming into their power may accidentally get a little overzealous in their passion for a human."

"Oh." Lindsey toed at the rock she was sitting on, wondering if that kind of death might be worth it.

"Don't worry, I'm well in control of my power, so if I were to seduce you, I would only drown you in pleasure, not kill you," Ebele said with a sexy wink.

Lindsey bit her lip as a wave of desire shuddered through her body. "That sounds very tempting."

Ebele looked into Lindsey's eyes and felt as if she were the one being lured by desire. She looked so beautiful with her thick curls framing her face and a dress that matched the color of Ebele's tail perfectly. She wanted Lindsey but was afraid that her desire wasn't solely based on physical need. Earlier that day as the storm moved in, she had decided to go for a swim. She loved to be in a storm-tossed sea. She likened it to the feeling humans got from riding roller coasters. Shortly after she got in the water, she felt a fear and panic from Lindsey as if it were her own. It was just as intense as her grief had been the previous night. Ebele closed her eyes and homed in on it. As soon as she picked up where to go, she shot off with a speed she didn't know she had. She felt her own panic starting to set in when she saw Lindsey's situation. She didn't even stop to consider the consequences of what she was about to do. All she knew was that if she didn't save Lindsey, a part of her would die. As soon as Ebele was able to get her close enough to shore to make it the rest of the way on her own, she left. The fear of almost losing Lindsey made her realize that there was more to their connection than Lindsey's grief.

"She is your heart and soul," Mami Wata had whispered on the wind when she had been praying for guidance moments ago.

Ebele knew there was no sense in fighting what fate had designed. She leaned forward and pressed her lips to Lindsey's, literally sealing their love with a slow, passionate kiss.

Lindsey ended the kiss and gazed at Ebele curiously. "How is it possible to feel like I've known you forever? Like I've been waiting my whole life for you?"

Ebele grinned. "As I said, we don't question Mami Wata's decisions."

Lindsey gave her a teasing smile. "Well, I wouldn't want to bring down the wrath of a goddess, but I will take the love of a mermaid."

Ebele stood and offered Lindsey her hand. She accepted it, and they walked toward the cottage. Later that evening, with Lindsey sleeping peacefully in her arms, Ebele wondered why her sisters' hearts were able to find one of their own to love yet hers always belonged to a human.

"Because they need your love and compassion more," the sea breeze whispered through her window. Ebele felt a sense of sadness that she would spend at least another half century without seeing her family again.

"Ebele, I would never ask you to leave your home and your family. To live someplace where you wouldn't be able to be yourself," Lindsey said.

Ebele looked over at her in surprise.

"I don't know how, but I can feel your worry and seem to know what it's about. I also don't know how it's possible after just a couple of nights to know that I love you and will do whatever it takes, or make whatever offering to Mami Wata needs to be made, to make this work."

Ebele felt a tear roll down her face. She had loved two other humans in the past, and neither of them had offered to change their lives to be with her. Ebele had to be the one to sacrifice.

"What about your family?" Ebele asked.

"Unless I have to become a mermaid and live under the sea with you, I can visit them, and they can come visit us. Of course, they can't know my new girlfriend is a mermaid, but I'm sure they won't mind some vacations on a Caribbean island occasionally," Lindsey said with a grin.

Ebele laughed. "Is everything you know about mermaids from fairy tales?"

"No, but I'm sure the myths and legends I've read are pretty much wrong about you as well. You have three more weeks to educate me before I have to go home and announce to my family that I'm selling everything I own to live in a cottage on the beach with a beautiful mysterious woman I just met."

Ebele tapped her chin in thought. "Three weeks, huh? I wonder how I can share all that knowledge with you?"

Lindsey gave her a sexy grin and shifted them so she was lying on top of her. "I can think of a few ways."

It was the last week of Lindsey's stay at the resort, and she felt as if the time had flown by much too fast. She and Ebele had been inseparable over the past two weeks. On weekdays, at Ebele's insistence, Lindsey stayed at the villa, and she would meet her there at sunset every night. Lindsey didn't mind because she enjoyed the group classes and activities. She felt centered surrounded by so much healing energy at the resort. She had even made some friendly acquaintances with a couple of other guests who were there for their own month-long retreat, and she'd befriended the resort founders,

Ramas and Sarita, as well. She never asked Ebele what she did during those hours they weren't together. She assumed it was whatever Mami Wata directed her spirits to do.

On the weekends she stayed at Ebele's cottage, where they spent early evenings discussing what was and wasn't true about the myths and legends of mermaids, as well as her recent internet searches about Mami Wata. Their late nights were filled with lovemaking and the days exploring the island. To Lindsey's surprise, some of the locals knew who, and what, Ebele was. They were people Ebele and her family had helped at one time or another.

Lindsey found herself laughing in amazement when she thought about the turn her life had taken within the past year. She thought she had been at her lowest when Rita broke her heart, but that was nothing compared to the shape she was in when she'd arrived at the resort three weeks ago. She had not only found a way to make peace with her grief and loss but also to love in a way that went beyond what she could ever imagine love to be. The day Ebele walked out of that water, Lindsey had found her soul mate.

A REVOLUTION OF MASKS

Brent Lambert

Comic books, SFF, and good cooking are the gumbo that is Brent Lambert. A full-fledged military brat, he is consistently struck by wanderlust and has a keen sense of things never really being permanent. A writer with an insurmountable TBR list, he remains forever determined to conquer it.

Having to bury his parents left Sable confused and dissatisfied with all the questions they never got to answer. An only child to parents without any living siblings, he buried them alone. His salary as a military financial adviser could cover the funeral costs. In a time of civil war, that boon couldn't be claimed by many.

Coming to this backwater part of Eyristul filled him with introspection. Nine years of missed opportunity since he last saw his parents. They weren't happy with him then and he didn't imagine they smiled at him from the afterlife of Okaru's Abode. He always joked they would be waiting for him with a frown when he died.

He stood on the porch of their estate and looked out onto the many acres his great-grandfather had bought from Red Mask Saborin. How brave did that man have to be to approach that monster? Even at this very moment, the Red Masks worked their oppressive magic on the country and the Purple Masks fought back. Neither side appealed to Sable, but it had been the Red that paid him.

Sable wished he could draw on some of his ancestor's courage for himself. He didn't want to be here alone. Everything he left behind was threatening to drag him into an emotional stupor. The war hadn't touched this small community the way it had so much of Eyristul, but he still felt like he was about to march into battle.

Loneliness wouldn't be his current truth if he hadn't been such a fool. He'd have arms wrapped around him telling him it would be okay. He'd have soft, dark lips against his neck. Now all he had was the cool night air and the shrieks of flocking Whiteseam birds migrating back from the southern ends of the continent. Okarudin custom said the Whiteseams were harbingers of death. Given the circumstances…

The door opened and Sable didn't look behind him. He already knew who it was. His parents' maid, an immigrant from the Southern Tears, was the only other person around to genuinely mourn the loss of his parents. "Aldamine, you really should get some sleep."

"So should you, Mr. Sable. Your parents would not look kindly on me leaving you to the night."

Sable laughed. It felt bitter and sad. "The night is black. Black is creation. What better place could I be?"

He wanted to scream. Every part of him demanded release. His flesh craved satisfaction. His heart sought an unattainable forgiveness. Mom always said he kept himself locked up in sorrow. He wanted to scream.

"They loved you. I should know."

Aldamine came to his side at the porch. Her hair was done in the style similar to his mother's; rich, black hair made into two long braids. Mom always said simple attire made for easy living. Aldamine seemed to have taken that advice to heart with her dress, jacket, and shoes being uniformly brown. The simplicity connected him in that moment to his dead mother. The one in the pair who always seemed on the verge of forgiving him for all his choices.

"I don't doubt they loved me. But I don't think I made them happy."

The first punch to their guts was when he told them that he was going to university in Relamoo. Mom laid out all the reasons she hated that city while Dad lamented against the military. He left without saying a word and they didn't speak for two years afterward.

His resentment for them was a mountain that took a long time to climb.

The second blow came when he introduced them to Borrin, the man he needed so badly with him now. They hated him. He was a government clerk, and Dad railed against the personal corruption it took to get such a position. Mom didn't like the expensive fabrics, the vibrant colors, and how they influenced him. But he loved Borrin intensely, and so they didn't speak for another five years.

Amends came slowly through tender letters and remembered milestones. The Okarudin religion said the fifty-fifth birthday for men was to be celebrated with great fanfare. Sable made sure he came, and all seemed forgiven, but he couldn't resist delivering the third blow. Borrin and him were married. It was the loudest Dad had ever yelled. Then came the nine-year gap. The last memory he had of his parents was their weeping.

Aldamine frowned. Sable might have felt more comfortable if he could point to the pungent sap of the zunga trees in the air as the culprit. He always hated his father making him help with the harvesting of it. But Aldamine was likely as nose blind to it as everyone else in this small town.

The financial adviser in him winced at all the lost money for not harvesting the sap. They never lacked for money when he was a child. As long as people in the cities wore makeup to hide the ugliness of their successes, the sap would bring people fortunes. Yet somehow his parents had no money saved. It baffled him, but he just didn't have the energy to try and unravel it.

"When did Dad let go of the staff?"

"A year or so ago," Aldamine said, her tone suggesting she wanted to talk about anything else.

It didn't make sense. Mom and Dad loved this farm. They took absolute pride in the history behind it. Liberty and independence were what Dad said it represented. A blow against the perceived tyranny of the Red Masks. Sable didn't think they'd give all that up for some big trip to Chasmek's beaches. Aldamine knew more than she was saying, but he didn't feel like he had the right to press. And if he was honest, he didn't want to run her away.

"I'm going to meet with the Leekoor tomorrow."

"All the more reason for you to go to sleep," Aldamine said.

Sable ran his hand through the tight curls of his hair. He didn't want to close his eyes. Every time he did, he saw Borrin. He saw that look of hurt. Those brown eyes drowning in the revelation of betrayal. The recognition that things would never be the same.

"Not sure if I can sleep," Sable said.

Aldamine rubbed her hand on his back and he stifled a cry. "You really should sleep, Mr. Sable."

"There are many things I should have done."

Sable did manage to get some sleep, but none of it was peaceful. His dreams were full of Borrin and…the other. Even saying his name felt like the deepest betrayal. He hated how his mind conjured images of him. Strong hands gripping him and pushing their lips together in furious, searching kisses. Discovering that hidden passion had left Borrin in pieces.

He woke in the bed that had once felt so familiar. The bed that carried him through childhood. His parents never changed it. The better part of Sable hoped it was because they wanted to preserve some of the good days. Times when they could love each other without having to build walls. He grabbed his sheets and pulled them to his face. He didn't want Aldamine to hear his anguish and emptiness.

"Mr. Sable, I made breakfast!" Aldamine called up from the kitchen. She sounded happy in her work.

The smell hit him halfway down the stairs. Oglutrich egg and steamed okra. It was always his favorite as a child. The eggs were more and more expensive since the Purple Masks had taken a few of the coastal cities. How much had this kindness cost Aldamine? He put it aside and tried to prepare himself to receive this generous act.

He smiled, though he imagined it looked painfully false, as he walked into the kitchen. His movement must have been quiet because Aldamine jumped and quickly stuffed something gold plated into her pockets. It looked like a medal. Probably something from the Southern Tears. He shouldn't pry.

A plate was set out for him. Scrambled oglutrich eggs, red pepper, salted okra, and a cup of mango juice. But it was just one plate.

"Are you not eating with me?"

Aldamine laughed. "Of course not, Mr. Sable. My place isn't at the table."

"Well, I would prefer to not eat alone."

She looked uncomfortable with what he was suggesting. He wondered what his parents set down in terms of rules. As tyrannical as his father felt the Red Masks were, he couldn't imagine him imposing strict rules of decorum on Aldamine. So her hesitance must come from her alone.

"Do you not trust me, Aldamine? I'm sure my father must have told you stories about what I do."

She wrung her dark hands, and the wrinkles on her face suddenly looked more pronounced. "I heard plenty about your father's political leanings, and yes, he had more than a few complaints about what you did. But never did he imply that you were anything less than a man of good character."

Sable used his fork to cut into his peppers. "You're from the Southern Tears. What does your country think of Eyristul's problems?"

"We are as divided as you. Some see the Red Masks as lawful and others see the Purple Masks as trying to assert what's right. It all depends on who you ask."

Sable continued eating, hoping that Aldamine would sit. "They say their leader, the White Mask, is something to behold. A madwoman in a fight."

"Yes, I have heard these stories."

He could see he was making her uncomfortable and sighed. "Where would you normally be after serving breakfast?"

A little smile crept on Aldamine's face. "I would tend to the flowers until your mother was ready to go to the nursing home and read stories. She was very punctual, and they always knew to expect us thirty minutes after the town breakfast horn. It was one of our favorite things to do."

Sable nodded, returning the smile. "Then perhaps you should head that way. The last thing I need is my mother scolding me from Okaru's Abode."

Aldamine walked by and put her hand on his shoulder. "Be gentle with the Leekoor."

❖

Sable wasn't sure why Aldamine had asked him to be gentle with the Leekoor—the man looked absolutely terrifying. His sunken face, wide eyes, and flat lips gave him a grave quality that probably scared little children. If anything, Aldamine should have said a prayer or two for him.

The Leekoor's sanctuary was a small place without much in the way of decoration. The walls looked like crumpled-up brown paper, the building having been exposed to too many years of humidity without repair. Strange that the religion of his parents dictated that no sanctuary be repaired. Something about the natural course of life being symbolic in the rise and fall of a sanctuary. Sable thought the practice foolish and not cost effective, but that was why he dealt with numbers and his parents hadn't.

The Leekoor was dressed in a long black gown with a thick gold rope tied around his waist. Smaller black ropes were tied around his wrists. If Sable remembered correctly, the ropes were supposed to be symbols of the struggle that the great hero Yutika faced when taking on the Forgotten White Dragons of Hakari Nan Below. It was said that sympathizers to the Purple Masks painted red ropes across the country to draw a comparison. Borrin called the graffiti pointless and detrimental to the overall character of the country. Love prompted Sable to agree and push his opinion of the matter to the side.

"Your parents will be greatly missed." The man's voice sounded as grave as he looked. Sable wondered how he kept any congregants at all, sounding so creepy.

"They were great members of this community," Sable said, trying to muster up a pleasant tone. He didn't want the hurt of his relationship with them to come through his words here. That was his business, and he didn't feel like sharing it. Dealing with Aldamine and her sad, demanding eyes was hard enough. He wanted to get this over with as fast as he could and return home.

The Leekoor looked hard at Sable and made him almost want to squirm in his seat. It wasn't a pleasant thing, being under that kind of scrutiny. The kind that made you question if someone could peel right through the layers of you and see to your core. That's why Sable avoided religious leaders. They all seemed to come equipped with that particular ability.

"I know your parents did not approve of who you loved. That could not have been an easy thing."

Sable could almost feel the color leaching from his skin. Just how much had his parents told this man? "Yes. I mean no, it wasn't an easy thing. But my father always had issues with the government."

The Leekoor nodded. "Yes, he had some significant problems with them. Spoke to me of the virtues of the growing Purple Mask movement in the days before the war."

Sable frowned. "Sounds like him."

"Do you know why he hated the government so much?"

"The Red Masks and my family haven't always had a pleasant history. The animosity stretches back a while."

The Leekoor moved to a corner and opened a small gray box. He pulled out a long black stick, put it to his lips, and it immediately was lit without a fire in sight. He went to one of the sanctuary's candles to pass the light on. A soft, vanilla scent wafted in the air as he approached Sable again. "You weren't raised in this religion, yes?"

"No, I wasn't. Mom and Dad found it when I was away at university."

"Yet you never wanted to follow them in joining?"

Sable shook his head. "Please take no issue with this, but religion has never been my thing."

The Leekoor laughed, and it was an expression far more friendly than anything else on his body. You would look at a man like him and not think him capable of such expression.

"Religion wasn't always my thing either, Mr. Sable. I'm not here to try to convert you."

Sable let out a breath that he didn't know he was holding. "I'm sorry for making assumptions about you. Just that in Relamoo religion is frowned upon for being outrageously false."

"Same could be said for most folks from the city. You have their clothes, but certainly not their temperament. This town has stayed in your bones, at least in that fashion."

A truth was in those words that Sable didn't have the capacity to deal with at the moment.

"So I would like for my parents to be buried in the Okarudin tradition," Sable said, reaching into his shirt pocket and producing a folded piece of brown paper. "These should be all the funds you would need to make that happen."

The Leekoor held up his hand. "Okarudin tradition does not allow payment for burial. It is a bad omen to do such. There is only one thing that we ask of you."

Sable felt a thick knot form in his stomach. "And what's that?"

"A relieving of the heart," the Leekoor said, taking a long drag from his black stick. "The one who surrenders Okaru's children to the earth must have a clear heart, or those children will be lost getting to his Abode."

Sable rested his hands on his knees. What would this little ritual entail? He didn't want to do this. He just wanted to grieve the way he felt best and be on his way. Why did trying to respect his parents have to be so damn hard? They always demanded so much from him, and even now from beyond the grave, he could feel their insistence on him doing this.

"So how do I relieve my heart?"

"Talk with me, tell me how you really feel. Then I tell you what to do about it."

Sable flinched. "I don't even know you."

"Sometimes strangers make the best diaries." The Leekoor smiled, skin going taut.

Sable closed his eyes, rubbed them, and then massaged his temples. His shoulders sagged a little. "Okay, let's do this. Let's... talk."

"Your parents. Why do you think they didn't like your choice in husband?" the Leekoor asked, taking a seat, and stretching his legs.

"Because he worked for the government. My dad assumes anyone involved with the government has got to be up to no good. It's why he was so damn mad at my occupation with the army."

"Financial adviser, right?"

Sable nodded. "He thought I was just going through a rebellious phase. Doing something to piss him off. I think me bringing Borrin home was the thing that solidified to him that I was really making a choice."

"And your mother? How did she feel?"

Sable scoffed. "Hard to tell if she ever felt at all, to be honest. She just went along with whatever my dad felt. I didn't think she really gave much of a damn about how I felt. She was just going through the motions."

"Why?"

Sable shrugged his shoulders. "Love. Loyalty. I don't know. I just wished she had been able to spare some of that devotion for me."

The Leekoor pointed his fingers toward the center of his chest. "Part of this relieving of the heart is for me to help you fill in the pieces you don't know. Not so that you're forced to forgive, but so you can have the full picture."

"Go on."

"Your mother was the secretary of a prominent Red Mask in her youth," the Leekoor said.

Sable rocked back a bit at the revelation. His mother had never once made mention of such a detail in her life. "How do you know this?"

"Okaru's children are called to confess all to him. I know quite a bit about your parents. The things they were scared to tell you and the things they wish they would have."

"But a Red Mask? I don't see how my dad wouldn't have ranted and raved about that."

The Leekoor raised an eyebrow. "He certainly did to me. But there were things he didn't want to make your mother relive."

Sable could feel his heart beating faster. "What things?"

"The Red Mask she worked for took a strong liking to your mother. He wanted her to marry one of his sons, a cruel, disgusting thing. Your mother would have no part of it and refused. But you know better than I that you don't embarrass a Red Mask."

Sable had heard enough stories to know how true that was. "I do."

"So this Red Mask used his resources and murdered your mother's family. That's why she didn't have any siblings."

Sable blinked hard as he tried to digest the words of the Leekoor. "But she always told me—"

"To protect you. See, she didn't want you to have the hate in your heart that she knew festered in hers and your father's. She wasn't being cold to you to be spiteful. She just wanted to shield you from herself."

Sable took a moment before speaking again. "But that's not fair. She should have told me."

"Perhaps."

"And what about my dad? What's the tragedy he hid from me?"

The Leekoor smiled. "No such tragedy, I'm glad to say. No, your father was just an idealist who saw all the things wrong with the world. He saw the sadness that never really left your mother and was infuriated by it."

Sable sighed. "So that's it? I don't feel like my heart is relieved."

"No, that's not all. We need to talk about exactly how they died."

Sable went cold. He was sure his blood was blue and icy. "What do you mean? I thought it was an accident."

"No, Mr. Sable, it wasn't. Your parents died in a fight."

"A fight? Come on, my parents never even lifted a shovel to smash a bug."

"As I said, your parents hid much because they wanted to protect you. Both of your parents spent time in the military. That's how they first met."

Sable felt like his whole world was crashing down all around him. This couldn't be a real thing happening. "Soldiers? But…"

"I know this is a lot, and we don't have to do this all at once."

Sable held up his hand to stop him. "No, we keep going. If I leave, I don't think I'll come back."

"Very well. Your parents were military and fought in the war against Chasmek, on opposite sides."

Chasmek? That's where Aldamine had said they died. On a trip, no less.

"Your mother got her fair share of awards. It led to a job with a Red Mask."

"Was she with my father then?"

"No, he was out and about in the world trying to find himself. The war left him in a broken place, and he wanted to make sense of it all." The Leekoor said the words whimsically, like he was missing an old friend.

"So they died in a fight? Fighting who?"

The Leekoor leaned forward and sat a hand on Sable's knee. "Your parents didn't just sympathize with the Purple Masks. They were among some of its top commanders."

Sable didn't speak. Couldn't speak. Too many puzzle pieces jockeyed to fit with one another in his mind. Finally, he bit his tears and let the words out. "They didn't hate me for joining the government, they were afraid for me."

"If they had ever been exposed, you would have been in very real danger. Fighting their fight and you being in Relamoo was torturing them."

"They should have told me!"

The Leekoor nodded. "As I told them many times, but they hoped that maybe you not knowing might protect you if worse came to worst."

"Where did they die?" Sable asked, a tear running down his face.

"And this is where I tell you what to do." The Leekoor stood up, hands folded in front of him. "Go home and talk to Aldamine. Ask for the ebony box."

Sable got up without a word and left.

Aldamine was sitting in the kitchen penning a note when Sable walked through the door. She looked up at him and sighed. "So you know?"

He wanted to be angry with her, but he couldn't find the strength for it. Next to the note she was penning was a gold medal. She had tucked it away quickly that morning. It must have been something his mother earned.

"I know enough of it, but not all," Sable said. "Why didn't you tell me?"

"I am a servant of this household and I loved your parents. Even in death, I abide by my oaths to them," Aldamine said with a firmness he had never heard from her before. She was such a gentle woman, and he knew in that tone just how much she loved his parents.

Sable felt like crumbling. "They let me hate them to protect me."

"Yes, and it ate at them for a very long time. But they loved you, my dear. They truly did."

Sable reached out and hugged her. "You have to show me where the ebony box is."

Aldamine nodded. "Come with me."

They went outside and out into the fields until they reached a wooden panel in the middle of it all. Aldamine bent down and undid the latch, pulling back the panel. In a small hole sat the ebony box. She stepped aside so that Sable could get to it.

He stepped forward, his heart threatening to beat right out of his chest. So much had been laid before him in such a short time, and he wasn't sure if he was ready for this. But his parents deserved to be buried, and that meant finishing this ritual. He'd have them in Okaru's Abode if it was the last thing he did.

Dropping to his knees, Sable dug past the dirt and unlatched the ebony box. He pulled out two purple masks, the ones his parents were out being revolutionaries in. Burn marks were on both, and a crack ran down one near the cheek. He held the masks close to him and rocked back and forth, the last vestige of his parents' love. He never wanted to let this go, couldn't let this go.

"What are you going to do now?" Aldamine asked from behind him, gentle as ever.

Sable looked up at her, full of resolve. He understood what real love was now. It wasn't the fleeting, lustful arrangement he had with Borrin. It was this. Love was sacrifice.

"First, I'm going to bury my parents. Then I'm going to see about finishing what they started."

BREAKING AND ENTERING

Gracie C. McKeever

A native New Yorker, Gracie C. McKeever has authored several novels, novellas, and series, most of which can be found at Siren Publishing under multiple subgenres beneath the erotic romance umbrella. Of particular note are her BDSM/GLBTQ/Interracial/Historical/Ménage/Paranormal/Western, *Three Men and a Bounty*, and her GLBTQ/Interracial/Paranormal trilogy, *Zara's Bois*.

Trey Reed told himself he was doing his duty, not as an officer of the law, not as a Good Samaritan who wanted to be a hero, but as a compassionate human being who knew right from wrong. He told himself the perps would be back to finish what they had started a few nights ago and it was best for him to be here and deter another attack.

When all was said and done, however, Trey knew he was lying to himself.

The only reason he was sitting outside this house without his partner and on his own time was the occupant inside.

The memory of smooth ivory skin stretched tight over lean muscle, sandy-blond waves brushed back over a proud, unblemished forehead, and high pronounced cheekbones had Trey salivating with longing.

He hadn't seen cheekbones like that since, hell, since he'd last looked in the mirror. All the Reed men had stereotypical high, prominent cheekbones passed down through generations of Choctaw.

The kicker, though, what made Trey's heart stand up and notice, was the long-lashed pretty blue eyes. Simultaneously innocent and wise, they were old-man eyes that had probably seen a lot, maybe even more than Trey had, which was a great deal, and more than most people bargained for.

He licked his lips at the vision of his mahogany limbs intertwining and melding with the paler skin of his prize. He was drunk on the contrasts and similarities. Drunk on the possibilities.

Trey shook his head to clear the lust. The last thing he needed was to let his libido roar out of control and get the best of him, something that hadn't happened in a very long time. Not since he had allowed Lore Marshall past his defenses.

Lore had been the closest thing to a boyfriend Trey had enjoyed back in college. Beautiful and well-endowed, athletic, and smart, Lore had it going on in many ways. What Trey had admired most was Lore's ability to assimilate. Both a good thing and a bad thing. Lore had assimilated so well he'd forgotten where he had come from and who he was. Not to mention he was so deep in the closet he could have shaken hands with the Lion and the White Witch in Narnia.

Trey had come out at thirteen. It hadn't been the easiest thing to do—it never was—despite having progressive, supportive parents. He hadn't been willing to go back in the closet, not for anyone, even someone as perfect as Lore.

They'd had a big fight over what Trey called Lore's cowardice, a cruel, judgmental term he'd later regretted using, no matter how accurate a description he thought it at the time. Insulting Lore hadn't been the best way to make him to see things Trey's way, and Lore had reacted in kind, calling Trey a self-righteous prick who didn't know how hard things were for Lore.

Trey had sarcastically boo-hooed, playing a tiny air violin and basically ringing in the death knell of his and Lore's relationship.

At the time he'd told himself he was better off without Lore. He didn't need someone who would deny his true nature, his heritage, effectively asking Trey to do the same. He didn't need someone who couldn't see the beauty in being different.

Trey came from a long line of men who didn't shy away

from their feminine side—indeed, they embraced it. His people in general had nonconformist views where gender and sexuality were concerned.

His grandfather, like several older males on the Rez where Trey had grown up, was a *hoobuk* and chose to live his life as a female. Hoobuk were celebrated and held in high regard rather than seen as deviant. This was probably part of the reason Trey had found it easier than most of his gay peers to come out at a young age. He thanked his parents and grandparents every day for allowing him that freedom, something Lore had obviously and unfortunately never experienced.

Trey glanced across the street, wondering about the man inside the house, wondering how out and proud he was. Wondering if Cameron Johns could understand Trey and all his facets, not just the gay and red ones but his primal ones.

Maybe he *had* been too hard on Lore and he was a self-righteous prick, as well as a hypocrite, since Lore hadn't been the only one denying and hiding parts of himself.

Trey reached for the leather strap around his neck, caressing the small wood carving that hung from it, garnering his strength.

The figurine portrayed a wolf with head tilted back, powerful jaws parted as if caught in the act of howling at the moon. It had been given to him by Minco, the tribal healer of Trey's clan. A hoobuk and kindred spirit, he had also given Trey one of his tribal names, Nashoba—wolf—long before Trey's first shift.

Trey had several tribal names, as was the tradition of his people. The first, Chito, meant handsome and had been assigned by his parents. One of the last, Nayati—he who wrestles—had been bestowed by his grandfather right before Trey had left the Rez for what he'd thought were greener pastures.

At the time, Trey hadn't understood the significance of the designation. Since he'd left for college fourteen years ago, however, it became clearer as he daily straddled the line between Indigenous and non-Indigenous cultures and, yes, wrestled with the repercussions of his race, his proclivities but, most importantly, his beast.

Trey fidgeted in his seat trying to find a position comfortable enough to accommodate his insistent erection.

Shit, he was officially a stalker, no better than the perps who had violated Cameron Johns's property a few nights ago. As soon as this thought formed, two shadows emerged from the side of the house as if summoned.

They'd come back just as Trey had predicted they would.

He peered into the darkness to get a better look at them.

Hoodie-wearing punks who reminded him of some of his Lakota brethren whose attitudes toward hoobuk—or the old Lakota word, winkte—ran the gamut from tolerant to homophobic. It hadn't been enough for these guys to break Cameron's windows and shout slurs, now they were preparing to spray-paint the man's front door.

Well, Trey had a little something for them.

He grinned, quickly and efficiently stripping off his clothes and treasured necklace. His body tensed and adrenaline sped through his system at the idea of an impending hunt.

He wouldn't hurt them...much. He would fuck with them the way they were fucking with Cameron. Maybe he'd take a little chunk out of their hateful, deluded asses while he was at it to really teach them a lesson.

It pissed him off that in this day and age he even needed to, but that's how things were in Trumpistan. In no unspoken terms the hatemongers had been granted the freedom to come out and spread their venom.

Dogged by an image of villagers clamoring and wielding pitchforks, Trey wondered how they would treat *him*, an aberration in so many ways other than his homosexuality.

Naked, Trey slipped out of his dark-blue SUV, enjoying the punks' reaction when he closed the driver's side door and approached.

Despite the ungodly hour and Johns's house being located in a current blind spot with no working street cam in the immediate vicinity, he was taking a chance of someone other than the perps seeing him. Their wide-eyed gazes alone, however, were worth the price of his calculated risk.

Can you say show-off?

"What the fuck?"

"Auditioning for the next *Terminator* movie?"

Trey heard the nervousness beneath the second punk's chuckle, nervousness bordering on fear. He could smell it on them both. They reeked, the telltale perspiration oozing from their pores.

He bared his quickly growing fangs and growled.

The two thugs dropped their spray cans and fled.

Trey willed the change on the run—dense, brown fur sprouting over his body, bones and organs violently rearranging and shifting until he was on all fours and in wolf form by the time he caught up with the perps a block from Cameron's house.

He hadn't given free rein to his animal in such a long time; the exhilaration of running wild proved intoxicating.

Trey leaped as the boys scaled a chain link fence, caught the back pocket of the slower one, denim material coming apart beneath his canines.

The punk screamed, gained the top of the fence, and landed on the hard concrete on the other side in a breathless heap.

Trey patiently watched his cohort come back to help him to his feet before the two of them took off down the alley.

A lupine grin of satisfaction spread across his features as he pondered the honor among thieves. And they were thieves as surely as if they had burglarized Cameron's house rather than vandalized it. They had stolen Cameron's peace of mind.

Mine.

Trey warmed at the thought, turned, and retraced his steps to Cameron's house, where he found the man of the hour standing just outside his open front door.

Shit, had Cameron seen him shift?

Fuck it, in for a penny, in for the whole buck.

Trey padded closer, expecting Cameron to back up and slam the door on his snout, but the man opened the door wider, silently rolling out a welcome mat.

He entered the house and walked in a tight circle several times before reminding himself that, no, he should not piss on the plush cream sofa in the well-appointed, earth-toned living room to mark his territory.

Get a grip, Trey.

Not before Cameron finished locking the door and turned to him did Trey shift back to human form.

The whole process took less than a minute, and when he was done, Cameron stood staring at him, a look of appreciation in his blue eyes that made Trey's exhibitionism worthwhile.

Not fear, not even shock. Appreciation.

How long would it last, though? How long before appreciation turned into vulgar fascination and resentment?

"Say something."

"You're as magnificent as I imagined you'd be."

Trey's cock throbbed at the adulation, a jewel of pre-come forming at the tip.

Why did it sound like Cameron had known what Trey was before witnessing his earlier shift?

He had long forgotten about their incompatibility. The thought of Cameron being in on his secret, however, added a whole new layer to Trey's desire, dimming his doubt.

He closed the space between them, cupped Cameron's face with both hands. He took pleasure in the feel of the other man's stubble against his palms, reveling in the contrasts between them. Like most of his people, Trey was relatively hairless except for the straight black hair on his head, which he kept short for his job with the OCPD.

"You're not afraid of me," he said, already knowing the answer. He didn't smell any fear on Cameron as he had on the punks earlier.

"Obviously."

"Smart-ass." Trey chuckled and relaxed when Cameron's laughter joined his. He had never felt so comfortable with anyone so fast, especially not someone outside his race. He and Lore had initially hit it off because of their heritage and outward similarities, but their inner differences and worldviews had ultimately been too much not to drive them apart.

With Cameron, he felt comfortable enough to tease and intimately touch. He didn't see that ever changing.

"You wouldn't hurt me."

Trey arched a brow. "How do you know that?"

"You're not..." Cameron paused to glance down at Trey's enlarged penis jutting between them and swallowed. "You're not like them."

"An understatement." There were no state laws in Oklahoma

addressing hate crimes based on gender identity and sexual orientation, but that didn't matter to Trey. Even if he wasn't a federal law officer, he'd do everything in his power to protect what was his. He considered Cameron his.

Trey firmly drew the other man's face closer. "My profession and desire for you don't preclude malicious intent."

"Unfortunately, I've had my share of guys like that. You're not like them."

"You trust too easily."

"You don't trust enough."

"You're so sure of what you're getting into?"

"If you're a dream, then I don't want to wake up."

"Obviously, you're a romantic."

"Better that than—"

"Letting the haters win?"

Cameron's grin was sad. "Now you're getting the picture."

Trey got the picture, and Cameron was right. He didn't trust enough. As a cog in the justice system, he was too jaded to believe everyone got what they deserved or what they wanted. He was too afraid to believe this—Cameron's affection and fearless faith—could be real. "What if I'm a nightmare?" Trey murmured.

"Any worse than the bastards who damaged my home?"

He had a point.

Trey hadn't been sure of much since he and his partner had been called to investigate the vandalism wrought on Cameron's property. He was sure he needed Cameron Johns in his life, though, preferably naked and wanting beneath him. He was sure Cameron was the part of himself he hadn't known he'd been missing.

Trey liked Cameron, liked him as much as he wanted him. He liked Cameron's body, but more, he enjoyed his spirit and quiet courage.

There weren't too many men, even larger and heavier, who wouldn't have been intimidated by Trey's aggression and broad-shouldered, towering height.

Cameron had seen him change from man to wolf and back again and still wasn't afraid of him.

Cameron tilted back his head slightly to stare Trey in the eyes.

He reached down between them and grasped Trey's cock, scooping pre-come from the slit with his thumb before raising the digit to his mouth and licking it off with slow relish. "You taste as good as you look."

Trey groaned at the husky tone of the other man's voice, heart speeding at the idea of Cameron's full lips wrapped around his cock.

Before he could object, Cameron slid down to his knees on the plush area rug, licking his lips as he stood eye to slit with Trey's engorged penis.

Trey slid his hands through Cameron's hair, enjoying the feel of the silken strands against his fingers, body so attuned to Cameron's it was as if he'd performed these moves with the other man countless times in the past.

Perhaps he had, if he trusted any of the soul mate and reincarnation philosophies his grandfather believed.

What would the old man say to the idea of his shapeshifting Choctaw grandson being attracted to a full-human White man? Which was worse? The White man part or the full-human part?

Trey closed his eyes, breath hitching in his chest when Cameron's teeth scraped a teasing pattern down the length of his cock and back up again before he was forcefully sucking the head of Trey's dick into his mouth.

All thoughts of his grandfather and soul mates flew right out of Trey's head at the exquisite torture Cameron inflicted on him.

He slowly pumped his hips, finding Cameron's rhythm and matching it as the other man licked and sucked his way down to the base of Trey's cock until the head bumped the back of Cameron's throat. "Oh fuck..." Trey fisted Cameron's hair, ground his pelvis against Cameron's face as he eagerly pulled him in.

He took Trey's balls in his hand, juggling them for a long while before sliding his hand back and teasing Trey's taint with the tip of his finger.

It had been so long since Trey had been with anyone, the manual titillation was enough to send him over the edge.

He gritted his teeth, balls drawing taut against his groin right before he exploded into Cameron's mouth with a hoarse shout.

Before Trey's body stopped shuddering, Cameron slowly stood, licking, and nibbling a wicked path from Trey's semi-erection to his hard nipples.

Cameron paused at the right one pierced by a tiny silver barbell. He arched a brow. "For a cop, you're a bit of a maverick."

"There's no 'bit of' about it."

Cameron grinned and craned his neck to take in Trey's face, a shy expression suddenly dawning in his eyes. "If you want to leave now, I'll understand."

"Who said anything about leaving?"

"It's just that I know you're on duty."

"I'm not on duty."

"Oh."

"And I'm not a douche who would leave you high and dry after you gave me head."

Cameron chuckled. "You don't pull any punches."

"What's the point?"

"Are you as out and proud with your sexuality as you are with your wolf?"

"What do you think?"

"I think, what man can resist mind-blowing head?"

"If you say so yourself?"

Cameron flushed and tried to step away, but Trey caught him around the biceps and drew him back.

"Where do you think you're going?"

"You don't owe me anything."

Trey frowned.

Who had hurt Cameron in the past? Hurt him enough to doubt his appeal and worth? Someone like Lore who wanted to keep everything on the down-low? Someone who didn't want to claim and enjoy every part of the gay sex experience? A douchebag who only wanted to hit it and quit it during wee-hour booty calls?

The idea made Trey's heart clench with some unnamable emotion.

"Whether I *owe* you or not has nothing to do with anything. If I didn't want to be here, I wouldn't. And it's not just my job."

"You're a mind-reader too?"

"Just a Cameron-reader." He caressed Cameron's cheek with his knuckles.

"Besides, we're not finished." He leaned in, holding Cameron's face between his hands again as he captured Cameron's mouth with his. Trey teased his parted lips before thrusting his tongue and tasting remnants of himself on Cameron's.

Trey felt like he should be repulsed, vestiges of Lore's oft-expressed disgust niggling. He wasn't repulsed, though. Nothing about Cameron repulsed him, and Trey wanted inside him in the worst way.

He backed Cameron against the nearest wall, planting lingering kisses from his lips to his jaw to his throat, pausing at the inviting pulse in his neck before he turned Cameron around. "Damn, I wish I had my cuffs."

"What…what would you do with them?"

Trey answered by capturing Cameron's wrists and drawing his arms overhead, imprisoning him beneath him and against the wall. He nudged the seam of Cameron's ass with the head of his cock. "I want you. Right here, right now."

"But we need—"

"I had my last departmental physical six months ago and I'm clean."

"How do you know I am?"

Trey knew Cameron was clean because he couldn't smell any illness on him. He was as healthy on the inside as he presented on the outside. In fact, his aura felt like a—

"Trey? Do you trust me?"

"I trust you." He bent his head to nibble Cameron's earlobe while Cameron gasped and trembled under his superior weight.

Trey shoved down Cameron's boxer briefs and wanted to lean down to bite his tight, round ass, it looked so enticing. But first things first—

"We need something else besides protection."

"Something…?"

"Lubricant. Or this could get pretty uncomfortable."

Trey mentally snapped his fingers in an oh-shit moment.

Truthfully, he thought the pre-come gathered in his slit might just be enough lube, he was so ready, but the last thing he wanted to do was hurt Cameron more than he had been hurt already. That *would* make him a douchebag. "Where?"

"Top drawer, left side—"

"Don't move!" Trey rushed through the house, found the bedroom and the drawer in question before dashing back to find Cameron exactly in the position he had left him. "Do you know how hot you look?"

"Even without handcuffs?"

"I'll just have to make do." He opened the tube of lubricant, squeezed a liberal amount into his hand, wary of touching himself for fear of prematurely shooting his load.

Next, he coated Cameron's anus, sliding a finger inside and groaning when his inner muscles clenched around his digit.

Trey covered Cameron's body with his, teasing his opening with the tip of his hard-on before sliding in on one long stroke. "Damn, you feel good!" He leaned in to nip Cameron's neck, enjoying the musky-clean smell of him. Shower gel and turned-on male, an irresistible combination. He had never felt such a tight squeeze before, Cameron's snug hole fitting him like a glove, turning him on.

"Touch me."

Trey knew what Cameron wanted and reached around to grasp his cock, pumping it in tempo with his own rhythmic thrusts.

Within minutes, Cameron was panting, arching his neck like an offering that Trey couldn't resist.

He nibbled and sucked Cameron's neck before Cameron let go on a loud cry of ecstasy, his come spurting against the wall as Trey milked him with his fist.

Trey's own release quickly followed, and he shot deep inside Cameron on a guttural groan that lasted as long as his climax.

Barely able to stand, he leaned in to lick the perspiration from Cameron's skin, whetting his appetite for more.

Cameron glanced at him over his shoulder, that shy and questioning look in his eyes again. "What now?"

"Now I continue my bodyguard and stakeout duties, only from inside your house."

"For the rest of the night?"

"For as long as you need me."

"What if I need you for a very long time?"

"You're not getting rid of me that easily, Cameron Johns." Trey turned him around, stared at Cameron long and hard so that he wouldn't miss Trey's meaning. Then he bent his head and kissed Cameron breathless before he pulled back and grinned. "Wolves mate for life."

"I know we do."

One Night in Brazil

Nanisi Barrett D'Arnuk

Nanisi Barrett D'Arnuk has written mysteries, romances, and erotica. Being of Aleut decent, she dreams of riding her Harley across Alaska and being five foot eleven.

I'd been in Manaus less than a week. Next time I'd have to plan more than two weeks if I was going to explore unknown-to-me regions of the world. Two weeks to explore Brazil and Argentina? What had I been thinking? Two weeks was far too short to even explore one of those countries. I had let my friend Andrea convince me it was all the time I'd need. That was the last time I'd listen to her. Brazil spoke to my soul. It reminded me of my grandmother. I didn't want to leave. Even a month wouldn't have been enough. This trip was semi-planned to include five days in Manaus, four more in the Pantanal, and four days in Buenos Aires.

My grandmother had talked to me about Brazil since I was little. It was where she'd been born and had spent the first nineteen years of her life, until she fell in love with Grandpa. He'd married her and moved her to the States, where she'd spent the next sixty-three years of her life. When I had the chance to finally go on a vacation out of the country, I'd chosen here. I wish Grandma was still around so I could share my adventures with her. She would have loved to talk to me about this.

This was the fourth day in Manaus and the fourth day I'd had to look at our tour guide, Michaella.

My God, she was beautiful, in a very Brazilian way. She had long, curly black hair that fell around her mocha-colored shoulders below her beautiful, chiseled features that accented her beauty even further. Her tight jeans showed a length of leg that would make anyone drool, and her shirts bulged out just enough to show she had exquisite attributes. I'd been ogling her for the past three days and fantasizing about her for the past three nights.

I sauntered down to the pool area of the hotel. My trip up the Amazon River didn't leave until two o'clock, so I still had a couple hours. Some friends I'd met on this tour were already sitting at a table near the pool, having a light lunch.

"Hey, Leah! Come join us," Eunice called to me. She and her husband were making a trip she'd planned as a fortieth anniversary celebration. Her husband Stan had just retired, so they were getting to do all the things they had talked about all their lives. I walked over and sat at the one empty chair at their table. Michaella, our delicious-looking tour guide, was there too.

"Boa tarde, Leah." Michaella greeted me with one of the biggest smiles I'd seen this week.

"Michaella was just telling us about this afternoon's trip. She says that the water from the Amazon and the Rio Negro are different colors and don't mix for almost four miles."

Michaella smiled. "We call it Encontro das Águas, the Meeting of the Waters. The Guainía river, or the Rio Negro, comes in from the north with its warmer, black water and meets the Solimões, with its cooler, sandy-colored water. They don't mix together for six kilometers. Many think that's where the Amazon really starts, although there are those who insist it starts in Peru. It's amazing."

"Grab yourself something to eat, Leah. We'll be gone until well after dinner," Eunice told me.

I ordered a Bauru sandwich. It was roast beef and mozzarella with tomato and pickled cucumber that was quite popular here. Grandma had made them for me as a treat when I was a child. The taste made me miss her more.

"Let me show you how we drink that here," Michaella said,

pointing to my Coke. "Hold on a minute." She rose and walked into the bar, reappearing just a few seconds later with another Coke, a glass, and a cold bottle of beer.

"Have any of you ever tasted it this way?" she asked as she poured Coke and beer into the glass.

We all gasped. Eyes darted from one to another as my friends and I grasped the concept of Coca-Cola and beer.

"It is wonderful!" she exclaimed. "Try it!"

Her exuberance was so contagious that we gladly sipped the concoction as it went around the table. I had to admit, as did Eunice and Stan, that it was quite tasty. Who would have thought that Coke complemented beer the way it did rum? I immediately ordered a beer for my Coke.

"This is going to be a great side trip," Stan exclaimed as he ordered more for himself and Eunice. Hopefully, we'd be sober enough to enjoy the boat ride.

Four other tourists came out onto the pool deck and joined us at the next table.

"What a wonderful day this will be!" one of the men shouted. "I can't wait! I've been reading about this on my iPad, and it looks amazing."

"It's more amazing in real life," Michaella explained.

"This is one of the reasons I came to Manaus," I told them. "My grandmother was from down near Bonito, so I want to see some of the things she told me about."

"It's beautiful down near Bonito," Michaella said. "There are places where the water is so pure you can see down into it for many, many meters."

"I want to see the birds, too, especially the jabiru storks."

Michaella laughed. "They're almost as tall as you are."

I was five four. "That's what I can't imagine. I've seen ostriches in the zoo, but never another bird that big."

"I hope one of them doesn't carry you away!" Bob, one of the other travelers, said.

"Think they could?" I asked.

"I imagine so. Just be careful." Everyone at the two tables laughed.

"They do a lot of spelunking here, too," Michaella said softly. "That is, if you're into examining deep, dark tunnels." She stared into my eyes and flicked her eyebrow seductively. What? Was she suggesting something? Was I misinterpreting that look in her eyes?

❖

Michaella made sure I was on the front bench of the tour boat and she was right beside me. As she pointed out the different sites, she grasped my hand to make sure I saw everything. She whispered little asides into my ear so I'd notice things she didn't tell the others. That didn't help, because it just drew my attention to her and not the river. Her bare arm brushing against me was disconcerting, and even the smell of her light perfume distracted my concentration from the trip.

I was even more distracted when she finished a sentence with "Leah minha." Her Leah? Good heavens. Was she claiming me?

It was a good thing the boat was pulling up to the hotel dock. I might have attacked that beauty right then...but my thoughts were interrupted by a voice behind me.

"The entire boat excursion up the river was extraordinary," Stan said. "It was weird to see the two-colored waters flowing side by side, and feeling the temperature difference was unbelievable. You could see the flotsam racing down one side of the boat and just drifting slowly down the other."

"I'm so glad we came here, Stan," Eunice said to her husband.

"And Buenos Aires is going to be just as wonderful next week," he replied.

When our boat moored, we got off slowly and walked from there into the main lobby of the hotel. We were directed by hotel staff into a side room off the main dining hall.

Dinner was waiting for us there; a plus from the hotel for booking so many of their excursions. The food was exquisite and exotic. Dinner gave us another real taste of Brazil. We all sat there filling our bellies and chatting happily to each other about our afternoon.

Michaella came over. "Have you ever tried a caipirinha cocktail?"

"Never heard of it," I answered. My stomach tensed at her nearness. Had she really sought me out again?

"It's a very famous drink in Brazil. You should try it."

"What's it made with?"

"Cachaça."

"Ca-what-seh?"

"It's almost like rum but smoother."

"Well, I love rum, so I should try it."

She handed me a glass. The liquid was dark.

I took a sip, thought about it, and took another. "This is really good," I said, amazed.

"I knew you'd like it. Remember how to pronounce it if you want it again."

"Ca-sha-sah?"

"Close enough."

Everyone laughed and commented on the day. The others asked what I was drinking, and in a few minutes, the whole table was indulging.

"This is my last night with you for a while," I announced. "I'm going to Bonito tomorrow, but I'll meet you in Buenos Aires on Wednesday. Save some good excursions for me to go on with you."

"We will, dear," Eunice promised. "Is that where your family is from?"

I nodded. "My grandmother was born there."

"Good luck, and travel safely."

"You, too."

I'd left the party to come back to my room, leaving some still drinking beer and laughing. My flight out was early tomorrow afternoon, and I hadn't started packing. Four days' worth of clothing, new purchases, and souvenirs lay across the bed and dresser. I'm usually not that messy, but the commotion of the past two days hadn't left me time to put each item away. Paper sacks lay all over the floor, where I'd tossed them as I inspected each of my new treasures. I carefully folded my clothes and stowed my purchases until I had almost everything packed. I'd have to do a batch of laundry when I got to my next hotel, but I was good for now.

There was a knock on the door. I opened it and my breath caught. "You left the party too early!" Michaella said as she stood there with a dark amber drink in her hand. She handed it to me. "Another cachaça?"

"Thanks." I sipped it. "I have a flight tomorrow and I haven't packed," I stammered. "I shouldn't have scheduled this much travel for just a few days."

"You'll be fine. Maybe I can help you," she said, staring into my eyes, that cute smile on her face. "May I come in?"

"Of course," I said, backing into the room to give her space to enter. "It's usually not this messy in here." I apologized as I pushed the door closed.

I turned around. She was barely a foot away from me.

"I didn't come here to worry about your mess. There was something I wanted to give you to remember Manaus."

I'm not sure what my face said, but my stomach was knotting itself into a tight ball. "You don't have to give me anything—"

"But I have been wanting to give you this all week," she interrupted. Then she leaned forward and planted her lips firmly on mine. One arm slowly circled my waist, holding me as close to her as possible.

I'm not sure how long it lasted, but when she finally backed away, my head was spinning and every ounce of liquid in my body had somehow found its way to my crotch.

"Wow," I said, licking my lips, my eyes barely open. I was frozen in place with my back to the door.

"May I stay awhile?" she asked, softly. Without waiting for an answer, she walked into the room, piled things carefully on the floor, and then turned and held her hand out to me.

Without thinking, I followed her and placed my hand in hers. Was this just part of my fantasies? Was I dreaming this?

She pulled me closer and gave me a slow, gentle kiss. Then she stepped back and lifted her shirt over her head. Her beautiful dark hair cascaded down around her shoulders as the shirt came off, followed by her black bra.

"Don't back away," she whispered to me, as she lifted my shirt and undid my bra. She slid it off and let it fall to the floor.

I hadn't backed away, I don't think. I was staring blatantly at her incredible tits. They were beautiful, large, firm orbs with nipples the color of dark chocolate and areolas the size of silver dollars. That was one of the things I hadn't imagined in my fantasies.

"You do want this, don't you?" she asked, with a shy look of doubt.

I looked up into her eyes, at a loss for words.

"Of course you do."

She pulled me closer. Our lips met again as she pulled me onto the bed.

"I wasn't sure you were a lesbian," I said when our lips parted again.

"I'm not." She smiled, looking deeply into my eyes. "But good sex is good sex, no matter where you find it. You do like good sex, don't you? It would be a shame to part without exploring it."

I must have grinned because she laughed as she covered my mouth with hers.

God, I had never expected this! Sure, I'd fantasized about it. But I never dreamed it would really happen. I'd thought her smiles and sexy looks were just innocent flirting. Now I had her in my arms. Now what?

For someone who wasn't a lesbian, she certainly moved like one. I didn't have a chance. My clothes…and hers…were on the floor before my brain even realized she was serious about this.

Her fingers roamed my body while her tongue urged its way into my mouth. My hands caressed her back and buttocks. It was the smoothest, firmest skin I'd ever felt. It was like gliding over silk stretched tightly across a painting frame. The feeling of her skin was unlike any I could remember touching before, but then, at that moment, I wasn't sure I could remember my name.

What I did remember was that I wanted to make love to her. I had all week, ever since I met her. I rolled her over onto her back. She didn't object and started to press her body up into me as her legs wound around me. I could feel her heat pressing onto my abdomen… or was it my own?

The smile in her eyes invited me to continue and I started my journey down her body. I slowly created a trail of kisses and nibbles across her beautiful chest. I went from left to right and back again, pulling, sucking, and nibbling. Her skin tasted wonderful. The hint of salty sweat, toasted under the Brazilian sun, created the most delicious sheen across her body.

I made my way between her legs. My thumbs ran up and down her thighs as I kissed her belly. Her legs were firm, just like the rest of her. It felt like she was a runner, or a dancer, or something to keep them this perfect.

Then, oh, heaven! There, within the thick hedge of black hair, lurked a pool of ambrosia. I could have feasted on it for days.

Her mewls and sighs erupted into loud moans and cries of pleasure. She grabbed my shoulders and sank her fingers deep into my muscles as her body writhed beneath me. I reacted by sucking and biting even harder.

I slid two fingers deep inside her. Pushing and rubbing, I finally found her sweet spot and she came unglued under me.

Her hands shook, her head thrashed back and forth as her body tensed. Suddenly, my face was awash with her glossy liquid.

I lay there for a moment, my head nestled between her legs until I heard her whimper, "Ah, meu Deus!"

I didn't need a translator. I looked up into her face. Her eyes were half closed, a small smile on her lips. How sweet.

She pulled me up to her and planted her mouth on mine. She kissed my lips and kissed my cheeks, and my forehead, and my nose. After a minute, she slid down to my chest.

"Oh, please!" I moaned as she took my nipple into her mouth. Her teeth bit into me and every nerve in my body responded.

As she sucked on my nipples, her hands roamed the rest of my body. It was almost impossible to remain still and let her gently feel me. I could barely breathe as she continued.

"You are so wet," she whispered as she found the space between my legs.

"Because I want you," I said.

"No, I want *you*," she replied as her hand delved into me. My God! Could she fit all that in there? Where were we? How did we get here?

"That's not too much, is it?" she asked as her hand twisted within me.

"It's wonderful," I managed to say as her hand explored me. When she reached my sweet spot, I stopped breathing. Was this the spelunking she'd mentioned earlier?

Then her tongue found its way to my clit and the world disappeared into a blaze of bliss.

❖

When I awoke the next morning, she was gone. Looking at the clock, I realized I had just enough time to finish packing and maybe grab some breakfast before I caught my plane. As I walked into the bathroom, I realized that my shoulders were tender. An inspection showed small fingerprints. I smiled to myself, remembering the delight she'd expressed and the joy she'd brought to me.

I grabbed a quick shower, threw all my remaining possessions into my suitcases, and called the front desk to send someone to bring my bags down to the lobby.

I also called her office, but there was no answer. Taking a last look around the room to make sure I hadn't forgotten anything, I picked up my carry-on and took the elevator down to the lobby.

I walked out to the pool to look for her, but she wasn't there, either. Neither was she in the dining room. I sighed to myself. I so wanted to see her just one more time. Maybe I'd have to come back someday soon…maybe very soon. Did I really need to see Buenos Aires?

I chose some fruit and pastries from the buffet and seated myself so I could see if she walked in while I was eating. My brain kept returning to the taste of her in my mouth. I pushed the breakfast away and walked into the lobby to catch a taxi. As I waited for my bags to be loaded, I looked back inside the hotel, but she still wasn't in sight.

My God, I wish so much that Grandma was still around. She would have approved of this adventure.

A Sunday Kind of Love

Yolanda Wallace

Yolanda Wallace's love of travel and adventure has helped her pen numerous globe-spanning novels, including the Lambda Award–winning *Month of Sundays* and *Tailor-Made*. Her short stories have appeared in multiple anthologies including *Romantic Interludes 2: Secrets* and *Women of the Dark Streets*. She and her wife live in Savannah, Georgia.

Tamara Washington refreshed the feed on her laptop screen to no avail. She was still the only participant logged into the online meeting. Sunday Hilaire was late. Not thirty minutes, "I didn't hear my alarm and overslept" late. More like two-hour, spoiled pop diva flexing her power late.

This wasn't the first time a celebrity had left Tamara hanging, but that didn't mean she had to like it. She stalked to the kitchen, poured herself another cup of coffee, and tried to decide how much longer she planned to wait. If the senior editor hadn't promised her a cover spread for the article he had contracted her to write, she would have bailed a long time ago and dared him to try to screw around with her advance check to boot.

Cover subjects were notoriously flighty because they knew the magazine couldn't go to press as planned without their cooperation. Guillaume Clément, Sunday's manager, had set up the time for the interview. Tamara texted him to see if he could tell her how much longer he and his client planned to have her sitting around twiddling her thumbs.

Sunday's running late, he texted back.

"No shit," Tamara said. "Tell me something I don't know."

She'll be with you in thirty minutes, tops, Guillaume wrote.

"I'll believe that when I see it."

Tamara reset her mental timer and decided to use the extra half hour to perform some additional research on the artist she was supposed to interview today.

Like most music fans, she was familiar with the basic details about Sunday Hilaire's life. She was a native of Martinique whose West Indian–tinged debut single was voted the unofficial song of the summer the year it was released. It was a light, frothy bit of pop perfection, and most critics had said at the time that she was destined to join the long line of one-hit wonders. Five years later, she was still pumping out chart toppers. Her new single was supposed to drop in a couple of months and the accompanying album would follow shortly after, but her record label had set that schedule before the headlines about her personal life began to overshadow the ones about her music career.

Tamara performed a quick internet search to refresh her memory on the details of the topic Guillaume had made great pains to say was off-limits, not only in today's interview but for any follow-up sessions that might be needed to fill in potential gaps in the story as well.

She flinched each time she saw photos taken the night Sunday had gone from pop princess to punching bag. Six months before, Sunday and her now-ex boyfriend had gotten into an argument while they were on their way to a late-night party at a mutual friend's house.

Justin Tate, the man Sunday had been dating at the time, was a music star in his own right, though his biggest hits had come when he was a squeaky-voiced teen idol. His post-puberty track record had resulted in only a few modest successes, but he had managed to grab Sunday's attention. Gossip columnists said it was due to Justin's rumored twelve-inch penis, but Tamara didn't want to speculate. Or view the pics that kept hitting the internet each time Justin's phone was allegedly hacked.

Neither Sunday nor Justin had ever explained what they had been arguing about the night all hell had broken loose, but no topic could have offered a sufficient excuse for the split lip, black eye, and broken nose Sunday had received as a result. Justin had gotten a career boost as a result of the incident as a slew of female fans were drawn to his newfound edginess, but his and Sunday's relationship hadn't survived the fallout.

Tamara had a bunch of questions she wanted to ask about that night—and the rumors that Sunday was seriously considering accepting Justin's very public entreaties for her to take him back. Guillaume had warned her that broaching either subject was a deal breaker, but how was she supposed to craft an in-depth profile of Sunday if part of the story was missing?

"I feel like I'm being asked to write with one hand tied behind my back."

The task would be difficult, but not impossible. She had navigated her way past more stringent restrictions over the years. She could navigate her way past this one, too.

She took a sip of her rapidly cooling coffee. She tried not to get too emotionally involved with the people she interviewed so she wouldn't be tempted to mistake their effortless charm for overtures of friendship, but she had to admit she had a bit of a soft spot where Sunday was concerned.

Like millions of others, she was a fan of Sunday's music. She'd been privileged to interview her as part of the publicity tour for Sunday's sophomore album. The suggestive photo on the cover of the magazine had made headlines around the world; the article inside had gotten Tamara noticed by people in the entertainment industry. Gigs for dozens of other magazines had followed. She had saved copies of each article for posterity, but only one was framed on her wall—the piece she had written about Sunday three years before.

She regarded the article now. She and Sunday had crossed paths only a handful of times since it was written. Sunday was practically a cottage industry now and had begun to rely on social rather than mass media to publicize her latest ventures so she could control the narrative instead of allowing other people to tell her story. Her record company, however, wasn't hedging any bets. Her upcoming release was her first album since the incident with Justin, and the music execs at her label were obviously making an all-out effort to win back the fans who had accused her of instigating the event. Those same fans had chosen not to question why Justin had felt the need to turn what had been a verbal altercation into a physical one. He had served his time—thirty days in jail and one hundred hours of community service, thanks to a skilled lawyer and an incredibly lenient judge—but Sunday was still being punished.

"Blame the victim. Happens every time."

Tamara poured the rest of her coffee down the sink. Old memories had left a bad taste in her mouth.

Her heart sank when her cell phone rang and she saw Guillaume's number printed on the display. She could think of only two reasons why he would be calling her: he wanted to either reschedule today's interview or cancel it altogether.

"Sunday wants to have a sit-down," he said. "Today. Are you available for a face-to-face?"

Tamara glanced at the launch screen of the online meeting that had yet to start. "Isn't that what we already arranged?"

"Apologies for the mix-up. She wants to meet with you in person. Text me your address and I'll send a car to pick you up."

"To drive me where?" Thanks to contactless delivery and a lightning-fast internet connection, she hadn't left her apartment in weeks.

"To Sunday's house. She wants to do the interview in what she considers a safe space instead of online."

"I'm not averse to that as long as it achieves the desired results, but why the change in plans?"

"I assume she wants to make sure no one Zoom-bombs your meeting. I didn't ask and she didn't tell. It's my job to give my artists what they want, not question their motives."

"Fine." Tamara flipped her notebook shut. She recorded all her interviews so none of her subjects could try to claim they were misquoted if something they said didn't go over well with their adoring public, but she liked taking handwritten notes for backup.

"Excellent. I'll have a member of her staff set up an area on the property that's socially distanced but also affords a bit of privacy."

Tamara almost laughed at Guillaume's last comment. Celebrities had way too many people in their entourages for any interview to ever be considered private. Perhaps in this case private meant Sunday would limit herself to one makeup artist, one PR person, and one personal assistant instead of two of each.

"Yeah, sure," she said, "whatever it takes to get the job done."

"Thanks for being flexible. I'll see you in an hour."

"Why don't we make it two?"

She had made herself presentable only from the waist up. If she was going to sit across from one of the most glamorous women in the world, she didn't want to do it wearing a pair of Scooby-Doo boxers with a hole in the crotch.

"You got it," Guillaume said. "See you when you get here."

Only time would tell how long she would have to wait when she arrived. "You're already on the hook for three hours," she said to herself after she ended the call. "What's three more?"

❖

Even though Sunday hadn't yet given in to the temptation most singers felt to take a crack at acting, the sprawling mansion she owned in the Hollywood Hills had once belonged to a pair of classic movie stars. The scene taking place outside it, though, was thoroughly modern.

An attendant wearing what could best be described as a hazmat suit met Tamara and her driver at the gated entrance. The person waved her out of the car, verified her identity, took her temperature, and asked her a series of questions that made her feel more like she was about to see a doctor than one of the most popular entertainers on the planet.

"Have you or anyone you know been out of the country in the last fourteen days?" the attendant asked.

"I wish, but no."

"Are you exhibiting any symptoms of Covid-19?"

"No."

"Have you been exposed to anyone who has tested positive for Covid-19?"

"No."

The questions were the usual ones and Tamara's answers hadn't changed since the last time she'd been asked them, so she responded by rote.

"Okay," the attendant said after he'd checked off all the entries on the form attached to his clipboard, "you're free to go inside. Follow the driveway until you get to the main house. Guillaume is waiting for you."

Tamara turned to head back to the car, but the driver must have thought his next fare was more important than his current one because he took off without bothering to ferry her the rest of the way. It was a good thing Guillaume had footed the bill instead of her because her rating would be far less than five stars.

If she remembered correctly, the front gate and the main house were several hundred yards apart. She'd gotten lazy during the lockdown and wasn't looking forward to making the long trek on foot. "It's a good thing I wore comfortable shoes."

Thanks in part to the steep incline, she was out of breath well before she reached the front steps of Sunday's palatial estate. She briefly lifted her cloth mask so she could draw extra oxygen into her burning lungs.

"I think it's time I started using my exercise equipment as something other than a spot to hang my dry cleaning." She felt disheveled, so she used the camera app on her cell phone to give herself a quick once-over.

The quarantine haircut she'd given herself three weeks ago had finally grown out. It looked halfway decent, in her humble opinion, though she planned to leave future trims up to the experts. She hadn't been able to recognize the person she'd seen reflected in the mirror for the first few days. Now she looked—and felt—like herself again.

She panned the camera lower. Most of her wardrobe consisted of old concert T-shirts. She hadn't donned one today because she hadn't wanted to risk offending Sunday by brandishing the image of an artist she might view as competition. She had opted for jeans, a button-down shirt, and a funky blazer she'd picked up from a vintage clothing store. She had tied the outfit together with a pair of tennis shoes that had more miles on them than an Uber. She had hoped to strike a balance between looking professional and looking cool without trying too hard to be either.

"Close enough."

She turned off her phone and slipped it into the inside pocket of her jacket. The bark of what sounded like a very large dog echoed through the house after she rang the bell. Guillaume opened the door a few seconds later. "Glad you could make it."

Tamara greeted him with a nod instead of the one-armed hug and pound on the back she had been forced to retire after handshakes became a thing of the past. Then she warily eyed the panting Great Dane sitting at Guillaume's feet.

"That's Bellefontaine," Guillaume said. "Belle for short. Ignore her. She's not as tough as she looks."

"If you say so."

"Follow me." Guillaume waved her inside. Tail wagging, the dog named after Sunday's hometown trotted behind him like a docile puppy. If puppies were the size of small horses, that was. "Thanks again for being so understanding about today. Sunday has a lot riding on her next album, and she wants to make sure every step of the launch meets her exacting standards."

"No problem."

What else was she supposed to say? When it came down to it, she was only the hired help. Sunday was the one calling the shots.

"We've got you set up in the garden," Guillaume said as he led her through the first floor of the house.

Tamara felt like she was walking through the many exhibits at the Rock and Roll Hall of Fame. A series of awards, glossy photographs, and gold and platinum albums lined the walls.

"If you'd like something to drink, we've got practically everything you could possibly want," Guillaume said. "Beer? Wine? Something stronger?"

"Huh?" Tamara dragged her eyes away from a display case featuring the six Grammy awards Sunday had earned over the years, including the one she'd won for Best New Artist the year she burst on the scene. "Oh, water's fine. Thanks." She didn't like to drink alcohol while she was working so she wouldn't be fooled into finding what had felt like genius-level stuff at the time turned out to be utter crap upon closer inspection.

Guillaume turned to the uniformed maid trailing them. "Two bottled waters, please. Make sure one's room temp."

"Yes, sir," the maid said before she scurried off to what Tamara presumed was the kitchen.

Like most musicians, Sunday had a rider a mile long when she was on tour. Tamara remembered that one of her requests was for room temperature bottled water because she felt cold drinks adversely affected the quality of her voice before performances. Was that what today was, a performance? Tamara had hoped for something real. She should have known better. Sunday was in the entertainment industry, after all. Her whole life was based on illusion.

Under a huge pergola in the garden, two patio chairs had been set up across from each other but spaced six feet apart. A small round side table sat next to each chair. Tamara could hear the relaxing sound of a water feature in the distance, but her view of it was blocked by the dozens of tropical flowers lining both sides of the walkway. The overall effect was cozy. Almost intimate.

"Does this work for you?" Guillaume asked.

"Yes, it does."

The new setup was a hell of a lot more personal than anything they could have arranged online. Perhaps it could provide the spark to a meaningful rather than superficial conversation.

"Cool," Guillaume said. "Sunday will be out in a minute. I'll leave you two to it."

"Aren't you going to be joining us?"

The maid placed Tamara's bottle of water on the side table closest to her, then disappeared almost as quickly as she had arrived, and the hangers-on Tamara had expected to linger on the edges of the scene had yet to materialize.

"I trust you to be professional," Guillaume said. "We've gone over the ground rules several times, so there's no need for me to stay."

Tamara had to bite her tongue to prevent herself from saying that had never stopped him from micromanaging her before.

"If you need anything, I'm just a phone call away."

The call would probably end up being long distance. The house was so large it practically had its own area code.

After Guillaume left, Tamara took a seat in the patio chair she had been assigned and placed her digital recorder on the side table. She flipped through her notebook to remind herself of the questions she planned to ask. She might not use them all during the course of the interview, depending on the expansiveness of Sunday's responses, but it helped to have a good starting point.

She took a sip of water. Her mouth was dry, and she felt uncharacteristically nervous. The hurry-up-and-wait routine had given her too much time to think. Now she was psyching herself out. Frightening herself into believing the words she counted on to make a living wouldn't be there when she needed them most.

The article wasn't due for several weeks. She had plenty of time to come up with something.

"Let's just hope it's something good," she said under her breath.

"Was that comment meant for me or you?" a French-accented voice asked.

Tamara looked up and saw Sunday walking toward her. Instead of the latest designer fashions, Sunday was dressed in leggings and an oversized sweatshirt. She didn't look like a glamorous, world-famous pop star. She looked like the girl next door. If the girl next door had the voice of an angel, a face and body as fierce as Naomi Campbell's, and her own athleisure line.

"I'm sorry I kept you waiting for so long, but I was rehearsing for a music video and was having trouble getting the steps down." Sunday folded herself into her chair with a loose-limbed grace that belied what she said next. "Dancing has never been my strong suit."

Tamara, who had stood to greet her, resumed her seat. "Says the woman whose string of number one singles on the dance charts is longer than my arm."

Sunday's emerald eyes sparkled. "Donna Summer was the queen of disco, but she's remembered more for her voice than her choreography."

"What do you want to be remembered for?"

Sunday glanced at the digital recorder on the side table. "Are you asking me on the record or off?"

Tamara hadn't started recording yet because the interview hadn't officially begun. "It's whatever you want it to be."

Sunday was quiet for a moment, giving Tamara time to regard her without appearing to stare. Sunday's long hair was pulled into a messy ponytail that straddled the fine line between casual and high fashion. Her light brown skin was devoid of makeup, which seemed to accentuate rather than dull her beauty. Plastic surgery had fixed the broken nose Justin had given her, and her green eyes were as luminous as ever. The only visible scar that remained was a fine line on her upper lip. The blemish was small and barely noticeable, but Tamara couldn't take her eyes off it. She felt a ridiculous urge to touch it with her fingertips. To trace it with her tongue. To connect with the woman behind the well-manufactured image.

The realization caught her off guard. She hadn't been starstruck since the first time she saw Prince perform live, but she was definitely feeling the same sense of wonder now.

"Let's leave it off for the time being," Sunday said. She responded to Tamara's question by asking one of her own. "Did Guillaume tell you I requested you be the one to conduct the interview?"

Tamara nearly dropped her pen. "We barely know each other. Why would you ask for me?"

"I consider you something of a good luck charm. Most music critics assumed my second album was going to be a flop because my style was allegedly too lightweight to sustain a lengthy career. Then the interview I did with you was published, the positive word-of-mouth began to build, and the album ended up going triple platinum."

"I think the success of that album had more to do with the five hit singles you released than anything I wrote, but thanks for the compliment. Is that why I'm here today? Were you hoping we could capture lightning in a bottle for the second time?"

Sunday's smile was as cryptic as her response. "Perhaps."

Tamara opened her notebook to a blank page. If the pre-interview was any indication, the list of questions she had prepared wasn't going to do her any good. "All set?" she asked as she reached for her digital recorder.

Sunday held up her hand like a crossing guard at an intersection. "Indulge me."

Tamara didn't point out she had been doing exactly that all day.

Sunday fiddled with her phone. "Do you mind if I play something for you first?"

"Of course not." Tamara sat up straighter in her seat. The songs on Sunday's upcoming album had been as closely guarded as the gold in Fort Knox. Now Sunday was offering to play one of them for her? She hadn't expected to be treated to a listening party, but there was no way in hell she was turning down the invite.

The song Sunday played was upbeat and catchy. The lyrics were clever and burrowed their way into Tamara's head with the speed of an earworm. Listening to it, she knew without a doubt that she was hearing a surefire hit. When the song ended, she was unable to hide her excitement.

"That was fire," she said, sounding more like a fan than a journalist. "Is it going to be your first single?"

"The label would like it to be, but I'd prefer to lead off with something else."

"Something like what?"

"Something like…"

Sunday hesitated, then pressed a button on her phone. She bit her lip as a ballad began to play. The song was so heartbreakingly beautiful it brought tears to Tamara's eyes. Most of Sunday's music was about good times and having fun. It embodied the innate confidence she projected. This song was different. It was the first time Tamara had heard her sound so vulnerable. Seen her look so, for lack of a better word, human.

After the last note sounded, Tamara could tell Sunday was waiting for her response, but she was so blown away she couldn't get her thoughts together. "What's the title?" she asked, buying time.

"'Phoenix.'"

Tamara nodded. Without being too on the nose, the title was a perfect match to both the lyrics' imagery and the sentiment they expressed. "Who wrote it?"

So many people were credited with having a hand in writing Sunday's songs that the liner notes on most of her albums were almost as long as an unabridged version of *War and Peace*.

"I did," Sunday said almost shyly.

"You did? Wow. That's just—Wow."

Sunday began to chew on a manicured nail. "That bad?"

"No, that good." Tamara leaned forward, lessening the divide between them. "I can easily see it taking its place in the pantheon of empowerment anthems. I'd play it twenty or thirty times in a row if I needed a pick-me-up."

"That's what I was hoping for, but the A&R reps think I should lead off with something that makes me look strong, not weak."

"There's nothing weak about that song. Or you."

Sunday's cloudy expression cleared. Her body language changed as the tension in her shoulders faded away. It was as if she had been waiting for months to hear those words. Even if she had to hear them from a relative stranger. "Like I said, you're my good luck charm." She set her phone down, letting Tamara know that the sneak preview was over. "The label thinks the song sends the wrong message. That it might make fans think I'm dwelling on the past instead of rising above it."

"Are you?"

The question might have violated Guillaume's edict, but what he didn't know wouldn't hurt him.

"I'm focused on my future, not my past. That's why 'Phoenix' means so much to me. It—the whole album, really, is like my coming-out story."

It took a moment for Tamara to realize Sunday was speaking literally rather than hyperbolically. She began to tingle with excitement. The moment wasn't as auspicious as when then–President Obama had summoned Robin Roberts to the White House so he could announce he had become a proponent of gay marriage, but close. Major artists often offered teasing comments about their sexuality in order to appeal to a wider fan base, but only a relative few had actually admitted to being part of the LGBTQ community. And most of those were on the downside of their careers, not at the peak.

I love my job. I love my job. I love my job.

Tamara had been out and proud for years. A fact Sunday—or more likely Guillaume—was obviously privy to. "Is that why you chose me to write this article?" she asked as she fought to maintain her composure. "Because you thought I, a Black lesbian, could do justice to your story?"

"That's one reason. I was also hoping that after I revealed myself to you, I might be able to convince you to do the same."

Sunday's flirtatious smile almost made Tamara come undone. Was this really happening, or was she being punked? No, the interest in Sunday's eyes was clear. The feeling was decidedly mutual. The article Tamara had been hired to write had suddenly become secondary to something much bigger. Something much more personal. She felt honored that Sunday had chosen to share not only her truth with her but perhaps her heart as well.

She reached for her digital recorder. "Shall we begin?"

"I thought you'd never ask."

VENUS IN AQUARIUS

Malik Welton

Malik Welton is a blogger, writer, and journalist from Hampton, Virginia. As a lover of the arts, he writes to reach others and tell stories about different cultures. As a public relations student by day and creative by night, he tells his stories through a world view lens.

I don't hate him. Let's get that fact straight. I never hated him. In fact, I always loved him.

"Sometimes love is not enough," I said.

"Then you don't really love me. Love can always be enough," Elias said.

I thought about that for a second. Maybe he was right, if I truly loved him, maybe it would be enough. Maybe I was never in love with Elias. But what was I feeling, then?

"Let's go to DC!" Adam says.

I can't lie, the thought of DC excites me. I've been to DC plenty of times before, but the nightlife there is something I never got to experience. I've always been bound by family trips or school field trips that never let me explore beyond museum walls.

"I'm so down," I say without even thinking about it, stopping in the middle of my beach painting. With everything going on, I need a break. "Jake, you have to be down."

Jake pauses for a minute. "I don't know, guys, where are we gonna stay?"

"Who cares! Let's just figure it out when we get there," I spit out.

"Since I was the one who brought it up," Adam offers, "I'll pay for the room."

I smile. Adam is always up for a party no matter the consequences or risks. I, on the other hand, am just in love with the nightlife. The thrill, the rush, the social area, the bass in the background. It's almost therapeutic.

"What about Elias?" Adam asks.

I wince thinking about this. Elias has been my boyfriend for a while now. Recently, Elias and I haven't been seeing eye to eye. Even Adam and Elias don't like each other, honestly. Petty drama started tension between them. To be *completely* honest, Elias doesn't get along with a lot of my friends. He accuses them of having "ulterior motives" for being my friend. He's constantly caught in disagreements with them for things he swears are never his fault. It's a never-ending cycle with him. Embarrassing, to say the least.

Two weeks ago had to be one of the worst weekends of my life dealing with Elias. He becomes a different person when he drinks, and that weekend things truly came to a head.

"Don't worry about him. He's already got plans," I lie.

"Great," Adam says. "I really didn't want him to go anyway. We need a boys' night."

I force a laugh out. As much as I like Adam, he has a way of getting under my skin sometimes as well. Why can't he just be supportive of Elias and me?

"What clubs are there to go to?" Jake asks.

I've heard about different clubs in DC, but I don't know the best ones to hit on a Saturday night.

We all go through different search engines trying to find the best spots for a night out.

"Harbor seems really cool!" I say. "But are they even still open? I can't tell by these Yelp reviews."

"Nah, it's not," Jake says. "I saw a friend of mine post about them closing a couple months ago."

"Here's one called the Roof, sounds hot," says Adam. "Strippers and pole dancers! C'mon, how many chances are we gonna get to go to a gay strip club!"

I start laughing. "Can I please get a classy moment? I'm trying to find the best place to dance with good air and good drinks."

"Very true," Jake says.

"Marcelo, I'm sure you know someone in DC who could give us the move," Adam says.

That is true. I'm probably the most social out of the bunch. My mind floats through different people. Who lives in DC that could give me the best place to go? It hits me eventually—my old friend Dan.

I spoke to Dan earlier this week about my military issues. I'm trying to join but can't because my eyesight needs more examination before I can join on the spot. He gave me advice about the situation, but the conversation was pretty short and just about the military. He hasn't actually even texted me back about my last question. Typical.

"I might know someone," I say. "Let me see if I can get a hold of them."

I scroll down my text log until I come across Dan's name. I'm almost stuck, not sure what to say, or if he'll even respond. I need this night out, though. I've got to truly clear my head. I muster up some courage and start typing.

Hey! Sorry to bother you again, me and my friends decided we wanted to go out in DC tonight and wanted to know if you knew any clubs that would be the best to hit?

I tell Adam and Jake that I'll let them know if I get any info. We decide to be dressed by seven thirty so we can get to the city at a reasonable time. I decide we'll all send each other outfit choices, then lie down to take a nap so I'll have energy to face the night's festivities.

❖

I wake up to my phone buzzing and lighting up.

Hey yeah, you should start at this bar Charlie's on C Street. From there you can find a bunch of fun places to hit.

I smile. Even though Dan is pretty fickle, he does respond when I need him to.

Awesome! I think me and my friends are gonna do that. You should come out if you're free! It would be nice to meet after all this time.

Me and Dan got to know each other about a year and a half ago now. We followed each other on social media and always liked each other's posts. It wasn't until he messaged me that I realized he didn't live too far away. We were talking for some time, then eventually he went ghost. I didn't hear from him for about six months, and it didn't necessarily bother me because I was pretty busy with school and work and was also seeing other guys at the time.

After that break he contacted me again, but this time it was different. He was adamant about seeing me, constantly telling me how he wanted to take things to the next step. Trust me, I enjoyed our conversations a lot; he had a great sense of humor and he was able to flirt with me while still being respectful. But by that time, Elias and I were getting closer and closer. Even though I wasn't sure what was going on with him, even in the beginning of our relationship. I didn't truly know if I could put all my feelings into Dan. What if he left again? What was I supposed to do then?

Dan pleaded to see me, and I told him I would see him when I was free. I said that maybe we could do something for my birthday in January. He was essentially my backup plan if me and Elias didn't work out. Eventually, Elias and I ended up becoming a couple in late December. That was four months ago. It feels like things are still as rocky with Elias as they were back then. It's kind of embarrassing to tell Dan that I have a boyfriend when we've been talking. I really don't know what to expect with Elias. My friends recommend I should focus on myself.

I walk to the gym. The sky is a cotton candy painting, lost in a sea of mangoes and blueberry flavoring. It usually doesn't look like that, or maybe I never noticed it before. It calms me a little, like it can ease all the tension I have. Like I'm in the right place at the right time. A text buzzes my phone and I smile when I see Dan's name.

Hmm, I'm interested. I could use a night out. I'm working late but I think I can make it. Who all is going?

I stop for a second. I didn't text Elias back earlier, so I'm not exactly sure what his plans are for the night. I'm sure he'll want to go, but... I wince at the thought. I'm not having another repeat scene like before, not tonight. I want it to be fun, I don't want my friends involved in our issues. He's probably already got plans. Going to TJ's to get drinks with the older crowd. It's my night this time, and I deserve it.

Just me and my two best friends. They don't bite lol. I shake my head and go to set my phone down when it buzzes again. It's Elias.

Hey, wyd?

I put it back in my pocket without responding. I grab two dumbbells and begin to do curls. Working out is one of the only things that makes me happy nowadays. One of the only things that seems to go right in my life. It truly keeps me sane. I can push, grind, and sweat out all my frustrations. I want to make sure I hit cardio today so I can look slim for the club. Gotta look your best, especially in the gay club.

Cool, I'll let you know how work goes then.

I smile and my stomach flutters, but I don't say anything else that might sound silly. I see Elias's message and feel guilty.

Just at the gym, what's up, what are you doing?

I get on the stairs. It's time to put in work! I push to the interval level and I go in. I push harder than before, sweating out everything I can. I push away everything that's wrong. School, work, my parents, my terrible relationship, all of it. I begin to feel my legs ache, but it's all a mind game. I push myself 'cause it feels like heaven once you're done. The only heaven I'm used to nowadays. When I finally stop, breathless and relaxed, I check Elias's message.

Nothing much, figuring out what the moves are for tonight. What are you going to do?

I bite my lip and ignore the stab of guilt. *Not sure yet, probably just hang with Adam and Jake.*

I walk back to my place. It's already six, and I know that Adam and Jake will be getting on the road soon to come pick me up to head to the city. I'll need to get dressed fast. I grab a protein shake and head up to my room. Maybe I should invite Elias. It can't be that bad, right? A different environment could be just the thing we need. I take a deep breath and text him.

Hey, we're going to DC for the night. Did you already make plans?

A few minutes pass. I start to look at different clothing options.

Yeah, I want to go. What time are they leaving?

Probably soon, it's a last-minute thing.

How soon? I can get dressed fast.

Yeah, but Adam is driving, and I don't know how y'all would work without me there.

His issue with me is his problem.

I tense up. I can feel what's coming next. *Elias, that's fine but y'all have unresolved issues that haven't even been talked out yet.*

Tell him I don't have a problem with him and I'm coming.

I place my phone down for a second. Why is he like this? I don't want to argue, I just want us to be on the same page. I attempt a compromise.

Well, how about you drive, and we can meet them in the city.

No, it would be better if we all just rode together.

I don't want to ask Adam if Elias can ride with him. Elias is so outspoken; he just doesn't get along with others well. Even Jake told me that even though he likes Elias, he doesn't like us together and doesn't appreciate that Elias can't get along with many of our friends. But that's the thing with relationships. Am I supposed to take advice from two of my friends who've never been in a relationship before? What am I supposed to do? God, I hate conflict.

Look, just forget it. Time is running out and we can all just go another day when it's planned.

Elias wants to video chat.

I sigh and answer. "Hey."

Elias begins to laugh. "See, this is my problem with you. You make things worse between your friends and I."

"How?" I say. "I've tried making y'all work better, but it doesn't happen."

"You paint me in a bad light," Elias says. "You complain about me to your friends and then you paint me as the bad guy in public."

"What are you talking about?" I spit out. "Their view of you is your fault, even though I complain to them sometimes. I say the good and the bad, and a lot of times the bad only comes out when I need advice. If they don't like you, it's because of your own behavior."

"No, but it's your reaction," Elias says. "You make yourself out to be the victim."

Speechless. Who says that to someone they date? I hate this. I hate this so much. "That isn't fair."

"It is fair," Elias says. "You're spoiled, you've never had to work for anything in your life. You come from your happy home and your parents help you go to school. You're not grown up. You cry when any little thing doesn't go your way. You're so used to everything coming so easy to you. You cry when I don't show you enough affection... like, why can't we grow into that? I ask you to ask me to dance like a man, you still can't do that. You just don't get it. Like two weeks ago, instead of making a scene, you could have held yourself together and just talked with me about it later. But no, Marcelo has to act out."

I hold back tears. He talks so fast I can't even get a word in. "You were dancing with someone else inappropriately..." I stutter.

"I was, and I've already apologized for that. But you need to stop acting out about things and making it worse for us," Elias said.

Silence. I can't think of anything to say and I don't want him to hear the tears in my voice. "If you wouldn't have done it, I wouldn't have had anything to react to," I say.

"You need to grow up, period point blank," Elias spits out.

"Okay," I say. "Cool." My voice is flat. I refuse to argue anymore.

"Have fun with your friends," Elias says.

How does he not even notice that I've shut down? Maybe he doesn't care.

"Text me when you make it home," Elias says.

"I will," I say. "Good night."

He frowns at me, the line between his eyebrows defined, and then shrugs and ends the call. I just sit there. I throw my phone as hard as I can on the bed. I begin to shake my head angrily. What am I doing in a relationship like this? Am I being stuck up? Am I spoiled? I catch a glance of myself in the desk mirror on my nightstand. A tearstained face stares back at me.

Maybe I should call back. No, what would be the point? I pace my room more and more. How is this my fault? *How can you blame me for reacting to your actions?* If he hadn't done any of this in the first place, none of this would have taken place. Where is the responsibility? Where is the love? Where are the things I'm supposed to be getting in a relationship? Where is my love? Where are the things we talked about? Where is respect?

I ultimately feel like I'm not enough for Elias. Nothing I can do will be enough. I'm always combated, unheard. There is always another step I have to take, another obstacle that I need to crush. Months of enduring this has taken a toll on me. Why is it that the one thing that's supposed to make me happy doesn't?

I pick up my phone, but then I stop in my tracks. This night isn't going to be about Elias. I undress and sit on my bed. I look back at myself again. It's not that I'm unaware of what I'm looking at, but I'm unaware how I got to this point. I force myself to get up and get moving. I let the hot shower water run against my back. I need to move fast if I want to make sure I'm ready to go out tonight.

I pick out one of my usual go-to outfits. Black jeans, black shirt, black boots. Something about black is safe. It's clean and effortless but stunning all the same. I pick some chains to wear so I can dress the look up. I add a black mesh shirt underneath to give my outfit more of a club feel. The six-foot cinnamon-skinned boy looking back at me in the mirror looks confident, almost ambitious. You would never guess that he wouldn't feel wanted. My phone lights up.

We'll be outside your place in 5 minutes!

I spray on some of my cologne and head out to catch the elevator.

"I cannot wait to be in the city!" Adam exclaims.

I begin to laugh, feeling lighter. We've been on the road for about forty-five minutes now and have about another forty-five minutes to go. The bottle of vodka Jake and I've been drinking while Adam drives has me feeling better. Maybe it's just the guys taking my mind off stuff. I pull out my phone and text Dan.

About 45 minutes away if you still want to come out!

"So," I begin. "I might have another friend coming out with us tonight."

"Ooh, who?" asks Jake.

"My friend Dan," I say. "We've been friends through social media for a long time now."

"Nice," Adam says. "The more the merrier, in my book."

I stare out the window and think. What's funny about Elias and Dan is that they resemble each other. Not just physically, but also professionally. They're both in the medical field in the military. Both on the shorter side, both have olive-toned skin. Their only difference is their eyes. Elias has gray eyes, while Dan has dark brown eyes. Elias always talks about how great his eyes are, but Dan never talks about his. Their resemblance is uncanny, and it would probably make most people feel like I have a type. If I'm being honest, they both truly just fell into my lap.

We eventually find parking along a neighborhood street. I'm so excited to be in the city, finally having a good time.

We walk up the street to the nightlife area. Did I ever mention that I am absolutely in love with the downtown city lights? The screens and lights are safe spaces for me, almost checkpoints to let me know I'm home. The only other thing that makes me feel safe is the beach. I grew up at the beach, so it's always a part of my life.

"You are so cute!" a girl exclaims, snapping me out of my daydream.

"Oh my God, thank you!" I say back. "I love your glasses."

"No, I love your whole outfit! You all look amazing," she says to my whole group.

"Are you a swimmer?" asks another girl she's with.

"Yes, I am!" I say, smiling. "How did you know?"

"You have the look about you, like you know the water well," she says.

I laugh at how absurd that is. We end up talking to the girls while waiting in the line. Eventually, we get up to the front to the bouncer. He doesn't really pay us any attention, looks at our IDs and lets us in. The downstairs area of the bar is sports themed. Lots of jerseys on the wall, televisions playing reruns of recent sporting events. Some people are sitting downstairs enjoying their drinks, but most people are making their way upstairs. We follow the crowd up the steps and eventually land in the dance floor area of the club. Low lights and loud music fly through the air, people squeezed together but smiles all around. I almost feel like I can breathe. There is nothing and nobody here to make me upset or to not listen to me.

Jake, Adam, and I begin to dance. We make our way to the middle of the floor and throw our hands up, having the time of our lives. It's the spontaneity of it all. A job well done; mission accomplished. We're about to have a great night. I can feel it in the air.

I see Dan from the rooftop area, walking up to the front of the club. I begin to laugh nervously. I can't believe I'm really meeting someone I've talked to for so long online. It then hits me this is how most of my dating life goes, meeting through a screen and then in person later.

I watch him as he gives the bouncer his ID and proceeds up the stairs to the rooftop area. I laugh as I watch him pull out his phone and then mine buzzes with the text to say he's here. I run to the front steps to meet him.

"Oh, hey!" he says over the loud music.

"Hey, you made it!" I say. "This is Jake and Adam."

They smile and hug him as I introduce them both.

"It's definitely time to get a drink, then!" Adam says. He's always ready for a drink.

We make our way over to the bar as a group. Different groups of people come by, compliment us, and make small conversation as we wait to get to the front of the bar.

"What will it be?" asks the bartender.

"What do you like to drink?" I ask.

Dan laughs. "You can't handle my drink."

"Oh really?" I say back. "What is it?"

"Rum and Coke." He smirks.

I burst into laughter. "I'm six foot four, I can handle a rum and Coke."

Dan turns to the bartender. "Can I get two rum and Cokes?"

We take our drinks. "Have you been here before?" I ask as we find a place and sit down.

"I haven't. I'm usually so occupied with work, but tonight I deserved to get a break, so it was nice you texted me," Dan says.

"Hey, that was a part of my plan! I'm glad it worked," I say, laughing.

"Did you think I was gonna show up?" he asks, one cute eyebrow raised.

"I wasn't sure," I say. "But I figured I should at least extend the invitation."

"Well, I'm glad you did. You look really good tonight," he says.

I haven't heard that in a while. I feel the alcohol start to slow everything down. I haven't felt this good in a while. So free, so I can be myself. What's so different about tonight?

"Thanks, you too," I say, smiling back at him.

I dare Dan to take a shot with me. His Latin pride doesn't let him back down as we down two shots of tequila each. Warmth flies through my body and pulses like blood as we head to the dance floor. The music vibrates bass in my ear, and I love it. The dance floor is electric with people. Different people come up to us, complimenting us, dancing with us, exchanging information. I've never received as many compliments as I do tonight. There's no tension, no drama, no issues.

Dan dances to the beat but not with a lot of rhythm. I haven't even noticed that he's wearing khakis and a hoodie. Who wears a hoodie to the club? It makes me laugh, though. That's Dan for you, eccentric and sweet.

My heart begins to beat faster. My vision starts to get a little blurry, but I don't care, I keep dancing to the music. All of a sudden, everything slows down. My thoughts slow down like moonlit beach waves over a starry night. I stare at Dan more intensely. Is that where I'm supposed to be? What are the chances this can happen tonight? Dan, right here by my side. Dan, right here respecting me. Dan, right here able to have a conversation with me. Dan, dancing with me, proudly. Dan, getting along with my friends. Dan.

I step closer to him. Everything speeds back up. He notices me coming in closer and does the same. Are his thoughts racing like mine right now? We lean into each other and slowly begin to kiss.

I kiss him. I'm kissing him. I kissed him. I kiss him with so much…force? No, not force, maybe something else, like hate. No, it isn't hate, either. It's a certain type of…velocity. An electric shock. A death sentence to everything I love and hate. Everything that brings me so much power and pain. How can my relationship be everything and nothing at the same time? He smells like driftwood. He reminds me of home.

I come up for air, dazed. My eyes glaze over not from the tequila but from the shot of what just happened. I take control. I make a mistake. I regain my confidence. I'm not even sure if I like the taste of it, whatever it is. I look back at Dan. He's smiling and laughing. Unaware of what is going on at the moment, the gears grinding in my head. I don't know if I'm getting sober or more wavy.

You know that moment when you've done something wrong and you begin to question it? That was me in this moment. I reason with myself. Am I really doing something wrong? Isn't this what I deserve? Is this choice something I'm supposed to make? I'm still in shock.

I look around at my surroundings. It seems my friends haven't noticed what happened. I dance along to the club music bumping in my ears.

"That drink was strong, huh?" Dan says.

I laugh while keeping a poker face. "Maybe a little. I'm feeling it."

The rest of the night seems to fly by. I lose myself in the music and ignore my thoughts.

The club eventually announces the last call. "Last Dance" by Donna Summer blasts through the speakers as the true partiers sing it out to their heart's extent. We sing as loud as we can. In this moment, everything is okay. I wish I could stay in this moment forever. Safe between these party walls, loved by random strangers I'll probably never see again. It is so bittersweet.

We walk back through the downtown DC streets. The fresh air gives us all a clear mind again. We decide we should get food and end up deciding on pizza. Dan suggests a place by his apartment so we can crash there and also get food. We decide to drive separately and meet each other there. Dan's bright red convertible looks like something out of a Barbie commercial.

"I like old-school music, just a warning," Dan says.

I look straight back at him, laughing a little. "I love old-school music." I look outside the window, caught in my own daze.

"This Masquerade" by the Carpenters comes on. It makes my heart melt. The cinematic drama of the music fits the mood perfectly. The soundtrack to my heart being pulled in every direction. Dan, like before, seems happy in the moment.

We drive through the city toward his apartment. We push past buildings and statues of American history. We pass college students eating ice cream and laughing. We pass a couple holding hands on a night walk. I bask in everything that's happening. I notice that Dan isn't as much of a talker as he is on the phone. He seems to know when to cut it on or off. It seems to me he's relishing the moment as well. I can tell from the way he's dressed that he doesn't get out much. That, or he doesn't care what people think about him. I sort of admire that about him.

"You think your friends are gonna be okay?" Dan asks.

I snap out of my haze. I almost forgot my friends entirely. "I'm not sure, honestly. I hope they decide to stay with us, though. I don't want them driving home drunk," I say.

"Yeah, I hope they know I don't mind. My brother won't care, either, since he stays upstairs in his own place anyway," he says.

"I'll try to knock some sense into them," I promise.

We eventually pull into the garage of Dan's apartment complex. He makes jokes about parking in DC and how it's expensive. We eventually meet up with my friends and we go into the pizza place for a slice. We laugh and talk about the different people in the club. Jake stares at me thoughtfully. He can tell I'm going through it. But he doesn't speak up and just lets me go through the motions. I love how he picks up on certain cues.

After eating, Jake and Adam decide they're going to head home. Jake blames it on "not wanting to drive back in the morning." Dan pleads with them to stay, but they don't listen. I take my overnight bag and head with Dan to his place, a modern-style apartment that looks like any young bachelor in the city would like it. I sit on his bed, worn out from the day's events.

"You know," Dan starts, "I'm really glad I came out tonight."

I smile. It's still a really fun night. "I'm glad you did, too. I needed this night as well."

"I wish I went out more, but I'm always so busy with work. It's not fair," Dan says.

"I wish I had more time to myself sometimes," I say. "It seems like I'm always running around."

"You should make more time for yourself, then," Dan says.

"Maybe," I say, thinking out loud. "I could probably spend more time with myself."

"I feel that," Dan says. "I miss home a lot, and the beach. The beach taught me that I didn't need anything but myself. I definitely put a lot of pressure on myself to be there for people when I should be there for myself, too."

"That's been me lately. It seems like everything I'm going for just doesn't want to work out. I'm staying positive but I'd like a win."

"You've got to start looking at the bigger picture. What's holding you back from what you want?" Dan asks.

I begin to ponder the question. After the past couple of weeks, a lot of thoughts have crossed my mind, and I think about the negativity that has surrounded me.

"If you've got negativity in your ear, Marcelo, get away from it." He looks at me seriously. "You are absolutely attractive, mentally, emotionally, and physically. Do you not believe that?"

I look at the ceiling, unable to look at him directly. He rolls from his side onto his back as well.

"I stay positive to bring positive things into my life. I'm just trying to make the best decisions I can," I say. "Sometimes, it doesn't feel like it's enough."

He pauses. He looks at me and then looks away. He seems to have something on his mind, but he doesn't want to say it. Finally, he glances at me. "Then why didn't you choose me?" he asks.

My heart stops. "I…I was scared," I stutter. "You left me hanging before. I just wanted something constant."

"I get it. But I'm ready this time, and I wouldn't have done that again," he says.

I'm not sure what to say. I sink quietly into the pillow next to him.

"I saw the shock on your face when we kissed," he says. "If you aren't being loved right, you need to go."

I still say nothing.

"We're going through the same things. We gotta make ourselves happy, whatever it takes. At the end of the day, it's just truly going to be you and what you've made of your life," he says.

We fall asleep shortly after, holding each other. I can't respond, but I know he's right.

The next morning Dan drives me home. We laugh and listen to 70s and 80s music. I get home and feel relieved. I call Elias to have a real conversation.

I never hear from Dan again. I move back to the beach and start living the life I want.

RECLAMATION

Virginia Black

Virginia Black writes women-loving-women romance and speculative fiction while sipping fine whiskey. She favors gritty stories of lustful angst with happy endings, including her novella *Big City Blues*, a contemporary romance set in Eastern Oregon. She lives in the Pacific Northwest and is always hoping for rain.

Rade blinked the grit of fatigue from her eyes as she tucked a small toolkit into a side pocket of her tight black cargo pants. The first official Reclamation Hackerspace computer security contest had ended two hours ago at midnight, after twenty-four consecutive hours of competition. Now Rade wanted to crash, but once everyone stowed their gear, the imminent after-party would rage until dawn.

She suppressed a yawn and removed the loosened screws from one of the computer servers in the waist-high freestanding rack.

"These are ready to go." Rade had to shout over booming downbeat electronica. The makeshift booth she'd shared with her twin brother sat beneath one of the speakers. The music added to the overall feel of the hackerspace event.

D'Andriq gave her a thumbs-up, then pulled empty milk crates from a stack and spread them side by side on the floor. "Man, this shit was lit. All those upgrades you made to the network paid off."

His rich brown skin and thick curly hair matched her own, and though he was a few inches taller, they were both lean and muscular. There ended the resemblance. His hair fell about his head and shoulders in strategically planned disarray, while hers was cropped close on the sides and back and left long on top.

Rade nodded. "Yeah, I can't imagine the old backbone could have handled all the back-and-forth rankings in real time." During the exciting final hour of the contest, several teams had taken turns in first place.

She glanced around the main hall at the sixty or so bodies packing up computer gear in what had once been a church. One of them, a tall figure at a booth across the room, captured her attention.

Like many of the attendees, including Rade and D'Andriq, the woman wore a sci-fi inspired costume, but her broad shoulders, muscular arms, and confident bearing set her apart from the rest of the ragtag crowd of hackers.

When a restless unease made Rade realize she was staring at the woman, she went back to unplugging components and stacking cables. She pulled a network switch from the server rack and handed it to D'Andriq, trying to hurry things along so strike-down didn't take half the night.

In Rade's peripheral vision, the woman walked over to the DJ area that filled most of what had once been the altar. The DJ leaned over to talk to her, but he didn't have to lean far considering her height. Their faces were highlighted by the projection of psychedelic graphics against a giant screen covering most of the space where the former religious focus point had been. The DJ's skin was pale and reflected every color of the projected light, but the woman who spoke to him was dark, darker than Rade herself, with short black hair and striking beauty.

"Damn, she's big." D'Andriq had sidled beside Rade while her attention was elsewhere. "What's her story?"

Rade ignored him, more from spite than from her inability to answer. She knew nothing about the woman except that she was a puzzle Rade couldn't solve. She stood out in the crowd, yes, but there was something else about her that drew Rade's attention.

D'Andriq leaned closer and lowered his voice. "Why don't you quit staring like a creeper and just go talk to her?"

Rade looked at him in alarm. "What are you talking about?"

"C'mon, Rade," D'Andriq said, exasperated. "You've been scoping her since registration Thursday."

"It's not like that."

At least, Rade didn't think so. She couldn't remember the last time she'd been interested in anyone, but she was sure it hadn't felt like this giant question mark of an emotional state.

Sleep would help, she was sure. Too bad she wasn't going to get any.

The rack was empty now, so Rade started sorting cables into stacks.

"Right," D'Andriq said, his tone suggesting disbelief as he moved the stacked items into the different labeled crates. They'd done this strike-down together so many times before that little communication was needed. "Anyway, she's been scoping you right back."

Rade stopped working to glare again. "Bullshit."

"It's true. She never took her eyes off you during the glitch meeting," he said. "Even though her team didn't have anything to report."

"So what? Lots of people came to that meeting."

He crossed his arms over his chest. "You only get pissy when you're into somebody."

"What the hell are you doing watching her anyway? Sounds like you're the creeper."

D'Andriq peered at her, squinting. "When was the last time you got—"

"Shut up." Rade knew exactly when the last time had been. Seven months ago, and it had been a mistake of epic proportions. She couldn't remember the last time she'd just…clicked with someone. It was better to be alone than with someone who didn't get her, or worse, didn't fascinate her at all.

D'Andriq muttered to himself, and she missed most of it until he spoke in a louder voice. "How you plan on getting any pussy while being such a chickenshit is beyond me."

Rade punched him so hard in the arm he squawked and rocked to one side before righting himself.

She ignored his whining. "Keep giving me shit and I'll tell Mom about your hacker handle, *Frederick*."

"Unnecessary," he said, raising his hands to ward her away. "And uncalled for."

"You sound like a douchebag." When she glanced back at the DJ booth, the tall woman had disappeared.

Rade felt like she'd missed something important, but she was too tired to try to decipher it. She turned her back on the room and stashed a laptop in a case. "Besides, I don't even know her name."

"Kira."

A low voice cut through the music and prickled along the back of Rade's neck. She spun around in surprise to see the woman in question. Dark eyes met hers, and Rade's mind blanked.

She planted her feet so she didn't fall over but didn't know what to do with her hands. She settled for tucking them in her back pockets—no easy feat while wearing a knee-length leather trench.

"You're Rade, right?"

This close, Rade saw more of Kira's costume, a postapocalyptic combination of tight black leather pants and a loose off-white linen tunic. A black leather bracer with an embedded micro-display and a small circuit board graced one wrist. Tiny wires connected the board to small sensor pads affixed to Kira's forearm. The sleeves of a dark overcoat had been ripped away, leaving Kira's biceps bare.

Rade had seen tall women, big women, try to make themselves look smaller, but Kira stood upright, powerful yet somehow unassuming. When she met Kira's eyes again, she caught Kira giving her the once-over in return. She wondered about the verdict.

D'Andriq kicked the back of one of Rade's boots.

Fuck. His interference rattled her out of her inaction. "Yeah," she said to Kira. "I'm Rade."

Her brother snickered behind her.

Kira stepped around the edge of the table, into the area of the booth itself. "I heard a rumor this is your place."

Her voice was richer than Rade expected, and accented. British, perhaps, or born of one of the African nations. It vibrated through Rade's body more thoroughly than the music's pounding bass.

"True," Rade answered, but then she didn't know what to say next.

Kira smiled, perfect even teeth behind perfect full lips. This close, she was a head taller than Rade, but her presence didn't feel imposing. It felt...protective. Kira's stature suggested royalty more than it did hacker posturing.

"Want a tour?" Rade heard herself say, and mentally congratulated herself when Kira's smile widened. With a glance and a gesture, Rade handed off the rest of the cleanup to D'Andriq. She ignored his knowing grin.

Kira had already spent time on the main floor, so Rade led her to a small doorway behind the DJ area.

"Watch your step," she said, briefly resting her hand on Kira's bare arm. Her skin was warm to the touch despite the chill in the room. She could feel her own heart pound in response to that simple contact. Attraction had never hit her so hard or so quickly, and she fought to keep it contained lest this woman think her insane. She closed the door behind them, and the loud music was reduced to a persistent thumping against the walls.

"This is the server room," Rade said, relieved her voice sounded normal. "It used to be the area where the church staff prepared for services, but I added the ventilation and cooling systems before I installed the racks."

"You really built all this yourself?"

"Well, I mean, I designed it, but I had help with the execution." She described all the enhancements she'd made, her voice growing more confident as she talked about her favorite subject. She was surprised to discover that she wanted Kira's approval.

"What gave you the idea to start a hackerspace?" Kira asked. She walked around the small, confined space, perusing the systems.

"This town needs one," Rade said. "I mean, there's one across town, but it's affiliated with a big tech company and gets a lot of government funding." Rade picked up a few snipped network cable ends someone had forgotten and tossed them in a nearby bin. "With that kind of oversight, it's tough to explore all aspects of computer security."

"True," Kira said, watching her closely now. "You've got some hardcore gear here." She ran her hands across the front plates on some of the higher-value systems.

"Only the good stuff." Rade didn't bother hiding her pride and was happy Kira had noticed. She pressed her hand to Kira's back as she passed her on the way to the door at the other end of the room. "Come on."

The door led to a long hall that ran parallel to the former worship room, and several access points led from one space to the other. Despite Kira's longer stride, they walked in rhythm, their arms brushing against each other every few steps. It'd been a long while since Rade had been this close to anyone, and though she tried to hide the reaction her body was having to Kira's proximity, she liked the feeling.

"Solid turnout for a new contest," Kira said.

"Twelve teams? More than I thought we'd get."

Kira frowned in question.

Rade waved in the direction of the hall. "It's the first local penetration-testing, capture-the-flag contest in years that isn't part of a computer security conference. Much more on-the-ground and with a lower barrier to entry."

The hallway ended in the foyer near the entrance, and they maneuvered through the line of folks waiting for the restrooms. The brief touches as they brushed against each other sent pulses that awakened parts of Rade's body. She tried to pull herself together as they walked past stacks of church pews leaning against the walls.

"So why in a church?" Kira asked.

Rade scoffed. This question she was accustomed to answering. "Crazy, right? Particularly for a heathen like me." She shrugged. "It hasn't been an actual church in over a decade. Back when I was a kid, this place was a community center. I learned how to program in some of the STEM classes they used to have. When the lease came up a few years back, I snagged it."

She stopped at the other end of the foyer. "The hackerspace is more of a collective, really. I mean, my name's on the paperwork, but the members run the space by consensus for the most part."

There was no doorway, just an entrance in the wall separating the foyer from the stairwell. Rade paused before she stepped through the door. "Low clearance here, okay? Watch your head."

Kira arched her eyebrow, amusement in her expression. Rade kicked herself for being overly courteous.

Movie and convention posters covered the walls of the narrow stairway, the only sound the creak of Rade's leather jacket and the muffled bass of the sound system. At the bottom of the stairs, fluorescent light revealed a linoleum floor and a small but functional industrial kitchen area. Beyond it, several tables with mismatched chairs provided a casual cafeteria. A handful of contestants sat at one of the tables, deep in conversation, and didn't acknowledge Rade and Kira's arrival.

Rade pointed to a widescreen television mounted on a far wall. "Smaller groups host movie nights down here." She shrugged in humble pride. "So ends the tour." Maybe next time she'd start with the kitchen and end with the server room. Stopping here seemed anticlimactic.

"You should be proud of what you've done here. I've never seen anything like it." Kira put her hand against Rade's sleeve while looking around the room, and Rade stopped herself from leaning into the touch.

Even the poor lighting flattered Kira, revealing the tiny perfect curls in her hair and the circuit design shaved into the sides. The soft curve of her cheekbones begged to be caressed, and Rade rocked on her heels for a moment as she fought off the urge.

Someone hit a pause button somewhere and the music stopped.

Kira's gaze was piercing, like she was looking for something. Rade stared back, not sure what to do next.

The sound system kicked back in, this time with louder volume and a faster tempo.

"Sounds like the party's getting started," Rade said as the few people in the basement common area headed for the commotion upstairs.

"So," Kira said, close enough only Rade could hear. "There's nothing else you'd want to show me?"

It seemed like Kira was asking an entirely different question, and when Rade didn't seem to understand, Kira looked disappointed.

Rade wanted to make that look go away.

"Not looking forward to the cheap beer and schnapps passing for whiskey?"

"Never again, thanks. I got enough of that at uni."

"Uni?"

"Sorry. University."

One word in a foreign accent shouldn't sound so provocative or set off tremors in Rade's body. She forced herself to function normally.

"How about something a little less juvenile?" Rade walked backward, holding Kira's gaze with her own.

"Are we about to raid your fridge?" Kira said, pointing to the dated monstrosity in the kitchen area.

Rade rolled her eyes, but the usual joke didn't land so poorly when Kira made it. "Ha ha. Not exactly." She beckoned with a tilt of her head. "This way."

Rade rounded the long counter and headed across the common area to another door on the far side of the room. She led Kira to a small mudroom with two more doors, one that led outside and the other to Rade's apartment.

"This is my place," Rade said, keying a few numbers into a mounted keypad. After a beep and a loud click, she opened the door.

Recessed lighting activated when Rade walked into the room. Warm low light bounced off the ceiling onto three off-white walls and one of exposed brick. A comfortable couch sat along one wall across from a gas fireplace. Wide entries on either side of a center wall led to the bedroom and a small bar area. The decor wasn't designer, but Rade thought it warm and welcoming. She didn't know what might impress someone as worldly as Kira, who was definitely more worldly than she was, since she'd never been out of the country.

A low tone sounded, and Rade realized that for the first time in a long while, she'd forgotten about Achilles.

"Hale and well met, Rade," a male computer voice said from

hidden speakers. "No messages. All systems green. Name your musical poison."

"That doesn't sound like an off-the-shelf voice service," Kira said.

"Please select from one of the programmed genres." Achilles didn't recognize Kira's voice.

"Achilles, disengage," Rade said as she turned toward another door across the room. "I didn't trust the big-name services, so I rolled my own."

"You built your own AI?" Kira sounded surprised.

It made Rade blush. She hoped it wasn't visible in the low light. "Nah, not really," she said. "I started with an open source software package and hacked it, but most of the command set and all of the personalization is mine."

"You've impressed me again." Kira assessed the room as she spoke. "A girl might find your aptitude intimidating."

Rade tried to hide her surprise, but she didn't think she was successful. That this goddess of a woman might find her intimidating was difficult to comprehend.

When Rade didn't speak, Kira looked her way.

"The name Achilles seems significant," Kira said.

Rade swallowed, trying to suppress her growing arousal even though she was melting in response to that crisp accent. "It's really not. I needed a name that wouldn't come up in common conversation."

Kira made a noncommittal sound and Rade wondered if it was judgment. Maybe she should have picked a more meaningful name for the computer voice. Maybe this was crazy, offering a stranger a drink in her personal space. Maybe she'd gotten all the signals wrong. It had happened before. She didn't even know if Kira found her attractive.

In that moment, her eyes met Kira's, and the receptiveness she saw reflected finally made sense.

Kira was in her apartment. Alone. At three a.m. And despite her unassuming posture, Kira was looking at Rade like prey.

Rade took a deep steadying breath. "I think I promised you something better than grog." She crossed the room and stepped behind the bar. While pulling a couple of rocks glasses from one of the open cupboards on the wall, she stretched her other hand toward the collected bottles on the low counter behind the bar but stopped before selecting one. "Bourbon all right?"

Kira didn't answer, and after a moment, Rade wondered if she'd said something wrong.

Without responding or severing eye contact, Kira followed Rade behind the bar. She slid between Rade and the counter, and with a tantalizing display of easy strength hitched herself up to sit on its surface. She took the glasses and set them on the bar.

"Not thirsty," she said. "For whiskey, anyway." She rested her hands on Rade's shoulders as she spread her legs and pulled Rade closer.

The music upstairs was reduced to a distant faint thumping that made the silence between them loud.

The earlier restlessness, the unease Rade couldn't define…all of it settled low in her belly the moment she understood. It had been so long since she'd wanted anyone, she hadn't recognized the feeling.

Kira raised her hand and teased her thumb along Rade's chin. "So, would you mind very much if I kissed you?"

Shouting her vehement consent seemed like a bad idea. Instead, Rade settled for kissing the thumb so tantalizingly close to her lips.

Kira didn't keep her waiting. Rade's nipples tightened at the sound of Kira's hands sliding into the lapels of her leather trench. Kira tugged, closing the distance between them, and when their lips met, Rade forgot to breathe.

Soft warmth and Kira's scent overwhelmed Rade's senses. Eyes closed, she felt and heard Kira sigh against her lips. The gentle pressure of Kira's kiss along with the solid presence of her body so close sent part of Rade soaring, and she wanted more. Before she could think to stop herself, she traced her tongue along Kira's lower lip, and with a gasp Kira deepened the kiss. The rhythmic pulse between Rade's legs stole her attention when Kira cupped her face and pulled her closer.

A tinny beeping interrupted them.

Kira chuckled as she pulled back, and the sound of it made Rade's diaphragm seize.

"Evidently, you're having some effect on my heart rate," Kira whispered as she raised her wrist and tapped the tiny screen.

Rade was glad it wasn't just her. It would be undignified for her heart to pound out of her chest.

They were back to staring at one another, but Rade had spent so much time over the last two days trying not to look at Kira that it felt like a privilege.

She raised her hand to stroke her fingertips along one of Kira's elegantly arched eyebrows. When those same fingers trailed down Kira's jaw, Kira leaned forward like she'd been released from invisible restraint. She pressed her lips against several points on Rade's lips as if one encompassing kiss wasn't enough. She stroked the side of Rade's head and slid her hands inside Rade's collar to the sides of her neck.

Kira's cool hands against her hot skin sent a shiver down her spine.

She followed the line of Kira's jaw with her lips until the scent of the skin beneath Kira's ear captured her. Sometime later—who knew how long and who cared—she followed the delectable lines of Kira's collarbones with her lips, then nuzzled aside the swaths of cloth covering Kira's chest.

Kira tipped Rade's jaw upward and claimed her lips again. Gentle and soft at first, the kiss soon turned wild and hungry.

When Rade dug her hands into the tops of Kira's thighs, Kira pulled back.

"We could do that whole get-to-know-each-other thing," Kira said. "But I'd really like to get to the part where you make me come."

Desire washed over Rade so strongly her knees trembled. Perhaps the late hour or her fatigue contributed to her rash decision making, but she wasn't going to let this woman walk out of her apartment now. Not without touching her.

When she didn't answer right away, Kira withdrew. For all her bravado, a hesitant tenderness emerged from her fathomless eyes.

In that moment, it was singularly important that Kira know just how much she affected Rade.

The tunic Kira wore was designed to lie flush against her chest, but when Rade tugged it from its neat home tucked inside a wide belt, the fabric separated beautifully. She reclaimed Kira's lips as she loosened the straps of the bra underneath, sliding them half over Kira's muscular shoulders.

Rade didn't care how cumbersome it might be to put the whole ensemble back together. All she cared about was how quickly she could expose Kira's skin, loosen Kira's belt, unzip Kira's pants, all while tasting Kira's exquisite lips.

Kira clutched at her shoulders, clasped at her head, moaned her approval and encouragement until Rade pulled back.

She looked down and her mouth watered at the beauty of Kira's breasts in her hands. Dark and full, nipples taut, the skin smooth and without blemish.

"You are so, so beautiful," Rade whispered, unable to stop herself.

Kira stopped pulling Rade closer, but only so she could take one of Rade's hands and press it low against her belly. "Touch me, Rade."

Wiry curls scratched her palm as Rade slid her hand past the clothes in her way until heat and wetness stole her attention. The call and response of her touch, what made Kira pull away, what made her moan and push into Rade's hand, taught Rade quickly. Every iterative stroke drew her ever deeper into the magic weaving between them.

Kira cupped a hand against the back of her neck. "Rade," she said, her voice tensed and hard.

"Yes?"

"Don't you dare stop."

Rade tried not to rush in her hurry to obey, her fatigue forgotten. She closed her eyes, rested her forehead against Kira's shoulder, and focused only on what she could feel. The dew of sweat on Kira's skin, the feedback loop of arousal in this protected space between them, the ringing in her ears—it was all open and honest for however quickly it had developed. She had forgotten this feeling, the power of pleasing a woman. To be welcomed by this particular woman unleashed something inside her, something as potent as rage but benevolent and giving.

She kissed her way down to one of those delicious nipples and pulled it between her teeth. She didn't need to see Kira's face. Her nipple tightened in Rade's mouth, her arms pressed harder against Rade's shoulders, her hand tangled and tugged in Rade's hair. Kira's slick clit swelled to fullness against Rade's fingers and she felt when Kira came before Kira even drew enough breath to cry out. Rade moaned, victorious.

When Kira's breathing returned to normal, she laughed.

"You're taking me to your bed now, right?" Kira's voice was a satisfied croak. "I can't return the favor properly on this bar."

Rade hummed against the skin between Kira's breasts. "I will definitely take you to my bed."

"Is it big enough for me?" Kira offered a wry, sated smirk.

Though a king-sized bed awaited them, Rade pretended to consider her answer. She pulled away to look into the dark depths of Kira's eyes. "Maybe if I'm on top."

HER MOTHER'S LOVER

Namrata Verghese

Namrata Verghese is a JD/PhD student in Modern Thought and Literature at Stanford. Her work has appeared in *Catapult*, *The Los Angeles Review of Books*, *Tin House*, *World Literature Today*, and elsewhere. Her first collection of short stories was published by Speaking Tiger Books in 2019.

It's strange, seeing Ash with makeup on. It makes her face look all wrong, a wax statue of herself—Ash, but not quite. All those times Rincy clucked her tongue, handed her daughter a tube of lipstick, and ordered her to go "freshen up." When it comes to Ash, Rincy has so many regrets, but, abruptly, this becomes first among them: she wishes she'd never handed her that lipstick. Something comes out of Rincy's mouth now, something between a gasp and a sob. She wants so badly to scream, can feel the scream building inside her, thrumming up her toes and stomach, but she stops it, digging her nails into her palms. Over the years, she has mastered the discipline of her unruly body. She can fall apart later, when everything is done and there is no one left to watch.

Sunil lays a hand on her back—a gesture of comfort or warning, Rincy can't quite tell. She never could, with him. The first time they'd met, at her pennukanal, he'd looked at her clinically, appraising her worth behind his gold-rimmed spectacles. Although she wasn't privy to the conversation between father and son-in-law-to-be that followed, she imagines it followed the rules of haggling at a bazaar: *How much to take her off your hands? No, don't be ridiculous. Will you settle for this instead?*

His smile long and tight, Sunil maneuvers her back into the pew just as the priest steps onstage. He swings metal chains of incense and the smell smears everywhere, leaking into her stomach, her brain. Nowadays, so many of her memories have lost their texture, but one breath of incense and she is five years old again, sitting in church for Christmas service back home in Trivandrum. She can almost feel the chalky baby powder she and Nita, her childhood friend, would put on their faces because they weren't allowed to play with makeup. The itchy dresses they would wear, with plastic roses on the sashes. Those damn roses. They always poked into their bellies.

Two rows behind them, Sania is already crying quietly. If Rincy turns around, she knows Sania will be holding a handkerchief up to her face, her mascara running just enough for her grief to be elegant. A wave of vitriol fills Rincy's lungs. She hates Sania. *Hates* her. Hates her for how she took Ash away, how she turned Rincy's own daughter against her. How, now, she weeps openly and proprietarily. How she is allowed to do so.

When Rincy married, Nita was only allowed to cry in secret. Rincy had to quiet her, harshly, right before the ceremony, saying that her tears would draw too much attention.

"I can't help it," Nita had replied, eyes like red spiderwebs. "I feel as though I'm leading a cow to slaughter."

Of course, Nita married Rahul, one of Sunil's friends from medical college, later that year. Of the two, Rahul was handsomer and more interested in his wife, but their marriage, over time, had eroded just the same. According to Facebook, Nita ended things with him about three years ago. She was always braver than Rincy, or maybe she was just more able to be.

The sermon has started. Rincy finds, not for the first time, that she can't understand much of it, beyond catching the priest using the name Aishwarya once or twice, making her cringe. Thank God Ash can't hear him; she would have walked out. While Rincy still speaks to Sunil in Malayalam at home, they haven't been to church in so long that the high register of the language now seems foreign to her, all hard k's and retroflex r's. Any other time, this would disturb her, but today she says a silent thanks to a deity she doesn't believe in for allowing her to not hear, not understand, the eulogy that should never have been necessary in the first place.

And then it's all over, and Rincy is alone in her bedroom. And she cries and cries and cries, and when she thinks she's done, she cries some more.

❖

Sunil started sleeping in the guest bedroom about five years ago. Rincy didn't object. Ash's birth was bookended by two miscarriages; after the second, Sunil stopped touching her altogether. Then, once Ash left for college, there was no one to perform for anymore.

On nights like this, though, with the rain so loud and the room so cold, she misses him. No, not him, but the warmth of him, his small snores, the way he covered the bed so completely it was impossible to sleep without touching him. In the dark, she could pretend that things were different. It has been two weeks since the funeral and six years since Ash left the house, but still it feels like each night has been stretched taut with a rolling pin, infinite and textureless. Inside her, that scream still thrums. She thought it would soften with time, but instead it seems to be spreading. She imagines it metastasizing to her limbs, freezing her slowly. She imagines being a statue. A corpse. She imagines grabbing a knife and slashing away at herself, at the loose skin under her arms, at the fat that spills, gelatinous, over her hips. Hacking and hacking, until her body becomes as unrecognizable as Ash's was the day she got the call from the police station. She wants to put her fist in her mouth and reach down, deep down, past her lungs and her veins and her organs. To pull out her intestines. To taste them, slimy and wet against her tongue. She wants to hollow out her stomach. To evacuate.

Rincy sits up, her breath coming hot and quick. Everything is vibrating and she needs it all to be still. The air fills with paper cuts; her skin prickles. She gets out of bed and starts walking in the direction of the guest room down the hall, heartbeat oddly fast. It isn't strange to seek out her own husband for comfort, is it? It is, in fact, strange not to. The carpet soaks up her footsteps like sand. Just before she opens Sunil's door—closed as reliably as hers is open—she stops. Boxer shorts, white and stained, lie bunched up on the floor, yanked halfway through the crack in the door.

Every night, for thirty years of marriage, Sunil has kicked off his shorts after showering and left them on the floor for Rincy to pick up. Every morning, for around twenty-five years of marriage, Rincy has scolded him about it, in increasingly muted tones. Tonight, the thought of opening the door, picking up that warm, fermenting underwear, and putting it in the laundry basket in the corner of the room feels Herculean. Potentially Sisyphean. Bile congeals in her throat. Rincy swallows, hard, and leaves.

Back in her room, the rain sounds as though it might fracture the window. When Ash was small and they had just moved to the States, she would climb into bed with Rincy whenever it rained, always dragging that tattered little teddy bear with her.

"Amma, I can't sleep," she'd say.

Rincy, irritated, would respond, "Why? Are you scared? Big girls don't get scared of a little thunder."

But then Ash would chew her lip—a habit she'd formed as a baby and, despite Rincy's best efforts, never shed—and Rincy's heart would melt, every time, and she'd pat the space on the bed beside her, the space that has now been empty for so many years.

It was later, much later, during a thunderstorm on a visit home from college, that Ash had offhandedly mentioned how much she loved the rain. They were watching an old Bollywood film while wrapped up in blankets, eating banana chips, and drinking chai from steel cups that clanked against their teeth.

"What? No," Rincy said. "You hate the rain, you always did. That's why you always used to sleep with me when it rained."

Ash looked surprised, then smiled. "No, Amma. I just used it as an excuse."

And then she'd lunged at Rincy, hugging her fiercely, and Rincy had laughed and batted her away.

Her stomach hurts. She feels bloated, tender—overripe. Pushing herself up on her elbows, she drains the glass of water on the nightstand. The water spills, rolling from her chin to her shirt. Lying back, cold and wet, she stares out the window. Thin straws of lightning. A fat red moon, hanging low in the sky. When it rains, the world bleeds.

❖

She must have been staring at the Facebook message for the past two hours. The timer on the oven has gone off three times. Her eyes are watering from the white light of her laptop screen.

Hi Aunty, the message reads. *I hope you're doing well. I have some things of Ash's that I think you might like to have. If you're open to it, could we meet?*

The little circle above the text with Sania's picture—actually, a picture of Sania and Ash—has paralyzed her. They were on their Europe trip, the one they insisted on taking together right after graduating from college. Sania stands behind Ash on a set of ancient stairs, her arms around Ash's neck. They both wear sunglasses and grin at the camera, teeth white and dazzling in the Athens sun. Rincy can't blink; she can't look away.

A few automatic response options pop up on screen: *Not at the moment, sorry. Yes, I'd love to! Of course, when works for you?* Her hands shaking only a little, Rincy clicks the last one and closes the laptop so fast it slides across the table.

They arrange to meet at the café two blocks away from Rincy's house, the one where Ash used to study for hours a day, infuriating the owner by ordering only one drip coffee that she would sip painfully slowly. The morning of the meeting, Rincy selects nice jeans, the ones that Ash always said flattered her butt, and spends some time fiddling with lipstick before giving up. She's nervous, she realizes, drawing on kajal and watching her hand tremble in the mirror with detached curiosity. She arrives over half an hour early, orders a chai latte, and stakes out a spot in the corner. Although she brought along a book to pass the time, it dawns on her, about fifteen minutes in, that she can't remember a single word she's read.

"Hi, Aunty," Sania calls out when she arrives, her voice rippling across the café. Even today, dressed in workout clothes, hair in an oily bun, she reminds Rincy of a tiger. Long and lithe and proud. "It's good to see you. You look lovely."

Rincy hates how good the compliment feels, how warm. She hates Sania for it, for everything, but she makes sure to hate herself more. "Thank you. You mentioned you have some of my daughter's things?"

Sania hesitates, chewing her lip in a way that makes her look, for a few disorienting moments, like Ash. "Yes, I have some of her things. I would keep them if I could, but I'm moving soon and can't take them with me."

"Why?"

"Well, it would be quite expensive to ship this across the Atlantic." Sania's tone is wry, but her eyes flash. Something in them feels familiar.

"You're moving to another country?"

"To England."

"Why?"

Sania's throat works. "I can't stay here, Aunty. I can't go to work, leave the apartment. I can't do anything. It all reminds me of her."

Rincy stays quiet for too long. "I don't think moving to England will help much, mol," she says finally. "If it did, I would have done it a long time ago." Impulsively, she covers Sania's hand with her own and squeezes.

Sania looks up, startled. After a few moments, she smiles and squeezes back.

❖

Later that day, Rincy starts to unpack the box that Sania gave her. She slices through the brown sellotape, pulls open the flaps, and promptly shuts them again. Her mouth tastes like vomit and she runs to the bathroom, leaving the box on the kitchen table.

It lies there, untouched, for two more months. She returns to it on Ash's twenty-fourth birthday. What would have been Ash's twenty-fourth birthday. That night, she forces herself to take one thing—just one, that's all—out. Just one thing. It shouldn't be this hard. Rincy takes exactly three deep breaths, closes her eyes, and dives in. She hits something cold and metal and knows before pulling it out that it is the jewelry box. Ash's forever favorite birthday present, from her grandfather on her sixth birthday. They'd joked for years afterward that they could give her all the expensive toys in the world, but nothing would compete with the joy that this silly little box gave her.

It had been her grandmother's. Sunil's mother's. After she passed away, when Ash was only a baby, it sat on the mantel for years. The first time Ash opened it, on an early visit to India, a thick coat of dust rolled off the top and into her mouth. Her baby lips puckered like she'd bit into a lemon, and she laughed and coughed and laughed some more.

Inside the jewelry box, a wind-up ballerina twirls on a velvet stage, moving her arm robotically to a bright, busy tune. Ash used to sit in front of the box, chin in her folded arms, watching the dancer spin for hours on end. About a decade later, Sunil would point to this infatuation and say, see? She used to be feminine. *You* ruined her. You made her *unnatural*. And there was a time when Rincy had believed him. Had blamed herself, too. It must be genetic, she reasoned. There was no other way it could have happened, not when they had done everything right, when they had bought her Barbies and given her makeup and even let her date boys. There was no other explanation.

The drawer under the stage doesn't close all the way, overstuffed with trinkets Ash accumulated over the years. Ash wore no jewelry, except for the hoop in her nose, so the drawer only houses such nonsense as a receipt from a long-ago dinner, a boarding pass from Atlanta to Berlin (the first leg of the Europe trip, Rincy thinks), and a stack of black-and-white Polaroids from the "emergency" camera Ash always carried in her backpack. She had a knack for stripping things down to their skeletal parts: a person, a place, a gaze. Most of the photos are close-ups of Sania's face—the beauty mark next to her lips, the inner corner of her eye, the shadowy space where her jaw met her neck—and so startlingly intimate that Rincy feels like an intruder.

The last one, to Rincy's surprise, features her. Taken during some long-ago trip to India, it shows her and Nita sitting in rocking chairs, the ones on the verandah of Rincy's childhood home, talking. Or, rather, Nita is talking, her hands a happy blur, while Rincy smiles at her. Nita wears a sleeveless kurta—red, Rincy remembers. She can almost see it through the grayscale. So striking against her dark skin—and a shawl wrapped twice around her neck. Her hair is shorn short; her eyes are smudged black from kajal. With half her face in shadow, she is at once sharp and soft. And, as always, impossibly beautiful.

Of the two of them, Rincy had been considered the looker, the one Nita was always compared to and found wanting. But Nita's softness emerges only when she smiles. When her face, all hard planes and angles, splits open to reveal her dimples. And her hair, so wild and curly—when they were children, Rincy used to make up excuses to braid it, to touch it, finding some small joy in the feeling of Nita's scalp underneath her fingers.

Ash must have taken that photo when she was younger than sixteen. That was the birthday when Sunil had explicitly forbidden them from seeing Nita, even when they visited Rincy's hometown. The birthday when Ash told them what they'd dreaded for years. The birthday Sunil hit her—both of them, actually—for the first and last time.

Something catches in Rincy's throat. It becomes difficult to look at the picture in a way that feels appropriate, so she turns away.

She thought she'd been so careful. She'd erased every digital footprint; she'd thrown away all those incriminating letters. Even then, in that stolen moment on the verandah, she'd thought she was being discreet. But Ash was looking at her. Maybe Ash was always looking at her.

The tears come, as she'd known they would from the moment she'd opened that damn box. Rincy lets herself cry, and when she's done, stands up and walks over to Sunil's door. She practices what she is going to say in her head—something calm and diplomatic, something like, *we need to talk*—but, when she gets there, she stops short of opening the door.

His boxers. On the floor. His *fucking* boxers on the fucking floor. Enough.

"I'm leaving you," she says to the closed door and walks away.

❖

Rincy hasn't seen Nita in almost a decade. Beyond Facebook stalking and wishing each other happy birthdays, they've hardly had any contact. Nita called her for the first time in a while earlier this year, after hearing about Ash. Rincy hadn't picked up the phone. She hadn't known what to say.

But this time, when Rincy is the one to call, Nita picks up on the second ring. And when Rincy can't say anything, can't do anything but sob over the line, Nita says, *Come home.* Like they are still living next door to each other; like everything is still simple and absolute. And Rincy does.

She books the first flight out, at four a.m. that Friday. She doesn't sleep the entire time, and twice watches the sun crack open the sky, oozing yellow like yolk. She eats three airplane meals but can't remember what they were. She thrums, all over, all the way from the Houston airport to the layover in Dubai to Trivandrum. When she sees Nita standing in the Arrivals area, she drops her bags and runs. They hug with the gate between them, metal bars pressing into thighs, their bodies curling into each other. Nita smells damp and familiar. Her eyes are dark like oil. Rincy buries her face in the crook of her neck and closes her eyes, unsure of where she begins and ends, unsure of whether the wetness she feels is tears or sweat, Nita's or hers.

"Finally," she hears Nita whisper into her hair. "I've been waiting for so long."

Rincy lifts her head just enough to kiss Nita's collarbone. "No more waiting," she says.

Inside her, the thrumming has stopped. Outside, it starts to rain.

BUTCH JEANS

Reginald T. Jackson

Reginald T. Jackson is a Black Same Gender Loving Male
living in Brooklyn, New York.

He awoke to find himself in a fetal ball in the center of his queen-
size bed. Everything, including the sheets, wrapped around his legs,
arms, and waist. Damp. "A shower, a long mellow one," he said as
he stumbled across the hall, picking up various little necessities like
some lube, a clean pair of bikini briefs, and a T-shirt without ever
opening his eyes. He liked to talk to himself; it kept him company.

"Mmm..." The hot water seemed to melt him slowly, weight
dropping with his thoughts. As he reached for the small tube of
lubriseptic gel that he had gotten the night before from a group
meeting to begin his morning ritual of masturbation and prayer,
the phone rang and rang and rang. Of course. This couldn't be just
another day in New York. Throwing a conniption fit, he leaped from
the shower. Walking on little more than wind and water, he whisked
to the phone, praying that it would just stop.

"Hello?...Mother?" he said, sinking into his bed. *This will take a
while*, he thought. "You'll be where?...My neighborhood? Today?...
Lunch at one? Okay, fine...See you then." He hung up. "Oh, my God,
lunch. Today?"

The thought followed him back to the shower and cut it short.

He sank still deeper into his bed, this time unusually calm and comfortable. Lunch was less than two hours away. *This is what they must mean by calm before the storm*, he thought.

"What shall I wear today, who shall I be today," he said to his full-length mirror. "I need a change, a little adventure. Jeans. I'll buy a pair of jeans today. Not just any jeans, my first pair of jeans in over ten years. Real butch jeans."

Not his usual Italian tailored suits, famously matched with shirts of silks and satins, mostly in bright colors. Form fitting and flattering to his slim modelesque frame.

He screamed silently, hoping someone, somewhere, would hear him and explain the meaning of his life. It was the late 1980s when friends were dropping like flies from this horrible disease called AIDS. He spent his every spare hour attending meetings for Gay Men of African Descent, or Other Countries: Black Gay Men Writing, or the AIDS Coalition to Unleash Power's minority caucus. Sometimes he felt like a professional homosexual, a professional Black homosexual fighting the good fight for his brothers. If he wasn't at meetings or work, he was at a funeral, which was worse. But he couldn't just stay home.

While sitting at the ridiculously small counter at Woolworth's with his mother, the moment before came back to him. How, while standing in front of Mays waiting for her, he spotted her, but she didn't spot him and walked on by. How he thought for a split second to let her keep on walking, to let her go. How he dreaded playing Saints and Sinners, a tired little game they played whenever the subject of his sexuality came up. Her, of course, being the God-fearing Saint and him the shameful sinner surely on his way to hell. He was who he was, which was no longer debatable. He planned to tell her. Now, on his turf, he was appropriately armed for a two-barrel, no-holds-barred fight with her. He looked at her from the corner of his eye. Was she well, angry, happy? He could never tell before, but it was worth a try. In her face, he saw humility. Its quality seemed out of place among her features. Her cheekbones high, skin buffed brown and red like the Louisiana clay she used to play in as a child. She had the look of the Black regal women wearing those fabulous hats when he went with her to church. Her face was smooth and soft, like she was much younger than her sixty years. She didn't wear makeup, but she was pretty in a common country way; only lipstick adorned her lips. She had a pencil-thin but noticeable mustache above her lip and a few stray hairs around her chin area. She has more facial hair than I do, he thought. She was definitely tougher as well, so it seemed fair.

"Excuse me," said the waitress as she shoved two oversized pleather menus at them.

"Yes, he's crazy. Someone is gonna catch up with him and put him out of his misery. Your sister Edis tried to talk sense to him, but he started with her. You know how he is. His car was broken, and he got mad at the world." His mother's words finally reached his ears ten minutes after she had begun.

"Uh-huh," he said while searching the menu and feeling his pocket for something he was sure wasn't there. Something he wanted and didn't have. *Who's buying*, he wondered. Should he order normal because she was paying or light and pick it up himself? She continued talking, with him adding pseudo-vocal grunts and nods in the appropriate places; even she wasn't listening, he thought. Surely she didn't come all the way from Queens to Brooklyn for this. What did she want? What should he eat?

"I'm just gonna find me a 'friend' to keep me company and leave him and the rest of them alone. Child or no child, I'm tired. Shit. He's a grown man. Yep, that's what I'm gonna do. Find me a 'friend'… man or woman," she said with a laugh. She then took her first real look at him.

His shoulder-length black hair was pulled tight under a red rubber band, a scarf spilling down his back, his legs ever so slightly crossed. He could easily be her daughter from the way he looked and acted. He was proper and delicate in his movements, something she didn't know where he had picked up, since she grew up in the rough and tumble dirt roads of Baton Rouge.

"Say what? Is there something you'd like to tell me, Mother?" he said.

"These days you have to be careful 'bout what you do and who you do it with, especially who you do it with. If you want to stay around," she said to the rings on her fingers.

"I guess so," he said while scanning the store aisles.

"I hear it's best to just give up everything, stop everything 'til further notice. You can never be too careful these days," she said quickly, as though someone had just punched her in the stomach.

"I guess not, but some of us have no choice," he said as cathedral bells went off in his head. First a positive plug for his "lifestyle," then a little health report. This must be about Alexis, or rather his recent death from *Pneumocystis carinii* pneumonia—"AIDS-monia" he once heard her say in jest while describing the "freaks" and other "street trash surely causing this world to end." *She's worried? Worried about me and AIDS?*

"Alexis," he mouthed and immediately saw him balled up in a hospital bed with more tubes sticking out of him than he thought was humanly possible for one body to hold. Memories of planning Alexis's twenty-sixth birthday party for the week after he was to come home; instead his relatives came with rubber gloves and face masks to throw away his clothes, some of which he had just bought and still lay in the packages.

Memories of calling home from the 42nd Street subway station for a prayer for Alexis. She wasn't home. He remembered falling apart on the phone for what was to be the third of many times.

"I just wanted her to say a prayer for Alexis, because I don't know any," he remembered squeezing out from between the tears, shakes, and mutterings to himself.

He remembered the sweet times when he sat with Mother and sang church hymns. She had quit school at thirteen to get married and start her family of ten boys and two girls over a thirty-five-year period, but she never lost her love of singing church hymns, something she shared with him. They sometimes sat on the couch and sang for hours as she taught one after another. She seemed different to him in those times. Like she was a real person, with hopes and dreams, not just his mother. She was so childlike and innocent; she often giggled, and her voice cracked with hesitation or fear of making a mistake. It made him love her even more. If there was one thing he could count on her for, it was her unceasing knowledge and faith in God.

"You're still working on weekends?" she said to the side of his head.

"No. Ten to four Monday to Friday, and some night classes," he said to his image in the window.

"You should see the neighborhood. They have really cleaned it up. They tore down all the old houses and expanded the college practically to my front door," she said, while searching for her glasses in her purse.

"Yeah." He shook his head at the things she pulled out of her purse, trying to find her glasses. She was a pack rat. It was clear he had gotten it from her.

"You should see the mall from my living room window at night. The guards patrol the grounds," she said, each description more overblown than the last. He smiled as he envisioned her as a used car salesman.

Suddenly a long pause. "If you are not too busy, you should come over. You could bring your 'friend' if you want," she said, playing her trump card. It was out, all of it. Now it was up to him to make a move, but he stood his ground, his eyes filled with the image of her squirming through a meeting with one of his "friends."

He had been hurt and wanted her to acknowledge that, acknowledge that he had a right to be what she birthed him to be. Stubborn was all it was, her not admitting it, he thought. Things weren't that easy. Even though the fear of him catching AIDS and dying brought her to him this time, what would it take the next time? He wasn't gonna ever be a butch thing like she wanted. Butch was something he feared, having grown up watching his father beat his mother and then girlfriend after girlfriend until he was thrown out of the State of New York. Butch meant brute power and danger. His delicate movements were a way of empowering himself to prove he was nothing like the man who had made him, the man who scared him to death and whom he wished dead.

"Maybe tomorrow or next weekend—I'm so busy with work and school and the group I belong to. I go every Saturday. It pretty much wipes out Saturdays. Maybe Sunday, next Sunday," he said.

Finally, the overnuked, underdone food arrived and was slid in front of them.

"You want my fries? I can't eat them because I don't have my teeth in."

"Well, I guess I could get some down," he said, ignoring the reference to her age and exaggerated frailty. She had buried two husbands and sent a third packing; a weak woman she was not, and they both knew it.

"How you feel?" she said, giving him a quick inspection with her eyes.

"Okay. A little tired. Fighting a cold, a chill," he muttered without thinking, only to realize he had slipped.

A long list of cures, down-home remedies, and potions flowed from her instantly.

"Enough. I can't eat another bite," he said.

While walking toward the bus stop, she gave him two different "easier" ways to get to Queens from Brooklyn by bus, including the way she was taking then.

"Maybe tomorrow you'll come by?"

"Or next week. Next Sunday for sure. I'll call you either way. Okay?"

"Okay. Remember, lots of vitamin C and chicken soup. Oh, you don't eat chicken, maybe the broth then."

"Bye," he said, shaking his head and waving goodbye.

Moments later she was gone. He found himself in front of the Mays department store.

"I definitely deserve to buy myself something. Why not jeans," he said to himself as a bright red coat pushed past him.

"Calm down, life's too short," he said to the coat.

He made his way to the men's department and its jeans section.

After a short time, the perfect pair of jeans appeared: 29 slim, acid washed with long, long legs. As he moved toward the cashier counter, he caught a glimpse of a dressing room in the corner where there was a mirror.

"It is all of two thirty in the afternoon and it is already someday," he said to his reflection as he posed in the mirror. "A 'friend'? Man or woman, Mother, please! That has to be the tiredest excuse for a hint I've ever heard. Why couldn't she just say it's okay that I am the way I am?" *Stubborn is all it is*, he concluded. But just the possibility of her having a genuine concern for his life moved him greatly. So what if it started out with a fear of AIDS? "I'll call her tomorrow. Make it easier for her."

"Hey, hey! What are you doing in there?"

He suddenly heard a voice vault over the saloon-style doors as he brushed his hair back into place.

"What are you doing in there?" said the blue-black face and badge peering over the doors.

"Trying on jeans, of course," he said without a glance back.

"This is the men's dressing room, you shouldn't be in there. This is the men's," insisted the face, which now had the company of other guards.

"I know," he said, tightening his jaw until it hurt.

"Why are you in there?"

"I'm a man," he managed to squeeze out from his painfully twisted lips.

"A what?"

"I'm a man and I'm trying on these jeans. Butch jeans," he said, taking in a deep breath.

"A man? No, you aren't. You hear this? She says she's a man."

"He. Look, I'm buying these jeans, men's jeans. Look," he said, trying again to find some sanity or reason why he had to explain himself to every fool God saw fit to put on this Earth, but there were none.

"You a man?"

As the guards laughed and chattered in Creole, he sauntered past them, jeans in hand. Now they had to be his. As he stood in line for the cashier counter, he tried not to hear the guards debate him and hand down the verdict: "Bodyman!" Creole for faggot.

"Cash or charge?" the saleswoman asked.

"American Express," he said loudly so the guards could hear. He was sure both were still staring at him, but he dared not look at them.

"Sorry, we don't accept American Express," the saleswoman said as though she was handing down the final sentence: forty days and forty nights of hard labor, or a minute more of listening to the guards curse him in the same tongue as his mother's.

As he fled the store, he was sure all eyes were on him. He even thought he heard "Fag in aisle two" come over the PA system as he twirled through the revolving door and bolted home. Still the freak. The exiled.

Finally, at home, he sank deeper into his bed as thoughts and fears and tears welled up in him. He had vowed to himself that he wouldn't end up just another tragic faggot dying in a nameless hospital with faceless strangers by his side.

After all, Alexis hadn't planned to die a victim either, but it happened.

Mother hadn't planned on her child being one of those freaks of nature, but he was, and nothing could change that; not even her.

"Those damn jeans!" he said to his pillow. He felt stupid and exposed. He had secretly hoped that butch jeans would make a difference, would shield him from some of those aimless attacks. He was so tired of fighting.

"Dear Lord, is death the only punch line to life?"

He thought of his mother again. It had taken a lot for her to come to him and try to do the right thing by him.

He picked up the phone and dialed her number. It rang for what seemed a lifetime, then her voice.

"Hello?"

"It's me."

"I just got in. I told you it only took—"

"I'm on my way over. I need to see you. Today. We need to talk."

An Engaging Isolation

Mayapee Chowdhury

Mayapee is a published author of both fiction and nonfiction with six book publications to her credit and publications in other platforms. Mayapee is also a Spoken word artist/Poet and has performed at various festivals in the UK. Her work can be found online and on social media.

Am I completely insane throwing my life away like this? That's what people will say. Walking away from a perfect woman like Seema who ticks all the boxes on an Asian parents' marriage recruitment form. Good looking, fair skinned, flourishing career as a university professor who has written numerous books and papers. This is an absolute match made in heaven for someone who is into women.

Here I'm in my mid-thirties still living at home. I have a successful career and make good money, but it isn't the career that I want. This isn't a forced or arranged marriage, just a very convenient arrangement that both our families suggested. I've been working on a way out.

Being a solicitor is my job, but music is what makes me breathe. I've continued to perform gigs in the evenings and get plenty of work. Josh and I've been spending a lot of time together recently working on new material, and we'll be going on tour. Everything is all set, and this is a good get-out from this engagement as well. I already pre-booked some unpaid leave from work. I didn't quit my job. I decided to still be a sensible little Asian boy with a career to come back to should this all go wrong. I'm still debating different ways of calling off the engagement with Seema. I could just leave the country without saying anything. I could leave her a note, I could dump her by text; the options are endless. I could even just talk to her directly about it, but then I know what would happen. She would go and speak to her parents, and my parents, and everybody would get involved. In the long run I'm doing the right thing by her. I can't subject her to a life of misery being with a man who isn't in love with her and has no chance of *ever* falling in love with her because she's the wrong gender.

It isn't that I dislike her as a person; I simply have zero romantic feelings for her. Only Josh understands where I'm coming from, and that's why he has supported me all the way with this tour. I wish I could live more like him, so open about who he is and his path in life, able to explore who he is. He feels by touring together it will allow me to do this. Since we were boys, Josh has always understood me and stood up for me. He keeps wanting me to explore that side of myself, and we've had a few intimate moments together. He's never pushed me into anything, though, and he said he'll wait until I'm ready, but it isn't a side of myself I can even think about while I'm living here. A twinge of the green-eyed monster has bestowed upon me a deep jealousy when I've seen him with other men. Yet I always worry about the shame and the scandal that it could all bring. I need to be in a place where I can be free, where I can be myself without feeling perverted or dirty; that's how my mother would describe it.

Anyway, I've not lost focus of our plan. Our tickets are booked, the flights will leave in a few days, and we'll be on tour. As I work out a getaway plan, I receive a phone call from Josh.

"Bad news, buddy. Flights are being canceled because of Covid-19, and it looks like ours will get canceled too."

"No, Josh, don't say that! It can't happen, it can't happen."

"Ravi, look around you. It's everywhere. It looks like the country will go into lockdown and everything is going to close, so we won't even be able to do any more gigs for a while. It doesn't change anything. Our plan is just postponed."

As I put the phone down to Josh I sweat and struggle to breathe, so I loosen my tie. When I look at my phone, I see a message from Seema.

I love you. Can't wait to see you tonight xxxxxx

I get straight on the internet and hear about school closures and businesses closing. Another text comes through from one of the partners at my law firm.

I take it your travel plans are canceled now and you no longer require the leave. Please get in touch as we could do with your help at the firm.

That's it, then! My life has been planned out over a space of a phone call and two text messages. I'm stuck here now and still engaged to Seema. Then again, with this lockdown maybe there won't be a wedding after all.

When I arrive home, I start drafting a message to Seema but keep pausing and redrafting the message. Am I giving her mixed messages, showing that I care one minute and being completely aloof the next? Mind you, this is the kind of concern I would show any friend too. As I'm about to message her I hear my mum on the phone with her downstairs, which is a very regular occurrence. It feels like there are three of us in this relationship, since she's always there. I strain to listen to the conversation.

"This is just awful; this is just awful! Okay, I'm on my way to pick you up right now. We can't have this situation for you, Seema. I will not let my daughter-in-law go through this."

"Daughter-in-law," I mutter to myself. We're only engaged, and if I've anything to do with it, even that will cease soon.

"We have to do something. We have to do something! Get in the car, now," Mum orders.

"Slow down, Mum. What has happened, exactly?"

"Well, the train services aren't running, so she isn't going to make it back to London tonight. I've said that she must stay with us."

"I'm sure she'll get another train, so one night won't do any harm."

"Ravi! It may have to be for more than one night, as it's very uncertain with this Covid-19."

"Mum, we'll be effectively living together before getting

married. Are you sure that's a good idea? You know how Indians love a good old gossip."

"Well, you certainly won't be staying in the same room, and don't get any funny ideas about sneaking into her bed, either."

"Oh, Mum, *please* can we end this conversation?"

"I'll give her the back room, and I will be keeping an eye on you both. This is about her safety, so it's final."

Living with us…what a disaster. Now the tour is called off, too. What will I do?

On the journey to the station, everything is drawn to a standstill, and the number of people wearing masks to cover their faces is frightening, like something out of a dystopian film. On the drive home it's like I may as well have not been there, both of them talking amongst themselves. Anyone would think it was my mum marrying Seema, not me.

When we get home, Mum goes straight into the kitchen to prepare the evening's dinner, and of course Seema is ever so helpful. How will I get rid of her now? She's already becoming so useful to Mum, and there's no way Mum would accept calling off this engagement. Let's hope she only stays for a couple of nights. Then I'll have time to think up another plan.

Days later, the train services still aren't running and the department at the university has said that she can work from home. Of course, Mum is insisting that she stay with us. She is getting her feet firmly under the table, cooking with Mum, helping with the housework, looking after Dad, the absolute perfect model daughter-in-law. The model child I never was. What am I going to do? How am I going to get out of this situation? If Mum could, she would probably bring the wedding forward and just have a very simple ritual in the house. What a disaster that would be.

I've been speaking to Josh about it in little chunks through messages. We've had the odd chat, but I've not been able to talk, as people have been around. He thinks I'm wrong to go along with it. What else could I do? When Mum makes a decision that's it, nobody says anything. We just have to go along with it, as our opinions, feelings, or whatever really don't matter. Even when I played the community and society card, that failed miserably. She turned it around with the

Good Samaritan card of not wanting to put her daughter-in-law at risk during a pandemic. Why does she keep referring to her as the daughter-in-law already? God, I hate it.

In some ways it isn't working out too bad, as I hardly see her. If she isn't busy with work, she's helping Mum. I thought I was avoiding the whole intimacy issue…until we had the place to ourselves.

Mum went shopping for essentials. I was surprised Seema didn't go with her.

"I thought you would be out shopping with Mum."

"I'm supposed to be at work. At least, that's what I told your mum."

Lying to Mum? That's very unlike her—there must be an agenda.

"I've realized since I've been living here that we've hardly spent any time together, which isn't very fair really, considering one of the reasons I moved in with your parents was because I thought it would bring us a bit closer."

She puts her arms around me. I freeze. I can't stop sweating and I get this lump at the back of my throat, so I pull away.

"We can't. We mustn't. This is my parents' place. Anyone could walk in at any moment."

"Come on, I think your mum is going to be gone for a while with all the queues everywhere at the moment, and your dad is downstairs watching his Bollywood channel. He can't even hear anything."

"Well, I don't feel comfortable. It's very disrespectful, so no, I'm not doing it. Not here. Sorry, Seema, this is wrong." I feel bad, a little, for making it seem like she's the one doing something wrong, when in fact, it's me who is lying.

That little girl puppy dog's pouty face comes out, but when it has no effect on me, she stays in her room for the rest of the afternoon. I hear intermittent giggling and just assume that somebody on a conference call made her laugh. At least I didn't make her cry, I guess.

When Mum gets home, she spots the tense atmosphere between us, and of course I get the blame.

"I know this isn't the ideal situation, but please make an effort, Ravi."

"You're the one who finds it disrespectful to even hold hands in public."

"It's not about that. You hardly speak to her or look at her. You're so lucky to get a girl like her. She even cooks really well, and she looks after your dad a lot. I don't want you messing this up for us."

"You act like she's marrying the family and not me."

She waves her wooden spoon at me. "I'm not being funny, Ravi, but you didn't exactly have a queue of girls looking to marry you, and she wanted you, so be grateful."

I walk away without answering, though I'd be more *grateful* if I could be who I am. Seema and I grow more and more distant, however, I notice she stops complaining about the distance. When she isn't sucking up to my mum, she seems to be getting very glammed up and having a lot of extra work meetings, and she's on her phone a lot as well. I'm not complaining, it means I don't have to be intimate with her and we can just stay away from each other. I know that sounds awful. I don't dislike her, but I do feel uncomfortable about her living here. I resent the decision being made without speaking to me. I resent my life being mapped out for me because of other people's convenience and society pressure that has nothing to do with what I want.

Unfortunately, I'm starting to resent Seema as well. She could actually be a very good friend, but she wasn't somebody I wanted to marry. She is a guest in our house, after all, so maybe I should start making her feel a little bit more welcome at least. When the time comes, I do want us to part as friends. I knock on the door and she takes ages to answer, then asks me in.

"Look, I'm sorry I've been distant, it's just been so full on living together, and it was sprung on us." I give her a hug and it's returned in a very hesitant way, not trying to be close to me or anything. I'm not complaining, I never wanted her. I'm only making amends because we're living under the same roof and it isn't her fault I don't want her and don't have the courage to say so to my family. Maybe she has accepted the situation better than I have. If things are amicable between us, then it won't be so difficult when it comes to ending things. However, I've noticed a lot of changes in her recently. I should at least start some sort of conversation about it with her.

"Seema, can we have a chat, please? In fact, let's go for a walk."

"Yes, you're right, let's go for a walk. Give me five minutes just to freshen up and get organized."

"Don't worry about preening yourself. You always look good, and we're only going round the block." I don't want to wait and give myself time to chicken out.

"Okay, I'll meet you downstairs. Let me just finish this phone call." She waves her phone, and I realize it's on. Did she mute us from whatever call she'd been on?

I head downstairs and get collared as I put a jacket and my trainers on.

Mum looks up. "Oh? Where are you going?"

"Seema and I are going for a walk."

Mum starts putting her shoes on too and grabs a shawl, even though it's not that cold outside.

"Actually, Mum, it was going to be just Seema and I."

"Oh, I get it. You two lovebirds don't need to hide from me, that's fine, you go for a nice romantic walk. You don't need me hanging around."

I'm not sure if I would call it romantic but at least it got rid of her. Seema and I head down the road, and there are awkward silences followed by Seema constantly stopping to look at her phone, which eventually annoys me.

"Okay, what was the point of us coming out for this walk if you're going to be on your phone all the time?"

"I'm just busy with work, that's all."

"Seema, what's really going on here? If you're not happy in this relationship, now is the time for us to talk about it." It's cowardly of me, but I hope she'll be the one to break this off and give me a chance at freedom.

She looks at her phone again without answering me, so I snatch the phone from her hand. I see about twenty missed calls from somebody called Jaden. Seema almost fights with me to get the phone back. "Who's Jaden?"

"Just somebody I work with."

"You've never mentioned him before, and he's ringing you at this time of night? It can't be that urgent. You're entitled to have a life, but if he's harassing you, do you want me to talk to him?"

The phone keeps vibrating and messages come through. A quick glance at one of them shows various emojis with love hearts. That's interesting.

"Give me back my phone," she shouts at me.

"Very professional, all these love heart emojis." I hold it out of her reach.

"We're friends as well."

"Come on, Seema, I wasn't born yesterday."

"Ravi, you've been aloof and hardly welcoming. You can't blame me for…for talking to someone else."

I look at her phone closely and look at the messages, and this time she doesn't even try to stop me. Then I notice some of the dates on the messages. "You're blaming me for this when some of these messages were from the end of last year."

She sighs. "Ravi, don't torture yourself anymore. Just give me the phone and let's decide what we're going to do about this."

"I'll tell you what I'm going to do about this. Let's go home now and speak to the family." I walk in front of her, wondering what to do. This is perfect, but there is no way that Mum and Dad would let her go out of my life just like that, even if it means we get married and I let her continue seeing this Jaden person. It's not like I'd be jealous.

"Ravi, what are you going to do? You can't tell your family! They'll tell my family and then everybody in the community will know. You *can't* tell the family."

"What were you planning on doing, then, Seema? Marrying me and then continuing with this guy?"

"It's not like you're heartbroken, is it? You've never been interested in this marriage either."

While we continue going round in circles, I hear windows opening and closing, then we realize Mum is eavesdropping. We look up at her at the same time, wondering how much of the conversation she heard.

"What's going on with you two? Are you lovebirds having some kind of tiff?"

"Oh, it's more than a tiff, Mum!" It's freedom, and a chance to escape, if only I can figure out a way to take it without hurting Seema or my family.

"I see my son is misbehaving. Well, you just sort him out. You don't take any nonsense from him. Come eat."

We stop talking and go inside. There are awkward silences at the dinner table, and Mum keeps looking at me, giving me the stare of disgust. After dinner Mum whispers to Seema when I go into the kitchen. I do wonder which one is meant to be her son.

I go back and whisper to her, "Let's go upstairs now. We need to sort this out and decide what we're going to do."

Before we settle down to chat in Seema's room, I open the door and see Mum standing outside the door with a feather duster in her hand. When she realizes she has been caught eavesdropping, she starts dusting vigorously. We lower our voices when we talk.

Seema takes my hand. "We can still make this work. It can work for both of us. You think I don't know that you've never been into me, or any woman? I'm not blind or dumb. You continue with your lifestyle, I continue with mine, and the family is happy. We don't even have to sleep together or be intimate or anything. We can make this work." She's practically pleading with me.

"Why don't you just marry this Jaden guy?"

"It's far too complicated."

She knows. She knows about me, who I am, and she's still willing to go through with it. "Then we're adding to the complication by being married when both of us want to be with other people. You think the pressure of my parents will stop when we get married? They will want us to have kids. I can't see how we can do that without sleeping together. And I can't imagine that if you get pregnant by him, he'll be fine with you pretending they're my kids."

"Hang on a minute, Ravi! Are you with someone else too?"

I shrug my shoulders and shake my head, unable to say it out loud.

"You want to be with someone else, don't you?" she asks again, softly this time.

I keep hearing Mum's footsteps as she keeps coming up and down the stairs with clean laundry, then looking for more laundry to do, her pace getting slower and slower as she gets nearer to Seema's room. I can't talk about this anymore. I'm overwhelmed and confused, and I leave Seema's room and go to my own.

All night, I stay up pacing, wondering what I'm going to do. Seema's suggestion isn't unusual; it's a well-known secret that there are people who do it, but I refuse to live that sort of lie. In the morning, I hear footsteps and decide to go to Seema's room before the chaos of the rest of the house starts. I knock on her door several times with no answer. I open the door. The bed is still made and hasn't been slept in, and all her belongings are gone. I head downstairs and I see her with her bags packed, wearing a coat and writing something, with screwed-up paper everywhere.

She looks up when I come in. "Ravi, I'm glad you're here before everyone else. All this is how I was going to tell your parents." She motions at the crumpled-up paper. "You're right. It would be too complicated, and neither of us should have to live that way."

She takes the ring off and hands it to me, and we shake hands, then hug. I'm relieved and exhausted, and I still have to face my family. But if Seema can be brave and choose the life she wants, then so can I. As the front door closes behind her, Mum comes down the stairs. My hand is still open with the engagement ring in it. Mum starts gasping for breath and gets a glass of water.

"What will become of us now? I knew you would mess this up, Ravi. We're all finished!"

I turn away and ring Josh, and all he hears is Mum screaming in the background.

"So, you finally had the guts to call off the engagement? Do you want to stay at mine for as long as you need?"

"We're still in lockdown. Even Seema has taken a risk going wherever she has gone."

"Ravi, this is an emergency. Your chances of being killed by this virus are pretty slim compared to what your mum will do if you don't get out of there now!"

"Thank God I didn't completely quit the legal profession. If we get caught, I may have to work on some sort of insanity plea."

While Mum is busy banging pots and pans, screaming at the top of her voice, I gather as many of my belongings as I can and make a quick getaway. I will choose the path I take, and from now on, I will choose to be myself.

GRANDDAUGHTER OF THE DRAGON

Victoria Villaseñor writing as Brey Willows

Brey Willows lives in the UK and believes that humor and a bit of fantasy can keep us all going. *Changing Course*, a sci-fi romp on another planet, won a 2020 Goldie Award.

"Abuela, tell me the story of the dragon and the blackbird."

I smiled down at my sweet granddaughter who had yet to understand what she would one day become. It was good she loved this story so; it was part of her destiny. "Get in bed, m'ija."

"Please!" She was nothing if not persistent.

I climbed up next to her and noticed that she wasn't far from my own height. So, she was going to take after one side of the family instead of the other. So be it. "Cálmate, m'ija. Lay down, and I'll tell you the story of the aloja and the víbria."

She snuggled under the light throw I'd had since I was a child, a magical gift I'd always treasured. The faint blue highlights in her hair shone in the moonlight sneaking in through the window. The moon liked this story too. She was always hovering when Lidia wanted a story of any kind, but especially this one. I glanced out the window and smiled at her, letting her cold passion fill me as it did so many nights.

I toyed with a strand of Lidia's hair as I thought of the story. "Once, there was a blackbird—"

"The most beautiful blackbird in the world," Lidia corrected me quickly.

"Once, there was the most beautiful blackbird in the world," I said, smiling at her. "Her name was Maria—"

"Like yours." Lidia tied a piece of her hair around mine, deep red threaded around deeper black.

"Would you like to tell me the story tonight, mi amor?"

She giggled. "No. You tell it." She snuggled deeper into the pillow.

"Her name was Maria, and she was a very special blackbird. She was an aloja." I tickled her chin. "What's an aloja?"

"A beautiful water woman who uses magic to make the world a better place. And she can change into a blackbird."

"Very good. Maria loved helping people, but she always had to be near fresh water. Salt water wasn't good for her because it got in her feathers and made them itch and break. And when she was in her female form, she liked to bathe in the warm water to keep her skin beautiful and young."

Lidia poked at me. "What did she look like as a woman, abuela?"

She'd never asked me before. "The aloja are small women. They're all very short and petite, and they have long red hair, so dark sometimes that you can't tell if it's red or black. Their eyes are blue like the water that gives them life. And they have beautiful smiles, and they stay young looking for many, many years."

She sighed happily, still playing with our hair.

"Maria had always liked helping people, but one day a terrible illness came to the village. Maria helped everyone she could, but many people began to die. They were angry and scared, and they turned on Maria, who had only ever tried to help them."

"Mala gente," Lidia whispered.

"They were mean to her, but they weren't *bad people*, not deep down. They were scared, and when people are scared, they can be mean." I caressed her head, hoping she'd never find that out for herself. "So Maria ran away, away from her beautiful lake, away from the scared people. It took her a long time to find a lake that was perfect, even though she tried many. Some were too cold, some were too sandy, some were even too hot. But one day, she found just the right one. There were no people nearby to get angry with her, and there were lots of trees for her to sit in and sing her blackbird song. Plus, there was a big cave—"

"Big enough for a dragon!" Lidia tugged on my hair.

"Do you want to ruin the story for the moon?"

Lidia rolled over and looked out the window. "Sorry, Luna!" She turned back to me. "She knows it as well as I do, you know," she whispered.

"I know," I whispered back. "Maria decided this would be her new home. She bathed in the perfect lake and let it soothe her dry skin. Then she turned into a blackbird and played in the water, letting it clean her beautiful feathers until they gleamed like the night sky once again. And the moon came out to play too and tried to catch the blackbird in its beams, but the blackbird swam, and flew, and hopped, and together they played through the night."

Lidia frowned and sat up to look out the window again. "Why can't I ever get away from Luna? She always catches me."

"Are you an aloja?" I asked, wondering what she'd say.

She tilted her head, thinking deeply as only a child can. "No," she said, confident in her answer.

I admit my heart sank a little, but I made sure not to show it. "Well, then Luna will always catch you. Only an aloja or a bruja can outrun the moon. Or a monster, but we don't talk about those, do we?"

She frowned and dove back under the blanket. "I don't like the monsters." She curled against my shoulder and resumed playing with my hair.

"Sometimes the monsters are just creatures people are afraid of. Like Maria, people don't understand them, so they say they're bad." It was important, *so* important, that she understand this.

"But there are real monsters, too. Like the dip."

"Sí. The devil's dogs are real, but you are stronger than all of them put together. What else is stronger?"

"The víbria!" She practically vibrated with excitement as she said it.

Other girls her age were interested in dolls, in playing house, in racing around the village playing tag and chasing balls. Some liked clothing, others television. But not my granddaughter. Her love of dragons surpassed everything else. I should have known, really, but the prideful part of me had hoped. I looked at the giant dragon poster on her wall, one with blue eyes and black scales.

"Maria loved her new lake, but she was puzzled when Luna couldn't light the inside of the cave, which was so dark she couldn't see three feet inside. Unafraid, she entered slowly so she didn't trip over anything, and then she turned into a blackbird, because they see much better in the dark. She flew deeper and deeper into the cave, which turned out to be very large, with a ceiling so high she couldn't see the top. And then she felt heat like she'd never felt before and something scraped along the ground, like a shovel gouging out the rock." I drew my fingernail along her arm, and she shivered.

"How big were its claws? Were they as big as me?" She scrambled from the blanket and stood on the bed, full height.

"Bigger!" I tickled her stomach and she flopped onto the bed, giggling.

"What next?" she asked, and the moonlight flickered as if to agree.

"Maria had never before seen what she saw that moment. A creature curled up, sleeping. It was white, so white it looked like the moon had come to life in the middle of night. Except for a line of scales down its back that were black with purple swirls like the very end of a sunset in winter. In blackbird form Maria landed in front of it, but not too close in case it woke and wanted to eat her. She hopped around it, looking at scales the size of her wings, seeing the purple shift and glow against the white body. She was mesmerized, dazzled. Unable to resist, she hopped up on the creature's back."

Lidia's eyes were wide with excitement, and she scanned my face the way she always did at this point. I always wondered what it was she saw, or what she was seeing, when she looked at me that way. But I didn't want her to become self-conscious, so I never asked. I did wonder, though, if she sensed what we were, all of us together, her heritage. Had she ever wondered if she would become like me? Was she looking to see if she could see herself in the faint lines finally appearing on my face?

"And then the dragon woke up!" Lidia said, breathless.

"And then the dragon woke up," I said, lowering my voice. "And its big, bright purple eyes opened, and a shudder went through its body, shaking the scales all the way down to the tip of its tail. And it said," I lowered my voice even further, to a growl, "'What is that on my back?' And Maria, startled, jumped off the creature's back and flew into the air. She landed on a rock and stared in wonder. 'I'm so sorry,' Maria said. 'I didn't mean to disturb you.' The creature lifted its enormous head and inhaled deeply. 'You don't smell like a human, and you don't smell like a bird.' Its voice was like melaza poured over un fuego. Hot, and sweet, and slow, and Maria thought she might be in love for the first time in her long, long life."

Lidia clapped and sat up once again, hugging her knees to her chest.

"The dragon sniffed again. 'I'm an aloja, a water woman,' Maria said. 'I met one of you, once. Hundreds of years ago,' the dragon said. Maria hopped a little closer and lifted her beak. 'What are you?' The creature grumbled and rumbled and shifted. 'I am Corona, the last víbria. Come with me into the light.' Maria flew from the cave, listening to the scraping and scruffling behind her. When she got to the lake, she returned to her human self and watched as the víbria left the cave."

"And she was magnífica!" Lidia continued to hug her knees, but now she looked outside, and Luna caressed her cheek, highlighting the blackish purple highlights in her hair.

"Maria had never seen something so magnífica. The víbria shone like diamonds under Luna's light, and when she was clear of the cave, she spread her great wings that were the whole width of the lake, and they blocked out the sky. And when she lifted her great triangular head and yawned, Maria saw her great big teeth and was frightened."

"But she didn't need to be," Lidia said.

"And why was that, niña?" I asked.

"Because the víbria is a good dragon, one who likes peace and quiet. But she's been very lonely because she's the only one." She leaned forward. "And she had a secret too," she whispered.

I nodded and stroked her head. "Like Maria, Corona could change shape. And in human form, she was as dark as Maria was pale, and her hair was black with purple streaks in it. They were night and day, dark and light, and they balanced each other perfectly. And Maria understood Corona's loneliness, because she, too, had no family or friends. She was all alone, and Corona was all alone."

"But they weren't alone anymore." Lidia sighed, her little happy sigh that meant all was right with the world.

"No, they weren't alone ever again. Corona was happy to share her lake and her cave with Maria, and Maria would hunt and bring back little treats for Corona, even though sometimes Corona had to fly away to get enough food to feed her dragon appetite. But Luna always guided her home, back to Maria."

Lidia snuggled down in her blankets. "And one day, many years later, Corona laid an egg, and when it hatched, they raised their daughter together. She was part aloja and part víbria, and she could be a bird, or a dragon, or a woman who loved water and could heal sick animals." Her eyes drifted closed. "She was the best of everything."

I stroked her head, my heart aching. "Yes, she was, my child. Sleep well." I got up and turned to the moon. "Protect her well, old friend."

I made my way to the deck and slipped off my sandals so I could feel my feet in the grass as I made my way to the lake. I hiked my skirt and tucked it around my waist so I could walk in up to my thighs. I tapped the water and watched the ripples flow to the cave at the other side, and soon heard the sounds that always made me smile as my love woke and moved from the form she was most comfortable in to the one she used whenever Lidia came to stay with us. She came out and plunged into the lake fully naked. Laughing as she came up, she pulled me, fully clothed, into the water. We tumbled together as we had for centuries, our bodies intertwined in a dance our souls knew perfectly. When we finally grew tired, we got out and she helped strip me of the wet garments. We lay together on the grass, drying beneath the moonlight.

She plucked a black feather from the grass. "You're shedding."

"I molt. You shed." I scratched at her shoulder blade, where I knew her scales had been bothering her.

"How is our granddaughter tonight?"

I sighed, thoughtful. "I think she feels the changes beginning. I can see it in her eyes. I wasn't sure if Gabriela's gifts would be passed on, but I think she's beginning to shift." Our daughter, the first of her kind, lived with her own mate, a human who accepted but didn't fully understand her nature. She'd been sending Lidia to us more often, and I wondered if it was because she feared for her daughter's safety or for her mate's.

Corona sat up, listening. "Gabriela. She's upset."

Moments later, headlights slid over the trees a few miles away. We got up and went quickly into the house to get dressed and then waited for her on the porch.

Gabriela flew in as a blackbird and changed to human form quickly as she rushed to embrace us. We held her as she cried, her shoulders shaking. She was taller than I, more like Corona that way, and I had to reach up to hold her tight. We didn't ask any questions, simply let her cry until she sagged against us, taking soft, ragged breaths.

I pulled away and went into the house, returning with a large soft towel. "Get in the water, my love. Heal."

She quickly undressed and ran into the lake. Self-consciousness was a distinctly human issue, and none of us suffered from it. My heart swelled when she dove into the water, staying under for a long while and then floating serenely under the night sky. I left the towel on the deck, and Corona and I went inside to wait. But she didn't come back in, and in the morning, Corona went to the cave to check on her. In dragon form, our daughter was solid black, like me in bird form, except for the white scales down the middle of her back. When she came in for breakfast, she looked tired, but the moment Lidia came bursting from her room, her eyes lit up once again.

"Mama!" Lidia leapt into her arms. "Luna told me you were coming."

"Did she?" Gabriela asked, glancing up at us. I could only shrug. "Well, Luna is always right. Did she say anything else?"

"She said that one day we'll play just like Maria played with her a long, long, long time ago." Lidia squirmed out of her mother's embrace and ran to my wife. "Abuela Corona, can we go treasure hunting today?"

"If your mama says it's okay."

Lidia looked at Gabriela, who smiled and nodded. "I used to love going on treasure hunts too. Of course you can."

Lidia yipped and ran back to her room to get dressed.

"You're still hiding treasure in the forest?" Gabriela asked.

"You know I built up enough over the centuries to hide pieces for another hundred years." Corona smiled. "I'll take Lidia out, and you can tell your mother what's wrong." She kissed Gabriela's head and her eyes flashed. "And if we need to kill anyone, just say so."

Gabriela didn't laugh, which she would have done once. Lidia and Corona left soon after, and I made us mint leaf tea, something we'd always loved, though Corona hated it. She said all dragons did, but I wasn't sure I believed her. Our daughter, after all, was one of them.

"Tell me," I said, holding her hand.

"I thought he loved me. I thought we could be like other humans. But he became strange and possessive, and he started saying I'd fly away and leave him and take our daughter with me. And the way he was acting with Lidia..." She began to cry once again. "I found papers, Mama. Something about shipping and cages."

She went on to tell me of strange people lurking about, and her sense of danger keeping her awake at night. Her lake felt wrong, too, like it had been smudged with oil meant to incapacitate. She stayed far from it, and her mate became frustrated and tried to force her into it. So she fled to safety, to us.

I felt Corona's anger like it was my own, a rage so deep, so hot, it would burn through the forest with nothing but a whisper from her lips. She heard what I heard, as was the way with dragons and their true loves.

"Our kind aren't meant to be with their kind, m'ija." I stroked her hair as she rested her head on my shoulder. Thank the goddess she'd found what she had and come home to us. Corona would make certain neither he nor any of his kind ever came near our daughter and granddaughter again. "You're safe now, and Lidia is safe."

She raised her head and scanned the forest. "Is she changing?"

I listened, aware that Corona was feeling something intense, something other than the rage she'd felt a moment before. It was... wonder. Just as she'd felt when Gabriela was born. I smiled, my heart beating out of my chest. "I think we're about to find out."

It wasn't soon, and we had to wait until the sun had set and Luna waited with us. Gabriela paced, wanting to know what was going on. She could feel Lidia too, but in different ways than Corona and me. But then we heard giggling, and shouting, and the trees around us bent and swayed as Corona, in all her bright white glory, rose above the trees, her wings beating slowly. And then below her rose a tiny dragon, wobbling and flapping, black scales with white tips catching the moon and sending rainbows of light dancing across the treetops.

Gabriela gasped and laughed, a full, open-hearted laugh, and ran to the open field, where she shifted and launched herself into the air to join her daughter and mother.

I held back my tears and lifted my face to the moon, who was just making her way over to us. Mi familia, mi corazón, played in the sky, teaching our young one to fly, to make her way in this world. None of us would ever be alone again, and we would always have each other. I shifted to my blackbird form and joined them in the sky.

Barbara in the Frame

Emmalia Harrington

Emmalia Harrington (she/her) is a disabled QWOC with a deep love of speculative fiction. When she's not reading or writing, she's often sewing, cooking, or managing cats. Her work can be found at *FIYAH*, *Anathema*, and other venues. You can find her on Twitter at @EmmaliaWrites.

Bab's stomach growled for the third time in five minutes. "You were right," she said, pushing away from her desk. "It's time for a break."

Summer classes meant papers and tests smashed close together. There was hardly time to get enough sleep, let alone shop on a regular basis. The only food in her dorm room was an orange. Bab picked it up and walked to her dresser, where the portrait of Barbara, her grandfather's great-aunt, sat.

She put a segment in her mouth and gagged. "Sorry," she said, spitting the fruit into her hand. She forced it down on the fifth attempt.

Aunt Barbara's portrait frowned and glanced at the bookcase. The clothbound spine of Auntie's handwritten cookbook stood out among the glossy college texts.

"You know it's too early for the kitchen." Bab kept her eyes on the shelves and away from her aunt. "Those girls will be there."

Even without looking at her, Auntie's disappointment made her wilt. Bab retreated to her desk to choke down the rest of her fruit. "I'm safer here," she said as she wiped her hands. "It's just you, me, and a locked door." She closed her eyes, imagining what diet could sustain her until the cafeteria opened for the autumn. Carrots lasted days without refrigeration, and if she soaked oatmeal overnight, it would be soft enough for breakfast.

Auntie's book said food was more potent when shared. The book had nothing like the recipes the other girls loved to make for their Soul Food Sundays. Placing succotash next to their cheese grits and fried okra was little better than exposing her whole self.

"Remember when I came home from the hospital?" Bab asked, turning back to her aunt. "I was so skinny Dad and Papa wouldn't let me see you." She gave a thin smile. "They thought seeing me would crack your frame."

Her throat shrank at the memories. The bureaucracy at her old college insisted on using the name and gender on her birth certificate and had stuck her in the boys' dorms. Her roommates alternated between hitting on her and punching inches from her head when she rebuffed them. One loved spiking her food with hot sauce and worse. After a few weeks she couldn't sip water without panicking; a full meal was impossible.

"None of that will happen here." Bab cracked her knuckles and tried to type as memories of the last year washed over her. This women's college's administration accepted Bab for who she was, name and all. She still felt safer keeping to herself.

That midnight, she entered the kitchen with cookies on her mind. She pulled out her baking sheet and spices before she came to her senses. Food never worked right in an unconsecrated space.

After several deep breaths, she was scrubbing the counter and attempting to meditate. Incense was not allowed on campus but would have done wonders to erase the pork and garlic scent left over from the soul food dinner. Even when her dormmates weren't there, they were reminding her what she wasn't. Curvy figures to her still-underweight frame. Cornrows and other cute hairstyles while hers couldn't grow longer than peach fuzz without breaking combs.

Bab bit her tongue. A clear mind was the best way to perform a ritual.

A pristine table and stovetop later, she was assembling Auntie's happiness cookies. Rice flour provided security and cloves purified the mind and heart. Cinnamon brought comfort and strengthened the power of the other ingredients. Mix with water to create a dough, pop them in the oven for fifteen minutes, and suffer from anticipation. Tidying right away added power to the food and gave it time to cool, even if the aroma of fresh cookies filled her mouth with drool.

Back in her room, there were things she needed to do before eating. She paid homage to Aunt Barbara, placing the nicest-smelling piece by her picture frame. Next was covering her desk with a clean towel in lieu of a tablecloth and folding a pretty bandanna into a napkin. A duct tape flower decorated the space. After a prayer of thanks, she took her first bite.

At first, it tasted like a cracker in need of dip. As she chewed, spices spread through her mouth and into her nose. Tension fell from her shoulders and neck. The more she ate, the more her cookie took on an extra flavor she couldn't describe. The closest she could get was "a hug from the whole family."

When she checked on her aunt, Barbara's cookie was gone, crumbs and all.

College was a never-ending battle between sleeping in and being on time for class. Bab had just enough time to pull on jeans and run to the Humanities Building, cursing herself with every step. Life was hard enough as is, she shouldn't make it worse by writing papers after two in the morning.

By pinching the back of her hand, she stayed awake all through the lesson. The effect faded as she headed to the bathroom, where she fought not to drift off on the toilet.

She was washing up when a familiar voice called out.

"I said, 'Hey!'" It was Jen, dormmate and political science/Africana studies major, standing between her and the exit.

Bab stretched her lips into a smile. "Not working today?"

Jen laughed and shook her head. The beads tipping her braids tinkled as she moved. Bab wished she had a scarf to hide her own hair. "My internship with the congresswoman is this afternoon. I'm between classes now."

"I wouldn't want to keep you." Bab hoped the other girl didn't notice the wobble in her voice.

"There's time yet." Jen headed for the water closet and paused. "You're the reason the kitchen smelled so good this morning?"

Bab forgot how to breathe. Nodding had to do.

"Will you come next Sunday? The three of us can't make dessert to save ourselves." Without waiting for an answer, Jen entered a stall. The sliding lock sounded like a guillotine blade.

It was all Bab could do to run to her next seminar. Terror percolated inside her, tightening her throat until she couldn't get a lungful. The Number Systems for Schoolteachers lecture passed in a haze of graying vision. At her next course, the professor took one look at her and ordered her to rest.

Back in her room, Bab spent an endless time curled on her bed, fighting for air. Clattering from the dresser pulled Bab out of herself enough to check the noise's source. Auntie's picture had fallen.

"Thanks." She returned to the bed, hugging the portrait like a teddy bear. Her heart bumping against the frame's glass made a double beat, Auntie's pulse moving in time with hers. Bab's airway relaxed, and her head cleared enough to grab last night's cookies.

"What should I do?" she said after filling Auntie in on the bathroom encounter. "Dad and Papa couldn't teach me Black girl stuff. Jen and her friends have way more practice than me." She took a bite. "If I change my mind, they'll know something's up, but if they get to know me, they'll be just like my boy roommates and…" Aunt Barbara was pursing her lips.

"You haven't heard Jen, Maria, and Tanya speak. Their majors are going to help them 'change the world.'" Bab stuck her chest out, superhero style.

Auntie raised her eyebrows.

"I know becoming a teacher's important." She sighed. "But tell that to people outside my department. Anyway, that's not the main reason they'll hate me." She glanced at Auntie's cookbook. "On Sundays the kitchen smells like those TV shows with sassy mothers who teach girls how to cook the 'real way.'" She made finger quotes. "Nothing like what we eat at home. They'll take one look at my food and treat me like my old roommates." Her stomach twisted. "I don't want to go to the hospital again."

Finishing the cookie kept the worst throat swelling away. She still felt like barricading herself until graduation.

Light glinted from the portrait. When Bab took a closer look, Auntie met her eyes. Aunt Barbara resembled a professor, stern but caring. If photos could speak, Bab would be getting a speech on conquering fear.

The eye lecture finished with Auntie glancing in the direction of her book. Bab crossed the room, picked it up, and flipped through the dessert section. She doubted Grape-Nut pudding would go over well. Apple-cheddar pie might work, but she wasn't masochistic enough to make crust from scratch. Hermits seemed easy enough, but the next recipe stopped her cold.

Froggers. Above the recipe, Aunt Barbara had written a few notes about Lucretia Brown, the inventor. Bab read and reread the page before saying, "They might like it."

❖

Summer lessons meant more homework and less time. Bab spent her free days camped in the library, reading hundreds of pages' worth of assignments before trudging back to her room to bang out papers.

She peeked from her window before going outside. Maria, a Soul Food Sunday girl, wasn't out running laps. Bab headed to the library, wiping sweat off her palms every couple of steps. If the pre-law/economics student wasn't marathoning, she was on work-study. Bab needed to find a secluded corner to avoid detection.

Maria was nowhere near the front desk when Bab checked out her classes' reserve texts. She walked the opposite way from the book return cart, in case the girl was shelving. Bab spent the next two hours in the clear until it came time to make copies. The other girl was bent over loading paper into the machine, looking more voluptuous than Bab could hope to be.

Bab closed her eyes, praying to avoid a repeat of yesterday. "Hey." Maybe starting the conversation would help.

The other girl yelped, whirling around and overbalancing. Bab rushed to steady her, half wondering if she'd landed in a romantic comedy.

Maria's face flushed redder than her shirt. "I didn't see you."

It was Bab's turn to freeze. She studied the wall behind the other girl's head as she tried to form words.

"Oh! You're coming Sunday." Maria sounded relieved. "We can talk then." She stepped away from Bab and hurried to the front desk.

Two hours and five textbooks later, Bab emerged from the library, dazed. Motor memory led her to the campus coffee shop, where she ordered a red eye. She needed the caffeine to unfry her brain and conduct decent extracurricular research.

Maria was nowhere to be found when Bab walked to the reference librarian's desk. There wasn't too much on Lucretia Brown, but what existed came from places like the Smithsonian. The state historical society had a series of frogger recipes as well as official documents on Brown's business. Bab's coffee went cold as she pored over the papers.

❖

"What do you think, Auntie?" Bab asked that night. "Those three might hate them because they have 'frog' in the name."

Aunt Barbara didn't react. Bab twisted her hands and continued. "I found a zillion ways to make froggers. Some I don't have to buy a ton of new ingredients for. One is similar to your happiness cookies and isn't very sweet. They'll think I was lying about making dessert. Another's fried, not baked. Those three..." She drifted off as Auntie wrinkled her nose.

"What do you think I should do?" Bab said, hoping Auntie wouldn't give the obvious answer. She gave Bab a hard stare. "I can't do that," Bab said, backing away. "I'm safer not making friends." She bumped into her bed.

Auntie looked miserable. Bab stroked the picture frame before returning to fretting. Silently, this time.

Every recipe called for allspice, which promoted luck, success, and health. It was also quite masculine. Bab wasn't keen on infusing virility in herself or the others. Liquor united the feminine elements of water and earth, but she was too young to buy the rum froggers required. Bab prayed rum extract with its high alcohol content was an acceptable substitute. Auntie's book had nothing to say about the power of molasses. Maybe it took after its sister sugar in terms of protection and enhancement. It could also be a soul food ingredient, though Bab was too afraid to check.

❖

Spices were never cheap. Bab spent the next few days outside of class in the city. Ethnic enclaves had spices at better cost than supermarkets, and she was going to find the best prices. She always went on foot to channel bus fare into grocery cash. Her feet swelled until she could barely pull her shoes off at night, but she got all the seasonings she needed, plus extra rice flour.

By Saturday afternoon, Bab had recovered enough to limp to the market nearest to the dorms. Butter was easy enough to find, but molasses and extract remained elusive, no matter how many times she wandered Aisle 5. Between her focus on the shelves and her still-complaining legs, she didn't notice company until she bumped into them.

Bab's heart froze when she realized who she'd crashed into. Tanya was Jen and Maria's buddy, a business/chemistry major and heir to a cosmetics firm that made products for Black women. She might have been in jeans and ponytail, but her skin glowed and her hair smelled of jasmine and coconut oil.

"I'm sorry!" Bab couldn't apologize fast enough. "I should have seen you—"

Tanya waved her hand. "I ran into you. Let me make up for it." She reached into her pocket and pulled out a wad of papers. "Have a coupon."

Bab reached for the offering, doing her best not to brush Tanya's fingers. She didn't want to piss the girl off by mistake. There were discounts on powdered soup, meal replacement shakes, frozen dinners…

"Mind if I have this one?" Bab held up a voucher for oranges.

Tanya shrugged. "It's not like I'll get scurvy."

Bab's grin felt foreign on her mouth. "They're also great for clearing the mind and cheering you up."

The other girl raised an eyebrow, something Bab had yet to master. "Isn't that what chocolate's for?"

Bab's cheeks burned, but before she could answer, Tanya said, "Maybe I'll get some chocolate peanut butter this week. They taste good with strawberry Caffeine Bombs." She waved goodbye. Bab couldn't decide whether to stare at her or her basket of white bread and neon drinks.

She resumed her search for the remaining ingredients, trying to imagine what Auntie would think of Tanya's cuisine. There could be disgust, terror, or horrific rage.

"Victory!" Bab announced later in her room. "Now I have everything for froggers."

She picked up the portrait. "Will it be all right?" Auntie beamed. "Of course you think that, we're family. I don't have that advantage for tomorrow."

Aunt Barbara looked Bab up and down before raising her chin.

Bab crossed her arms over her bust. "They're prettier than I am, and I don't think a padded bra would help."

Auntie's eye narrowed.

"What's worth knowing about me?" Her voice wobbled. Auntie glanced at the mirror. Bab stood in front of it for ages, trying to see what Aunt Barbara did. It never appeared. Whenever she turned away, Auntie nodded for Bab to return. Her throat ached from not shrieking her frustration.

Her reflection continued to show someone who did not have the looks, goals, or background that the other Black girls in the dorm did. She had bits and pieces of other kin in her appearance, like Papa's forehead, Grandfather's nose, and Auntie's love of frilly blouses. Bab straightened her back and assumed the formal pose of Auntie's portrait. She still couldn't find what Auntie saw, but her urge to scream faded. Maybe one of these years she'd be as awesome as Auntie believed.

❖

If Bab was going to bake undisturbed, she was better off starting at midnight. The cookies wouldn't be the freshest, but she half remembered one recipe saying froggers grew tastier with time. Or she could scrub the kitchen for so long, Monday would roll by before she finished.

Giving the counter, sink, and other surfaces the once-over wasn't going to be enough if she wanted to win the trio's favor. Bab scoured until her arms ached, shook them out, and started again. She filled her head with prayers for the cookies' success and her continued safety. Whenever her mind wandered, she bit hard on her tongue.

Now that she thought about it, froggers might taste better if she rewashed the baking sheet. As she worried it with a sponge, she caught a glimpse of herself on the aluminum. She was nothing more than a blobby outline, but it was enough to remember the afternoon. Auntie thought she was worth something, and Bab needed to act the part. She preheated the oven and pulled out the measuring cup.

Auntie's recipe didn't specify rice flour, but she could do with its protection. The spices that went into happiness cookies went into the mixing bowl, along with lucky nutmeg and ginger's love. Macho allspice went in after all, to impart success.

Wet ingredients went into another bowl before she combined everything to make a sticky dough. Nothing a bit of flour couldn't fix. She rolled everything out with the side of an empty glass, used the mouth of the same cup to cut out froggers, and stuck them in the oven.

Baking and cooling times stretched until every second felt like forever. Despite her best efforts, no amount of tidying would speed things. Sweat oozed from her face and armpits.

As soon as she could move the cookies without burning herself, Bab fled to her room. "I did it!" She hitched her shoulders in lieu of a fist pump. Dropping the froggers now would mean baking them later in front of an audience. Once they were safely on her desk, she fell to her knees.

"I thought of you as much as I could and how you want me to be." On the floor, she couldn't meet Auntie's face. "I'm still not there, sorry." Even through her jeans, the tiled floor felt so cool, but passing out here would mean a stiff back in the morning. "Just a minute."

It took a few tries to lurch off the floor and back to her feet. Bab placed a frogger by Auntie's picture. "What do you think?"

Between one blink and the next, the cookie vanished. Auntie's smile threatened to push her cheeks off.

❖

It was ten when Bab woke up, and eleven before she rolled out of bed. She only had a few hours, and laundry wouldn't do itself. Typical for Sunday, all the machines were full, but one just had a few minutes left to run. She buried herself in a textbook, wondering if she could drop out of dinner, saying she had a test tomorrow. Auntie would be disappointed in her.

The afternoon vanished in a flurry of chores, grooming, and actual homework reading. Bab shaved, brushed her hair until her arm ached, and smoothed out the wrinkles in one of her nicer shirts. Whenever her throat threatened to swell, she turned back to studying.

An hour before the event, Bab's heart thrummed in her ears. She had one last thing to do before she was ready, but it meant going to the kitchen, possibly in front of everyone.

The room was filled with cell phone music and off-key singing. Tanya and Maria's backs were to Bab as they chopped away. Jen hadn't arrived. Bab was free to cover the table with a freshly washed sheet, though she ached to clap her hands over her ears. The file quality, song genre, and the girls' lack of skill made it Vogon poetry in human mouths. She placed her duct tape flower in the center of the table before retreating to gather the froggers.

When she returned, the pair was belting out what might have been "Baby Come to Me." Bab prayed "4:33" was next on the playlist as she arranged cookies on her largest plate. She couldn't do anything more artful than a pyramid of concentric circles, but it looked good enough for a magazine.

A shriek stole the last of her hearing. "Bab, when did you get here?"

Bab turned to Tanya, rubbing her ears. "I didn't want to interrupt."

Tanya laughed. "It's either sing or put up with Maria's preaching."

"Soul food *isn't* vegan," Maria hissed.

"Aren't you making peas and carrots?" Tanya said.

"Doesn't count, I use butter," Maria said.

"See what I mean?" Tanya said to Bab with a hammy sigh.

Bab's smile shook around the edges. "Why not vegan?"

"Thank you!" Tanya abandoned her cutting board to crush Bab in a hug. "You understand."

"Does that mean no cookies tonight?" Bab winced at her lack of subtlety. "They have dairy."

"Of course cookies." Tanya stepped back, giving her a hard look. "Cookies need butter, chicken needs salt, and collard greens are better with orange juice instead of pork."

"Blasphemy," called a new voice from the doorway. Jen walked in, arms full of cans and equipment. "Smoked pork is food of the gods."

As the trio rambled amongst themselves, tension fell from Bab's shoulders. She set the table, making sure everything was picture perfect while the others worked by the stove and countertops. Aside from the odd comment thrown in her direction, they left her alone until their food was ready.

"What did you do?" Jen breathed as she took in Bab's handiwork. "It looks like a real Sunday dinner now."

"Ahem," Tanya said, looking in the direction of the garbage bin. An empty tube of biscuit dough and a gravy can sat on top of the trash.

"I was busy—" Jen started, but Maria cut her off.

"I forgot salt, gravy will help the peas and carrots." She plopped her dish next to the duct tape flower. "Let's start?"

No one commented on Bab sitting in the spot closest to the door. They were too busy saying things that threatened to stop her heart.

"How's the food? Maria used fresh carrots this time." Tanya wiggled her eyebrows. Maria, Bab's bench partner, turned the color of rust.

The taste was on par with cafeteria food. Bab liked safety too much to say it aloud. "You're right, it does go well with gravy."

Maria stared at her plate as more blood rushed to her face.

"You know what would be great? Bacon," Jen said. "Everything it touches turns to magic."

Bab opened her mouth, closed it, and lowered her head so no one could see her face. Auntie's cookbook never limited power to a single ingredient. The other girls were too busy arguing which brand of cured meat was best to notice Bab's silence.

It wasn't long before the serving plates emptied. With competition out of the way, the froggers perfumed the table and made full stomachs grumble.

"Are these the cookies you made last week?" Jen asked.

Bab shook her head. "It's a diff—"

The trio snatched froggers for themselves and went to work reducing them to crumbs.

Jen's first bite took out a third of her cookie. Her eyes widened. Tanya chewed slowly, lost in thought. Maria closed her eyes and clasped her hands like a church lady. "What did you say these were?"

"They're molasses cookies." Bab coughed, but her throat kept tingling. "Froggers."

"Made with real frogs?" Tanya said, her smile wry.

Bab took a deep breath and wished her lungs were bigger. "A woman named Lucretia Brown invented them." All eyes were on her, none of them hateful. She looked at Tanya. "Lucretia was a Black woman who ran an inn and made perfume and other things to sell." To Jen and Maria she added, "She was born in 1772 Massachusetts and owned property."

No one spoke. They were too busy considering their froggers. Bab took one for herself and bit in deep. Spices spread through her mouth and seeped into her being. Her throat relaxed enough to ask "Maria, mind if I jog with you tomorrow?" before she realized it. A second mouthful of cookie kept panic at bay.

Maria's ears darkened, but she said, "I'd like that. Front door at eight a.m.? Wear good shoes."

Bab took a second frogger, but when she reached for a third, all she found was an empty plate. Hearing the trio tease each other as they helped with cleanup almost made up for it. The lack of singing certainly did.

With four people helping, dishes and everything else were done in no time. Bab trailed the other girls out of the kitchen, itching to tell Aunt Barbara about tonight. It was too soon to tell how they'd take knowing Bab's whole self, but for now they added warmth she couldn't get with cookies alone.

Books Available From Bold Strokes Books

Arrested Pleasures by Nanisi Barrett D'Arnuck. When charged with a crime she didn't commit, Katherine Lowe faces the question: Which is harder, going to prison or falling in love? (978-1-63555-684-1)

In Helen's Hands by Nanisi Barrett D'Arnuk. As her mistress, Helen pushes Mickey to her sensual limits, delivering the pleasure only a BDSM lifestyle can provide her. (978-1-63555-639-1)

21 Questions by Mason Dixon. To find love, start by asking the right questions. (978-1-62639-724-8)

Charm City by Mason Dixon. Raq Overstreet's loyalty to her drug kingpin boss is put to the test when she begins to fall for Bathsheba Morris, the undercover cop assigned to bring him down. (978-1-62639-198-7)

Masquerade by Anne Shade. In 1925 Harlem, New York, a notorious gangster sets her sights set on seducing Celine, and new lovers Dinah and Celine are forced to risk their hearts, and lives, for love. (978-1-63555-831-9)

Femme Tales by Anne Shade. Six women find themselves in their own real-life fairy tales when true love finds them in the most unexpected ways. (978-1-63555-657-5)

Silk and Leather: Lesbian Erotica with an Edge, edited by Victoria Villaseñor. This collection of stories by award-winning authors offers fantasies as soft as silk and tough as leather. The only question is: How far will you go to make your deepest desires come true? (978-1-63555-587-5)

Escape to Pleasure: Lesbian Travel Erotica, edited by Sandy Lowe and Victoria Villasenor. Join these award-winning authors as they explore the sensual side of erotic lesbian travel. (978-1-163555-339-0)

Heart of a Killer by Yolanda Wallace. Contract killer Santana Masters's only interest is her next assignment—until a chance meeting with a beautiful stranger tempts her to change her ways. (978-1-63555-547-9)

Comrade Cowgirl by Yolanda Wallace. When cattle rancher Laramie Bowman accepts a lucrative job offer far from home, will her heart end up getting lost in translation? (978-1-63555-375-8)

Changing Course by Brey Willows. When the woman of her dreams falls from the sky, intergalactic space captain Jessa Arbelle had better be ready to catch her. (978-1-63555-335-2)

Spinning Tales by Brey Willows. When the fairy tale begins to unravel and villains are on the loose, will Maggie and Kody be able to spin a new tale? (978-1-63555-314-7)

A Turn of Fate by Ronica Black. Will Nev and Kinsley finally face their painful past and relent to their powerful, forbidden attraction? Or will facing their past be too much to fight through? (978-1-63555-930-9)

Desires After Dark by MJ Williamz. When her human lover falls deathly ill, Alex, a vampire, must decide which is worse, letting her go or condemning her to everlasting life. (978-1-63555-940-8)

Her Consigliere by Carsen Taite. FBI agent Royal Scott swore an oath to uphold the law, and criminal defense attorney Siobhan Collins pledged her loyalty to the only family she's ever known, but will their love be stronger than the bonds they've vowed to others, or will their competing allegiances tear them apart? (978-1-63555-924-8)

In Our Words: Queer Stories from Black, Indigenous, and People of Color Writers. Stories Selected by Anne Shade and Edited by Victoria Villaseñor. Comprising both the renowned and emerging voices of Black, Indigenous, and People of Color authors, this thoughtfully curated collection of short stories explores the intersection of racial and queer identity. (978-1-63555-936-1)

Measure of Devotion by CF Frizzell. Disguised as her late twin brother, Catherine Samson enters the Civil War to defend the Constitution as a Union soldier, never expecting her life to be altered by a Gettysburg farmer's daughter. (978-1-63555-951-4)

Not Guilty by Brit Ryder. Claire Weaver and Emery Pearson's day jobs clash, even as their desire for each other burns, and a discreet sex-only arrangement is the only option. (978-1-63555-896-8)

Opposites Attract: Butch/Femme Romances by Meghan O'Brien, Aurora Rey & Angie Williams. Sometimes opposites really do attract. Fall in love with these butch/femme romance novellas. (978-1-63555-784-8)

Swift Vengeance by Jean Copeland, Jackie D & Erin Zak. A journalist becomes the subject of her own investigation when sudden strange, violent visions summon her to a summer retreat and into the arms of a killer's possible next victim. (978-1-63555-880-7)

Under Her Influence by Amanda Radley. On their path to #truelove, will Beth and Jemma discover that reality is even better than illusion? (978-1-63555-963-7)

Wasteland by Kristin Keppler & Allisa Bahney. Danielle Clark is fighting against the National Armed Forces and finds peace as a scavenger, until the NAF general's daughter, Katelyn Turner, shows up on her doorstep and brings the fight right back to her. (978-1-63555-935-4)

When In Doubt by VK Powell. Police officer Jeri Wylder thinks she committed a crime in the line of duty but can't remember, until details emerge pointing to a cover-up by those close to her. (978-1-63555-955-2)

A Woman to Treasure by Ali Vali. An ancient scroll isn't the only treasure Levi Montbard finds as she starts her hunt for the truth—all she has to do is prove to Yasmine Hassani that there's more to her than an adventurous soul. (978-1-63555-890-6)

Before. After. Always. by Morgan Lee Miller. Still reeling from her tragic past, Eliza Walsh has sworn off taking risks, until Blake Navarro turns her world right-side up, making her question if falling in love again is worth it. (978-1-63555-845-6)

Bet the Farm by Fiona Riley. Lauren Calloway's luxury real estate sale of the century comes to a screeching halt when dairy farm heiress, and one-night stand, Thea Boudreaux calls her bluff. (978-1-63555-731-2)